TOWERS

THE EXIGENCY CHRONICLES: BOOK 1

TERRY SCHOTT

TOWERS
THE EXIGENCY CHRONICLES : BOOK 1
©2020 by Terry Schott
All rights reserved.

Aboot Spelling...

Throughout this book you will find words that might look to be spelled incorrectly if you are living in the USA.

For example, Travelled, Honour, Centre, Colour, etc....

Don't panic! The spelling is correct if you live outside of the USA, which I do.

I dedicate this one to my amazing daughter, Sydney.
This story would never have made it out of my head, were it not for your encouragement.
Thanks, Kitten.
I love you!

PROLOGUE

WILL FORCED HIS WAY THROUGH THE TIGHTLY PACKED bodies in front of him, cell phone pressed to one ear and other hand extended straight out to help him move people aside.

Screaming and explosions sounding all around, he tilted his head in an attempt to hear the ringtone as it chirped across the distance between him and his wife. "Come on, Malena," he muttered. "Pick up the damned phone."

There was a clicking noise, a pause, and then.

"Hello?" The woman's voice gasped the word, followed by a sharp intake of breath and another pause before she spoke once more. "Will? Is that you?"

Will ducked into an empty doorway and turned his back to the street, hunching his shoulders and lowering his head to try to drown out the cacophony around him. A loud explosion cracked loudly from his left, followed a second later by a wave of intense heat that washed past him and then disappeared.

He tucked himself tighter into the corner and cupped his hand around the phone. "Malena! Yeah, sweet girl, it's me. How are you doing? I got your message. The baby's coming?"

"Yes—" Malena gasped and then screamed.

Will winced, waiting until the scream faded and was replaced again by short, panting breaths. "That's right," he said. "Take those sips of air. Just like they showed us in class." Will began to make exaggerated breathing sounds to match those of his wife. He heard a second woman's voice in the background and felt a rush of relief. *Good,* he thought. *Her mom is with her.*

"The baby's coming, Will." Malena's voice was stern, but he heard the fear in it. "I need you. Come home. Now."

He blinked back hot tears and used the heel of his palm to wipe them away. "I can't... I can't come home yet, sweet girl."

"No. No, no, no." The volume of Malena's voice increased with each repetition of the word. "We made a deal, Will. When the baby was coming you would be here with me. You promised."

"I know, but—"

"The baby's on the way. You'd better be, too."

Will looked up as two people locked together in a chaotic tangle tumbled into the doorway. They were struggling, fighting each other for something in their hands that Will couldn't make out. One of them lost their footing and bumped against the frame of the door before finally tripping. Both bodies fell to the ground at his feet with a dull thud, but neither let go of the other and they continued to struggle.

Will frowned and placed one hand over the receiver of his phone. "Stop it!" he hissed. "Get the hell out of here!"

The pair ignored him and continued to fight.

Will placed a heavy combat boot against the backside of

the person closest to him and shoved with all his strength, sending the combatants rolling back into the street. Seconds later they disappeared, swept away in the flood of panicked people all moving as fast as they could in the same direction.

Will placed the phone back to his ear.

"Did you hear me, Will?" Malena panted the words.

"I heard you, Babe, but it's out of my control." He swallowed hard. "It's happening. Everything's falling apart."

"What? No. Not—"

"Yes. Right here. Right now."

There was silence. Will thought the line had gone dead, and then, "Oh, god, no." Malena whispered.

"Yeah." Will closed his eyes and dropped into a crouch, leaning forward until his head pressed against the cold brick wall.

"Where are you?"

"New York City."

"God damn it!" Her voice rose halfway through the sentence as another contraction came. Moments passed before she spoke again. "What am I supposed to do, Will?" He heard something in her voice that he'd never heard before.

Panic.

"Have the baby and get as close to the main tower as you can." Will's voice remained calm as he checked his watch. "I figure you have about twelve hours before the power goes out where you are. Get to Jack and let him know what's going on. He'll take care of what he can, and the rest can wait."

"But there's so much to do." She was speaking faster than before. "If it's happening now, we have to—I have to make sure everything and everyone is safe. I—"

"Listen to me, Sweetness," Will interrupted. "The only thing you have to do at this moment is focus on our baby."

A long pause. And then, "Okay."

Will closed his eyes. "I will make my way to you, Mal. It's gonna take a bit longer than we'd thought, but I am coming to you."

There was silence on the line.

"Malena?"

"I know," she whispered.

"You'll be fine. All of you will. We made a good plan, with excellent people. Do your best to keep everyone on track. I'll get there as fast as I can. And I'll bring whatever help I find along the way."

Silence.

"We don't give up."

"I know."

"We can do this."

"You're right, Baby. We can do this. We will."

Will pressed his lips together as he nodded, hot tears dripping down his cheeks as he gripped the phone tight. He knew he should hang up, get going while he could. But he didn't want to hang up. Didn't want this moment with her to end. *How the hell am I gonna get back to her?* he asked himself. *And even if I somehow manage it, it'll take me months. Maybe years.*

"I miss you." She was crying.

"I miss you too, Sweetness."

The clarity of the connection faded into a crackle, then a hiss, and finally a loud whistling noise. "Malena?" he shouted into the receiver. "My phone is going out. The signals are dropping."

"It's a girl, Will." Her voice came over the line, clear and calm. "You have a baby daughter."

Then the line went dead.

Eyes wide and tears streaming down his cheeks, Will lowered the phone from his ear and stared at it. Seconds later, a deafening explosion sounded from close by, and people began screaming in fear and pain.

Will powered his phone off and tucked it into the breast pocket of his long, black, leather trench coat. He stood and let one hand brush against the butt of the gun holstered under his left arm. Then he reached into his pocket and withdrew a bracelet made of polished gemstones, round and multicoloured. He stared at it for a long moment and then slid it onto his wrist.

The lights around him flickered and went out. People began to scream hysterically as darkness enveloped them.

Will stepped onto the street and melted into the crowd.

1

"LUNA!"

Luna jerked upright in her chair, pulse drumming like a hammer in her ears as the *BANG* sounded against the front door. Recognition set in as she stood up from the table and cast an apologetic glance toward her mother.

"Sorry, Mom."

"That boy." Her mother shook her head, brows furrowed as she raised a forkful of eggs to her mouth. "Tell him that he woke me up with his banging and screaming."

Luna smiled. "That'll scare him. The last time he woke you up wasn't fun."

Her mother grinned as she chewed her bite of food and Luna walked to the front door.

"Luna!" More loud banging. "For the love of—"

Luna swung the door open and took a sudden step outward. "Gage!" she hissed.

The boy's eyes widened and he drew back a step.

"What's the meaning of this?" The girl frowned, doing her best to imitate the look her mother gave when she was not happy. "It's too early to be screaming and banging on my front door. Actually, there's never a good time to be screaming and banging on—"

"Stylar is leaving," Gage blurted.

Luna's frown deepened. "What do you mean, *leaving*?"

"The line. He said he's gonna cross the line."

Luna felt her breath catch in her stomach, like it had when she'd fallen from the tree last spring. Her head shook from side to side, mouth moving while she waited for her breath to return. "That's not even one bit funny, Gage."

"It's no joke. He's at the edge of the Sampsons' field now, so close to the line that he'd cross it if he fell forward."

"You're lying."

The boy's head whipped back and forth. "I'm not. I know he's played at this before, but this time I think he means it, Lune. We've gotta stop him."

"Wait here." Luna spun on her heel. "I'll get Mom."

———

A crowd of sixty or so people had gathered by the time they arrived at the edge of the Sampsons' field. Luna sensed from the expressions of those gathered that what Gage had said was true. She continued walking with her mother and friend, her eyes coming to rest on the lone figure of a boy standing alone near the edge of the field, about thirty feet away.

The crowd parted for Luna's mother, some casting worried glances at her but no one speaking. Her mother nodded in silent reply and came to a stop beside a tall man with a goatee and long, salt-and-pepper hair tied back in a pony tail that hung halfway to his waist.

"Morning, Mal." The man addressed Luna's mother without taking his gaze from the lone figure of the boy.

"What's this about, Jack?" Luna heard anger and worry in her mother's voice.

"Not sure." Jack's grey-black hair swung back and forth as he shook his head.

"Stylar," Mal called toward the boy. "Come away from there. Back to where we are, please."

Stylar ignored her, head bowed and body unmoving.

"Now!" Mal snapped loudly. Luna felt her muscles jerk to attention. The tone in her mother's voice was one she had learned to obey without hesitation long ago. Everyone in the village knew to obey Mal when her patience had run out.

Luna looked to her friend, certain he would come running toward them.

But Stylar didn't move. Instead, he kept his back to them, head down as he shifted his weight from one foot to the other.

"Jack," Mal sighed, shaking her head. "Get over there and grab the boy."

"I tried that already," Jack said. "He was standing where we are now when I got here. He slipped out of my grip and then ran to where he is now."

"He's right at the line now," Mal murmured.

"And he screamed he'd step over it if we come any closer."

Mal closed her eyes. Luna's gaze slid to Gage, and he nodded.

"Luna?" Mal did not turn to look back at her daughter.

"Yes, Mom?"

"Go get him."

"But—"

"He's one of your best friends, right?"

"Yes."

"The other children all seem to listen to you. Go do your thing and bring him away from that line."

"I don't think he will, Mom. Not this time."

Mal turned toward Luna, her eyes tightening slightly at the outer corners. "Did you know he was thinking about this?"

"What?" Luna scowled. "No way. This is crazy. I can't believe he's standing that close to the line, even now. He's never mentioned doing something like this. Not to me, anyway." Her eyes slid to Gage and he looked down.

Mal noted the gesture. "Gage ..."

"Me neither ..." He looked up and gulped. "I mean, not until last night."

Jack swore and shook his head.

Gage's eyes widened. "I'm sorry. I didn't think he was serious. Figured he was just angry. You know." The boy paused.

"About his mother," Mal said.

"Yeah." Gage nodded.

Mal sighed and closed her eyes for a brief moment before opening them and gazing back toward Stylar.

"He thinks she's out there," Gage said. "Past the line."

"Well, she isn't," Jack said.

"I know, and I told him that." Gage's eyes shifted to Luna. "We've all told him. More times than we can remember, I think."

Luna nodded.

"Stylar," Mal called out once more. "Come over here we can talk about this. I know you miss your mom, but this isn't going to help anyone. Especially not you." She waited for the boy to respond.

He didn't.

Mal turned back to the group of people. "Everybody leave."

No one moved.

"Part of what's keeping him there is the crowd. If we make a big deal about this, then he will be more tempted to do something stupid."

"I think he's gonna do it whether we're here or not," one of the men stated, and others nodded in agreement. "He's gonna step over."

"No, he isn't," Jack said.

"Regardless of what happens,"—Mal held up one hand —"He gets no more attention from the village over this." Her gaze hardened and she stared at individuals one by one until they looked away. "Please, folks. You're only hurting the boy by standing around. Help us out and leave."

There were grumbles from a few, but the group slowly stirred, and individuals began walking away. Luna looked in Stylar's direction to see if he would notice, but the boy continued to stand with his back to them, head tilted toward the ground.

Once the crowd had left, Mal nodded at Luna and jutted her chin toward the boy. "Go bring him back, Dove."

Luna pursed her lips and looked at Gage. He nodded, and she began to walk forward.

"Heya, Styles."

"What's up, Lune?"

Luna couldn't help but smile. He sounded fine; calm and comfortable, as if the two of them were meeting up in front of school before a regular day. "Not much, how 'bout you?"

He looked up and lifted his chin toward the open field of green grass and hills in front of them. "Thinking about heading over there for a visit."

"I don't think that's a good idea, bud."

He shrugged.

Luna's stomach churned at the thought of stepping over the foot-wide, silver line on the ground in front of them. "I'm kinda scared, Styles." She heard the quaver in her own voice.

He looked up and met her eyes. Then he frowned and reached out to place a hand on her shoulder.

"Whoah!" Luna jerked her shoulder and took half a step backward.

"Wait—" Stylar's eyes widened. "You didn't think I was gonna try and shove you over, did you?"

"What?" Luna shook her head. "No. Course I didn't."

"You gotta know I wouldn't—I would never—"

"Dude," she held a hand up between them. "Right now I don't know anything for sure."

Stylar blinked. "What?"

"Look where we're standing." She pointed at the ground. "I'd have said we would never be this close to the line. Especially not in the morning, with you thinking about crossing it."

"You don't understand—"

"Of course I don't understand!" Luna shouted. "And you don't either, or you wouldn't be here. This is nuts, man. Freaking nuts." She realized what she was saying and froze. "I'm sorry."

Stylar laughed and shook his head. "No, you're right."

She frowned.

"You're totally right. This is crazy." His smile faded and

his expression became serious. "But I'm not crazy, Luna. I promise you, I'm not."

Luna considered her friend for a long moment and then sighed. "I believe you, Styles."

"You do?"

She nodded. "Of course."

"I'm glad for that."

They stood quietly for what felt like a long time.

"Let's go back," Luna suggested. "My mom isn't gonna give you any trouble about this."

Stylar snorted.

"I promise, she won't."

"I've broken a pretty big rule, Luna. Especially for kids like us."

"We're almost adults."

"Almost. And adults aren't allowed any closer to the line than kids."

"Yeah."

"Never go near the line. Stay away from the line."

"That's the rule," Luna agreed.

"Remember when Gage did this?"

Luna laughed. "I do."

"We were six."

"And didn't know any better." Luna's smile faded. "Still, Gage never got this close to the line, Styles."

"Oh, I know." The boy laughed. "But it sure felt that way, didn't it?"

"It sure did."

"Remember the trouble he got into?"

Luna chuckled. "He couldn't sit down for a whole day from the spanking his dad gave him."

Stylar smiled, but his eyes were sad. "I guess I won't have to worry about a parent punishing me, at least."

Luna took a step closer to her friend and slowly reached out her hand. He did not flinch away as she laid it on his shoulder and gave it a gentle squeeze. "I'm sorry about your mom. Everyone is."

"Doesn't seem like it." He reached up and wiped a tear from his eye. "No one even mentions her. It's like she never existed."

Luna said nothing.

"I miss her."

"I know." Luna paused. "But that's the thing, Styles." She pointed toward the field on the other side of the line. "She's not out there."

"I think she is."

"She isn't." Luna shook her head. "You saw what happened. She—"

"Yes, we all saw." The tone of the boy's voice hardened. "She stepped over the line and ... and ..." he bowed his head. "We all saw."

"Nobody wanted that for her, Styles, and we certainly don't want that for you. Why don't you just—"

"I don't think it's what we thought."

Luna frowned. "What do you mean?"

"That." His arm jabbed forward, finger pointing at the field beyond the invisible barrier. "I don't think the barrier is real."

"What do you mean it isn't real?" Luna's brows furrowed. "Of course it's real."

"No." He shook his head, eyes hard as he stared at the scenery. "I think it's just an illusion."

"Stylar—"

"It's taken me a while to put it all together," he said, "but I know I'm right."

"Styles, you're scaring me."

He turned toward her and smiled. "Don't be scared, Luna. This is a good thing."

"You're wrong. It's real."

"That's what they want us to believe, but they've been lying."

Luna shook her head.

"All this time, and they've been lying." He stepped away from her, eyes wide as he looked toward the field. "And the only way they will know is if I show them."

"Styles." She lunged toward her friend, her hands gripping his wrist.

Stylar twisted his arm and slipped away. "See ya on the other side, pal."

"Stylar!" she cried.

Stylar took one big step and crossed the line.

As he did, there was a sudden bright flash of energy and a loud *CRACK* that split the air and knocked into Luna like a wave.

Blinking rapidly, Luna stared in horror as her friend disintegrated into a cloud of black dust that remained in place for a few seconds before floating away on the light breeze.

2

A LIGHT RAP SOUNDED AGAINST THE DOOR, FOLLOWED by her mother's voice. "May I come in?"

Luna rolled onto her back, resting one arm under her head. "Yes."

The door opened with a tiny creak and her mother's face appeared.

Luna sat up and leaned against the headboard as Mal came to sit on the edge of the bed. She reached out and rested her hand on her daughter's knee. "How are you feeling? Hanging in there?"

"I guess." Luna nodded but pursed her lips, breath shuddering from the effort of holding back tears. "I can't believe he's gone."

"I know."

"And like that." Luna shook her head, one hand moving to wipe newly formed tears from her eyes.

Mal nodded, her expression sombre.

"Did it ..." Luna blinked and took a deep breath. "I keep wondering if he felt pain."

"He didn't."

"You can't know that. Not for sure."

"You're right." Mal's hand reached up to brush a strand of hair from her daughter's face. "I can't be positive that it didn't hurt, but even if it did ..."

"It was over quick."

"That's right."

Luna's head nodded up and down, her eyes on the wall across from them.

"No one is to blame for what happened," her mother said.

"Someone is always to blame." Luna repeated the words that she'd heard so often growing up. Not just from her mother, but teachers, other parents; it was a common sentiment among the adults of the village. Someone was always to blame.

"This life can be hard on the soul," Mal said.

"It wasn't always, though was it? So hard? There was a time when we weren't stuck in the village. When we could go anywhere."

"That's true, but it doesn't mean life was any easier then."

"Is that why his mother did the same thing as him?" Luna's eyes moved to her mother's, watching for some clue as she broached the subject. It was forbidden to speak about anyone who crossed the line. Stylar and his mother were the only two that Luna could remember having done it, and she barely remembered when his mom had done the same thing —walked to the edge of the village and stepped over the silver warning line to die in a flash of black dust.

Mal lowered her head and sighed. "Maybe." She scooted up so that she was sitting beside her daughter and leaned forward to touch her shoulder to Luna's. "We don't speak about things like this because it's not productive. No one knows why anyone does it." She shook her head. "It just ... happens on rare occasion."

"Their blood must have been weak."

"Luna."

"What?"

Mal frowned and then tapped her daughter's leg. "You're probably right, but that isn't something you should say outside of this house. I know you mean no harm by it, but others could take you for being cruel."

"I won't say it to anyone else."

"Good. That's good."

They watched the candle burn on the night table near the door.

"I don't understand why he killed himself like that." Luna leaned her head against her mother's shoulder.

"I don't either, Dove." Mal's voice was soft. "And I hope neither of us ever do."

"Why do you say that?"

"Because if you can fully understand such a mindset— the rationale which would allow you to step over the line and into oblivion—then you are in danger of doing so as well."

LUNA WOKE THE NEXT MORNING TO THE SMELL OF coffee and fresh bread.

She rolled out of bed, threw on her clothes from the day before, and made her way downstairs to the kitchen.

"Good morning." Mal smiled at her daughter over one shoulder and then turned back to crack an egg into the bowl in front of her.

"Good morning." Luna walked to the cupboard and

retrieved a mug. Then she poured herself a cup of coffee, kissed her mother on the cheek, and went to sit at the kitchen table. She took in the breakfast items already sitting on the table and smiled. A full jar of strawberry jam, a plate filled with toasted bread, a small dish of butter, and a pitcher of orange juice. The loaf of bread sat on the cutting board, a long, serrated knife resting beside it. Luna's eyes rested once more on the small dish of yellow butter near the cutting board and her smile widened. "Fresh butter?"

"Mhmm." Mal turned toward the stove and poured blended eggs into a frying pan. The eggs hissed as they made contact with the hot surface and began to cook. "I've got cheese and mushrooms for the omelette as well."

"Wow." Luna spooned a measure of brown sugar into her cup and stirred. She noted the third place setting at the table. "Who's joining us?"

"Your uncle Jack."

Luna groaned as her eyes slid to the calendar on the wall.

Mal laughed.

"I forgot it was the end of the month," Luna grumbled.

"It's the one day of the month you get to miss school." Mal stirred the eggs, scraping them from the bottom of the pan and turning the fluffy, cooked parts onto the top of the rest.

"I like school," Luna took a sip of coffee. "The monthly meetings are boring."

Mal sprinkled chopped mushrooms and cheese into the eggs as she stirred. "But necessary."

"For you and Uncle Jack, maybe."

"For everyone in the village. And definitely for you."

Luna groaned again.

"It's important for you to learn all of this, Dove."

"Why?" She set the cup down and shook her head. "You always say it's because I will run the village someday, but you know that isn't guaranteed. Just because you always win the yearly election doesn't mean I will in a million years when you're ready to step down."

Mal smiled and lifted the pan from the heat. "I'm confident that when the time comes you will win." She used her spatula to guide the cooked eggs into a bowl, then returned the pan to a cold burner and made her way to the table. Setting the bowl in front of her daughter, she leaned over and kissed the top of Luna's head. "Knowing how to do the job will be an advantage for you. No one else gets to sit in on these meetings and learn the ins and outs of how things are run. It'll be one of your selling points for getting the job of mayor." She made her way back to the kitchen counter. "In a million years."

Luna shook her head but knew there was no point in disagreeing. Her mother ran the village and she had intended for Luna to follow in her footsteps since the day she was born. The young woman took a drink of orange juice, her eyes drifting to the fresh loaf of bread once more.

At least she'd get to eat some tasty food to help her through the boredom of the next hour or two.

3

Luna managed to pay attention to the little meeting at her mother's kitchen table for almost the entire first half-hour.

But after the bread and eggs were finished and her belly was filled with two cups of coffee and three glasses of orange juice, the words droning from her mother's mouth and Jack's began to muddle together. It made her want to lay her head on the table and drift off to sleep.

She battled the urge by doodling in her notebook. She drew various sizes of lines and circles—the extent of her artistic ability—and occasionally added a note about crops, or a number to record remaining supplies of one sort or other. Mostly, she was bored because nothing being covered was new. She'd been sitting at the table for month-end meetings as far back as she could remember and had come to the conclusion that running a village was mostly mundane and routine. Important, her mother often reminded her, but boring nonetheless.

"When do we expect the next trader visit?" Mal asked.

The question cut through Luna's mental fog and she

looked up from her notebook, eyes focusing on her uncle with interest.

Jack noted the look and chuckled. "It should be soon. I thought he was supposed to arrive two weeks ago."

"Me, too," Mal frowned. "Should we be worried?"

"Nah." The village's second in command shook his head. "He's likely changed the order of his route a bit. You know he does that every so often to fight the boredom." Jack smiled at Luna.

"Oh, please," Luna said with a laugh. "I don't see how being a trader could ever get boring."

Jack raised one eyebrow. "Is that so?"

"How could it be?"

Mal grunted and shook her head. "You only hear the romantic or dangerous stories. I'll have to remind him to tell you about the boring times as well."

Luna smiled. "I bet he won't have a single boring story to tell."

Mal scowled and Jack laughed.

Luna opened her mouth to say more, but her mother changed the subject with her next question. "How are our reserves of essential supplies holding up?"

Luna turned to a fresh page in her notebook, interested in the answer to this question herself. Trader visits relied on this number more than any other. Essential supplies were things that could not be produced in the village and had to be brought in. She paid attention to this figure because it usually indicated when to expect a visit from him. The lower the essential supply number was, the sooner he would appear. It was a mystery how he always seemed to know when essential things were getting low, but he had always done so without fail.

Luna's pencil scribbled the information down as fast as

she could while Jack recited the list of supplies and current stock levels. When he finished, Luna's eyes danced over the figures and she frowned.

"What do you see, Dove?" her mother asked.

Luna looked up from the notebook, her gaze meeting Jack's and then sliding to her mother. "Many of the quantities are below normal levels."

"You're right. Very good." Mal smiled, showing pleasure at her daughter's conclusion. "How do you think we should we handle this?"

"Um." Luna looked back to the list and made checkmarks beside half a dozen items. Then she slid her list across the table for the two adults to see. "We should ration these items immediately."

"Correct," Jack agreed.

"Is this a test?" Luna asked the man. From time to time, the two would provide inaccurate data to see how their student would handle the situation. This suddenly felt like that sort of thing.

"No," Jack shook his head. "The numbers are really this low."

"Then ..." she frowned.

"It's okay, Luna," her mother said. "The village isn't in any danger without a trader visit yet. This is why we monitor the levels of our supplies as often as we do."

"Yes, but if he doesn't return—"

"He always comes back, dear." Mal smiled. "It's only the time between visits that varies every once in a rare while. The same thing happened ..." she frowned and looked at Jack. "Was it two years ago?"

Jack nodded.

"I remember," Luna said and looked at the numbers in

her notebook. "But we didn't get this low on supplies then. Especially the charging crystals."

Mal pursed her lips and then reached out and touched her daughter's arm. "There's no need to be worried."

Luna searched her mother's eyes and then Jack's. "Okay, if you say so."

"Next item of business," Jack said. "We have two cows ready to give birth at the same time. That's going to be a bit tricky, but I think if we ask—"

Luna continued to listen as the meeting went on, but the concern that she'd kept to herself tumbled around in her head.

What if something bad happened and he isn't coming back... ever?

4

"I think you're worrying over nothing." Gage tossed a pebble into the air and watched it disappear from sight.

"Huh?" Luna's attention drifted back to her friend as she turned her eyes away from the waving grass, trees and hills that lay in the far distance beyond the line, only faintly visible from where they were sitting.

"The trader." Gage plucked another pebble from the ground and flicked it through the air.

"Oh. Yeah, I'm sure you're right."

"I hope he brings some good stuff." Gage leaned close and nudged her with his shoulder. "I've been saving up to buy my best friend a birthday present."

Luna smiled. "You don't have to do that. I don't need anything."

The boy laughed. "What makes you think I was talkin' about you?"

Luna shook her head. The two had been best friends their whole lives. Some said it was because they were the only two of the same age and they had no choice in the matter, but neither saw it that way.

The village population was three hundred and twenty-six, including forty-six children under the age of sixteen. Luna and Gage were older than the rest by at least five years and, while it was true there was a short time when they'd had no other playmates, they never seemed to tire of each other and had remained fast friends over the years.

"What sort of things do you hope he'll bring?" Luna picked up a stone and tossed it at the cliff face.

The boy laughed. "Nice try."

She frowned. "What?"

"You want to know what I'm thinking of buying you."

"No I don't."

Gage laughed again. "Don't worry, I know what you like. We'll just wait and see what he brings this time round. I'm sure there will be one or two things that will work."

"I guess I should do the same."

"Why?"

"For your present."

Gage shook his head. "My birthday isn't for another three months."

"Yeah." She shrugged and ran her fingers through the dirt. "But who knows when he'll be back? He's pretty late this time around ..."

"Stop worrying. He'll be here any day now."

Luna didn't respond.

Gage frowned. "Did you learn something in the monthly meeting with your mom and Uncle Jack to think he won't show up soon?"

"No." Luna shook her head. "They're saying the same thing you are. That he's just a bit late, and there's likely nothing wrong."

"Good." He nodded and then frowned. "Wait a

minute." He leaned toward her and lowered his voice. "You didn't *see* him in trouble, did you?"

"Gage!" she hissed, looking left and then right. "You're not supposed to mention that in public."

"There's no one around," he whispered. "I'm not stupid."

"I know, but there are times when you're careless."

He grinned. "No one would believe if they heard, anyway."

"Maybe." She shrugged, her temper cooling now that she was more certain no one else had heard Gage mention her visions.

"So?" he prompted. "Did you?"

"No." She rolled her eyes. "I haven't seen him in trouble."

"Good." Gage picked up another pebble and cocked his arm back to throw. Then he paused and nudged her with his shoulder once more. "Didn't happen to see what gift I was gonna get for my birthday, did you?"

Luna laughed and knocked the stone out of his hand.

5

Most of Luna's visions came to her as dreams.

Three days before her sixteenth birthday, she lay in bed, tossing and turning for hours. Frustrated, she had found herself staring at the ceiling, counting pigs in hopes of boring herself to sleep, when a loud boom sounded from downstairs.

Luna froze, her ears straining to detect any other noises. A few breaths later, there was another loud boom, this time so forceful that it made the bed frame shake beneath her.

She waited, hoping to hear her mother getting out of bed to investigate, but there were no telltale sounds of floorboards creaking in her mother's room to indicate such a thing was happening. She remained still, wishing that whatever was banging at the house would go away.

BOOM!

A small cry escaped from her lips. Luna sat up in bed, ears straining.

A shadow appeared beneath the crack at the bottom of the door, blocking the faint line of light coming from the hallway. Luna held her breath, eyes wide, still as a statue.

A light, rapid scratching noise sounded from the hallway floor. Luna raised her hand to her mouth and pressed tightly to resist the urge to scream. The skittering sound continued. She prayed for someone to come and save her before whatever was in the hallway made its way in.

The noise stopped as suddenly as it had started. A second passed. Then ten.

Light appeared under the doorway once more as the shadow moved away.

Luna lowered her hand and frowned as it brushed against something at her side. Looking down, her confusion grew as she noticed that she was standing and no longer wearing her pyjamas. Instead, she was dressed in matching dark brown pants and shirt, and there was a black gun in a holster strapped to her belt.

"I'm dreaming," she mumbled and cast a quick glance at her bed, nodding in confirmation. It was empty of covers and dusty, as if it hadn't been slept in for years.

"This is a dream." She took a deep breath, then drew the pistol and moved toward the door.

Luna opened it with care, cracking it open a bit at first and then wider when nothing happened. She stepped into the hallway, gun pointed in front of her with the confidence of someone who had done it countless times before. A small part of her marvelled at this sense of familiarity, but not the part of her that was in control.

She made her way down the hallway, checking door-ways and rooms along the way for signs of an intruder. Finding none, she moved downstairs, taking note of the dust and disuse. It was obviously her house, but it looked as though it had been abandoned long ago. Part of her wondered how long it been empty and why it had become so.

BOOM!

Luna swivelled, no longer frightened but prepared to act. She moved to the front door and threw it open, gun aimed and eyes scanning for a target.

Seeing no one, she made her way to the barn. The consciousness that was dreaming marvelled at how calm and certain she now seemed. She caught a glimpse of herself as she passed a window and barely recognized the person in the reflection.

I'm older, she thought. *Taller. A woman. More serious.*

Luna was halfway to the barn when there was another boom. She nodded, guessing that whatever was making the racket was near the back of the barn, near where the horse stall used to be.

A dozen steps later, she was at the front door of the barn, which was standing open far enough to step through. Her eyes flicked to the hammer of her gun, verifying that it was cocked and ready to fire. Then she stepped into the barn, weapon extended and eyes searching.

The creature stared at her from across the barn. It had bare, sinewy arms and legs that were longer than a human's. Its torso was bare as well, naked except for what looked like dirty shorts. The beast was on all fours, its hips jutting into the air, forcing its head close to the ground. Dirty, matted hair hung from it like thin ropes. Its eyes were narrow but emitted a luminescent green light.

The dreaming part of her knew that grown-up Luna was trying to squeeze the trigger, to unload everything she had into the creature while she still had the advantage of surprise. But the girl watching through the woman's eyes was somehow exerting control over the body, preventing the shots from being fired as she considered the beast in front of her.

There was something familiar about it, although she could not put her finger on exactly what ...

The creature threw back its head and let loose a high-pitched shriek, a wet, raspy wail that sounded as if it was torn from the creature rather than voiced. Then it began to close the distance between them, bounding forward on all fours with a speed that surprised her. There was fifty or sixty feet between them, but the creature was halfway to her after only three great strides.

She stepped back, raised the gun and took aim. The beast kept coming, gasping and panting, its eyes filled with anger or hate and locked on her with an iron focus.

Ten feet away now, the man-thing leapt into the air, arms stretched forward and ragged, clutching nails extended. It sailed toward her, mouth open as it emitted a high-pitched scream of pure hatred reflected in the thing's eerie, glowing eyes.

No longer able to control the body she found herself in, dreaming Luna could only watch as the gun fired in rapid succession, red explosions punching into flesh as the bullets hit their mark. Luna took one giant step backward and emptied the last of her shots into the attacking monstrosity.

The screaming stopped as abruptly as it had begun. Two rapid clicks filled the night air as Luna pulled the trigger twice more for good measure on the emptied gun. A heartbeat later, there was a dull thud and the creature fell dead to the ground in front of her.

Luna stared down at it for a long moment. Then she stepped forward, flipped it over with her foot, and knelt close to get a better look at its face.

No longer filled with rage and hatred, the beast looked peaceful in death.

Familiar, the dreamer thought.

And then recognition hit her like a hammer strike between the eyes.

"No!" LUNA SCREAMED, SITTING UP IN BED AND panting as she looked around her room. Then she lay down, rolled onto her side, buried her head in her pillow and wept.

THE FLOORBOARDS CREAKED DOWN THE HALL. THE door to Luna's room opened and Mal entered, making her way to the edge of the bed to lay a comforting hand against her daughter's back.

"It's okay," Mal whispered. "It was just a dream. You're safe, Dove. Nothing is gonna hurt you."

Luna sat up and Mal joined her on the bed. The two hugged, Luna crying as her mother rocked her gently back and forth.

It took a few minutes for Luna to regain her composure. When she did, the young woman sat up and wiped her eyes with the back of her hand. "I'm sorry," she said.

"There's nothing to be sorry about. You had a bad dream. And it sounds like it was a bad one?"

"Yes." Luna nodded, wiping at her face again. "It was."

"Do you want to sleep in bed with me for the rest of the night?"

Luna's lips pursed and she nodded as fresh tears began to flow.

Mal stood, wrapped her arms around her girl, and led her to bed. She tucked Luna in on one side, then slid into the other. Her hand reached out and stroked her daughter's hair.

"I'm here, Baby," Mal whispered.

Luna nodded and stared at the wall.

Twenty minutes later, Luna was finally able to close her eyes and sleep. As she drifted off, the last image in her mind was of the face of the beast that had attacked her in the dream. The creature she'd been forced to kill before it could end her life.

The beast's face was that of her best friend, Gage.

6

For a teenager living in the village, day-to-day life was both busy and boring.

Every morning, Luna woke to the sound of an alarm and spent the first hour or so doing household chores that included feeding and watering the cows, horse, sheep, pigs, and chickens. Twice a month, she would thoroughly clean out every animal's stall, but that meant doing one or two stalls every few days. She hated mucking the stalls.

When morning chores were finished, she almost always met up with Gage—either at his house or hers, depending on the day—for breakfast.

After breakfast, they walked together into the village, where they attended school for the next six hours. At 3 p.m., school let out and the children dispersed through the village, to help out wherever their assistance was required. This was most often decided by their parents and the various village professionals.

Children were considered the most crucial part of the village, the key to the future and continued prosperity. For that reason, many adults went out of their way to spend time with the children whenever possible, taking every opportunity to teach and nurture them in the hope that one or two would show interest and aptitude for their particular specialty and ask to apprentice with them as they came of age. Everyone knew that, without those skills successfully being passed to the next generation, the village could not endure.

And enduring was the primary goal of this and every other village.

There were some days that helping the adults with their chores required children to work in pairs. When that happened, Luna and Gage made an effort to be assigned together. Helping the tower technicians was always a task for more than one kid, and the day after her latest nightmare, the friends were slated to assist Thomas on one of the towers.

LUNA SWUNG HER LEGS OVER THE STONE LEDGE AND watched fat white clouds float past across the blue sky above them. Every so often, she would glance at Gage for a few seconds and then look back up at the sky.

Gage sat beside his friend, back straight and legs crossed, his eyes closed. His brows were furrowed in concentration, lips pressed together to form a thin line.

Finally he made a loud huffing noise and opened his eyes, shaking his head. "I can't do it."

Luna smiled. "Try harder."

Gage laughed. "I am. I have." He shook his head again. "I'm sorry. I know it's so obvious to you, but I just can't hear it."

She shrugged. "Well, I haven't given up hope that it'll happen. Maybe it will after your birthday."

Gage leaned back and rested his hands in the dirt. "I appreciate you trying, Lune, honestly I do. But I don't think I was born to be a technician like you."

"I wasn't born to be a technician, either." She snorted. "You know that."

She turned her head toward the tall metal tower at the bottom of the hill they were sitting on. It rose high into the sky, a great crisscross of interlaced grey metal bars. It was a familiar structure to all in the village, and it looked identical to the dozens of others that circled the perimeter of their village. Up close, it was beast of a structure, with four wide, flat, metal feet that were bolted into a great square slab of solid white concrete. The tower extended hundreds of feet into the air, and at its top were six round, flat, white dishes. The dishes were positioned diagonally to one another, each facing outward in a different direction.

Gage might not be able to hear the sounds coming from the tower, but Luna certainly could, even from where they sat right now. "It's a slight humming sound," she said. "When I heard it for the first time it was real faint, almost like a background buzz that disappears when you try to focus on it. It took me some practice to be able to pick up on it." She frowned at him. "Are you sure you don't hear anything?"

He laughed again. "I'm sure. You've been dragging me all over the fringes of the village whenever you detect that a tower is humming. I sit and do my best to hear it, but never do. We've been doing this for years now." He stood and brushed his hands against the faded denim fabric of his shorts. "The towers don't talk to me like they do you."

She shook her head. "Well, that sucks."

"Heyo, you two." A voice called out from behind them and the pair turned to see a man approaching.

Both smiled and raised their hands in greeting.

"Heyo, Thomas," Gage shouted back. Luna stood and dusted herself off as the tower technician approached. Thomas was a middle-aged man with a bushy head of black hair that always appeared dishevelled. His blue eyes glittered with a tinge of amusement as he strolled towards them at a slow but steady pace, the toolkit of his trade swinging rhythmically from a wide leather strap that hung over his shoulder and tapped against his hip with each step. A canvas harness with dull metal clips and a single iron ring was slung over his other shoulder. He stopped beside the two friends and dipped his shoulder, letting the toolbox slide to the ground with a gentle thud.

He turned to Gage, eyebrows rising. "Did you hear it this time, pal?"

Gage shook his head from side to side. "I didn't."

"Aw, I'm sorry to hear that, lad." He turned to Luna and smiled. "Looks like you might have to leave your buddy behind when you apply to technician school, Luna."

Luna laughed. "There's still time. His birthday isn't for another couple of months."

"But yours is in a few days." Thomas squinted as he looked up at the tower. "It's a shame they made you wait this long, if you ask me. You could've been finished training if they'd let you apply when you first felt the calling instead of waiting until now." He glanced sideways at Gage. "Although it did give you a chance to catch up, didn't it?"

Luna laughed. "You know the rule. Kids can't apprentice until they turn sixteen and choose their profession."

"Yeah, well." Thomas's eyes returned to hers and he winked. "I think the Council should've made an exception for you."

"There are a lot of good options ..." Luna pretended to

be interested in the tower. "Maybe I won't choose to become a tower technician."

"What? Why not?"

"I don't know." She shrugged. "I might be afraid of heights."

Laughter. "I just saw you sitting on the edge of a cliff with your legs swinging like it was nothing."

Luna turned back to face him and smiled. "That's different than climbing a tower. I won't know how I'll deal with that until I get a chance to try it, right?"

Thomas laughed again. "You've climbed plenty of towers."

"Sure." Her grin widened. "But never to the top."

The technician's smile faded. He considered the tower, then her. Then he shrugged. "Okay." He picked up his toolkit and started walking toward the path that led to the base of the tower.

Luna's jaw dropped and she turned to look at her friend. Gage's eyes were wide, a smile on his face as he nodded.

"Really?" she called after Thomas.

"Sure, why not? You've more than earned a trip to the top. If that'll help you decide to apprentice with us, then I'll bend the rules." He cast a look at her over his shoulder and winked. "But only 'cause you're special."

Luna laughed and trotted after the technician, with Gage following close on her heels.

7

WHEN THEY REACHED THE BASE OF THE TOWER, Thomas set his toolbox down and let the harness fall from his shoulder onto the ground.

Luna's eyes took note, and she laughed. "There are two harnesses."

"Of course there are." Thomas grinned. "Like I said, I had a suspicion I might need to sweeten the pot in order to get you to consider choosing the tower technicians."

Luna giggled and clapped her hands with excitement. She had proven herself capable to many, and quite a few of the profession elders had indicated they would be thrilled should she choose them.

Thomas handed a harness to Luna, and she slid it over her shoulders with ease.

The technician watched her prepare for the climb while he donned his own harness, but spoke to Gage. "Wanna try again, Gage? Sometimes you need to be closer to pick up on it."

Luna met her friend's eyes and nodded, with an encouraging smile.

"Okay," Gage sighed and closed his eyes. Thomas looked at Luna and raised an eyebrow.

She shrugged her shoulders and waited.

After thirty seconds, Gage opened his eyes. "Nope."

"That's okay, lad." Thomas clapped the boy on the shoulder. "If everyone could hear it, us techs wouldn't be as special as we are."

"And you wouldn't get some of those village perks that no one else seems to enjoy," Luna said.

"Exactly." The tech smiled. "And be sure to keep those perks in mind while deciding which profession you will choose, young lady."

She grinned for a few seconds and then frowned as a thought occurred to her. "Couldn't Gage be a technician anyway? He's taken to almost all of the other duties that you're responsible for. Does he really need to be able to hear the towers if someone else is able to do it for him?"

"Oh, dear girl." Thomas's head shook from side to side. "It's crucial that a tech be able to hear and understand the language of the towers. If even one message was heard too late, or even missed altogether ..."

"The village could be in trouble," Luna repeated the words she had heard more than once from every technician she'd ever spent time with.

"Exactly so." Thomas reached into his pocket and withdrew a large metal key, which he used to unlock the gate around the tower's base. He stepped through, waited for the friends to follow him in, and then closed the door and re-locked it from the inside.

Luna reached for one of the cables that ran from the top of the tower to the ground and slipped a metal clasp over it. Thomas did the same and then jutted his chin toward Gage. "I'm sorry, man, but if you can't hear the towers speak then you can't do the job. I wouldn't worry too much, though." Thomas closed the clasp and screwed it shut with his thumb and forefinger. Then he turned toward Luna, inspected hers, and gave her a thumbs-up. "If you follow in the footsteps of your family, you'll have a very good job in the village."

"And you might even get to be chief of security someday," Luna smiled at her friend. "Like your dad is now."

Gage rolled his eyes but smiled back.

"And don't forget that being accepted into technician training is only the first of many steps along the path." Thomas ruffled her hair and took a step toward the tower ladder. "As it stands right now, you can only hear *some* of the tower signals. Not all of them."

Luna frowned. "You mean it's possible I could fail the training too?"

"Indeed it is."

"That would be terrible," Luna moaned.

It was Gage's turn to laugh. "Oh, yes. What a horrible fate it would be to follow in *your* family's footsteps, Mayor Luna."

Luna laughed, and so did Gage.

"Come on." Thomas was smiling. "Let's head up there and see what's wrong, shall we? It'll be dark in a couple hours. I'd like to be on the ground before then."

8

Luna felt her smile growing with each step she took up the tower ladder.

She glanced down, guessing that they were a hundred feet off the ground at this point.

"A quarter of the way up," Thomas called down from his place a few rungs above.

Luna smiled and nodded, pleased that her guess had been right.

The grey metal rungs of the ladder were smooth and cold to the touch. They were always kept clean and free of obstruction; safety and care were both paramount concerns for the tower technicians in every aspect of their work. This was for both the well-being of the techs and to ensure the proper functioning of the towers, upon which the entire village's existence depended.

Luna noticed that the square base of the steel-lattice tower looked smaller from this height, but it was still broad and wide compared to towers that were visible far away from the village at different spots. Not all villages were surrounded by square towers, like her home, even though these were the most secure and sturdy of all the types. Tower height also varied among villages, according to the instructors, ranging from two hundred to four hundred feet. Luna grinned as she tilted her head back and glanced toward the peak, glad that the towers protecting her village were the tallest, all four-hundred-footers. Aside from the extra protection they provided, it would give her more climbing time today.

Slowly, methodically, she climbed the ladder a few rungs behind Thomas. Every ten or twelve rungs, she would see a safety clip attached to her rung. She would stop, hook that one to her safety clip, and then unhook and allow Thomas to pull the one she had been using up to where he was. When the other rung was secure, Thomas would tug lightly and she would resume her climb behind him.

They weren't moving very fast; a snail's crawl compared with the speed at which technicians normally made the ascent. Luna didn't feel bad about it, though. She knew that full-fledged techs learned advanced climbing techniques and employed a floating harness system that moved upward without needing to be unhooked and reattached like hers did. That, along with years of practice, allowed them to climb up and down much faster. Veteran tower techs had agility and speed so impressive that it was common for nearby children and adults to stop whatever they were doing to watch a tech make the climb.

Slow and unimpressive though it might look to Gage on the ground below, Luna was thrilled with the experience and found it to be both fast enough and exhilarating. She laughed as she reached Thomas, who was waiting for her on the two-hundred-foot platform.

"Well, we're halfway there." He was grinning, too. "What do you think so far?"

Luna stepped past him, gripping a piece of steel framing for support as she looked out at the land beyond and below. "This is the highest I've ever climbed."

"Looks pretty awesome from up here, wouldn't you say?"

"Oh, yes." Luna nodded, her eyes scanning the ground and then moving out toward the horizon. "There is so much land out there."

"Aye."

Luna's gaze focused on a dark grouping of trees. "Which forest is that?"

Thomas laughed. "You tell me. It's important for a tech to know such things."

Luna frowned, remembering which tower they were standing on and what her study of maps might have taught her about the landscape in this direction. After a few seconds, she shook her head. "Sorry."

"That's okay. This is all a bit exciting for you, probably."

Laughter. "Yeah, probably."

"It's Laynard's woods."

"Right." Luna nodded. Her eyes moved to the left of the woods and scanned the horizon. "Another village is in that direction," she pointed. "Right?"

"Very good."

"I thought we'd be able to see it from up here. Or at least its towers."

Thomas shook his head. "At the top of the tower we can see about 24 miles to the horizon. There are no villages that close."

"What is the closest village?"

"That's something you likely have a better idea of than me."

TERRY SCHOTT

Luna frowned. "Most people don't seem to care about things like that. I thought you would."

"Why?" Thomas sat on the platform and let his feet dangle. "It's not like we will ever visit one."

"I know, but ..."

"Life gets too busy to worry about things that will never matter, kiddo." The technician sat down and patted the thick steel plate beside him. Careful to have one hand always gripping a piece of steel for support, she made her way to him and lowered herself to a cross-legged sitting position.

They sat quietly for a few minutes. Thomas was the one to break the silence. "I can tell you a lot, but most stuff I know revolves around my job as a tech and the goings-on of the village. Beyond that ..." he spread his hands. "I leave the dreams and fantasy to people who have time and the imagination for such things." He grinned. "Like you."

The two stared at the world beyond for another few minutes, then Thomas stood and held a hand out to Luna. She took it and got to her feet.

"Ready to keep going?" he asked.

Luna nodded.

9

Luna stepped onto the platform at the top of the tower, held both arms out to her sides, and turned slowly to look at the world from an altitude that most would never reach.

This was the most of her world that she had ever observed at once, and, although Thomas was right and there were no villages to be seen, it was still the most incredible sight she had ever experienced. On the ground, there had been a slight breeze, but up here it was a medium-strength wind; not powerful enough to blow her off her feet, but strong and persistent enough to make her bend at the knees and take care with each step.

She looked at Thomas and smiled. He was leaning against a large metal strut, his posture relaxed and body language at ease. It was obvious the man felt at home up here, where only a handful of people were allowed to tread.

After a while, the wonder of seeing everything look smaller than it normally did faded somewhat. Luna took a step closer to Thomas, raising her voice so that she could be heard over the wind. "What do we do now?"

Thomas pointed toward a zig-zagging set of narrow metal steps that led even higher. He moved toward them, one eye on Luna to make sure she didn't stumble or lose her footing. Then he led the way up twenty-two narrow steps to a smaller platform, which rested an arm's length away beneath the great white dishes.

"They're huge." Luna looked up at the closest one, eyes wide.

"Bigger up close, that's for sure." Thomas set his toolbox down and knelt beside it.

Luna tilted her head, eyes narrowing.

Thomas flipped open the lid of his toolkit and then looked at her again, frowning as he noted her expression. "What is it?"

"I hear a different sound than before."

"Good," the technician smiled. "Describe it to me."

Luna listened for another few seconds and then shook her head. "It's too complex to describe."

"Sing it to me."

She smiled, then loudly hummed a pattern of beeps, hisses, and finally a long sigh. She repeated the sequence four times, careful to match the cadence of the sounds that she was hearing. She knew that the speed and beat of a signal were as important as the actual tones and noises themselves.

"Wow." Thomas laughed, beaming as he clapped his hands together. "Very good, Luna. That's an advanced signal. Many don't hear this one until they've spent months being in close proximity to the dishes."

Luna smiled. "What's it mean?"

Thomas shrugged. "It can mean a lot of things, depending on what other sounds come before and after, and also how long the pattern of each lasts during the sequence."

"Oh." Luna frowned.

"Aatun only makes a few dozen patterned sound sequences, but they form a very complex language."

"Is it Aatun right now?" Luna frowned. "Or the individual tower?"

Thomas's smile widened. "That's an excellent question. We refer to each tower as Deandria, and the entire network as Aatun. The individual brothers—we refer to each of them by the same name, Deandria—all sing together to create the entity known as Aatun, or the mother. No one knows for sure how much comes from the single towers versus the total collective. We refer to the overall message as always coming from Aatun, though. To keep things simple."

Luna grinned. "It doesn't sound simple."

"It will after a few months."

Luna laughed and then reached out, her hand extending toward and stopping a few inches from the white dish's surface.

"Go ahead," Thomas said. "You're grounded, which makes it safe to touch."

"Grounded?" Luna frowned and shook her head. "We're nowhere near the ground."

Thomas laughed and tapped the metal platform they were standing on. "Any energy from the dish will harmlessly pass through your body and into the metal we are standing on. From there, it will rush all the way to the ground below."

"Through the metal of the tower?"

"That's right. If your feet weren't on the metal, then it wouldn't be safe to touch the dish."

"Why?"

"Because any energy from the dish would enter you and be stuck inside your body."

"And that would hurt?"

"It sure would."

"Grounded," Luna repeated the word and nodded. "I think I understand."

"You'll learn more about that, too. As you train."

She grinned and Thomas winked before grinning back, reminding her that the main purpose of this climb was to entice her to join the technicians.

Luna relaxed her body and reached for the dish. Her fingertips made contact with the cold, smooth surface and she gasped, eyes widening as the world around her disappeared in a powerful flood of white light.

Sound rushed into her like the leading edge of a wave, crashing with tremendous force as it moved through her body. As it did, bursts of colour blossomed across her eyelids; every colour she could imagine and many that she'd never dreamed of appeared in a flashing symphony, pulsing and ebbing with an intensity that matched the rhythm of countless clicks, beeps, whistles and sing-song tones that seemed to exist both everywhere and no place at once. She opened her eyes and found herself floating, suspended in some sort of magical landscape of wonder.

Luna had no idea how long she bobbed and moved along like this, but eventually a single sound rose above the others. She turned—not sure if she was actually doing so in real life or only in her mind. A great bird levitated directly in front of her with its wings spread wide. The creature was blue—the deepest of cobalt and indigo shades—with great pearl-coloured eyes and a yellow-orange curved beak.

Luna reached out and touched the bird's wing as she looked directly into the gaze of the magnificent being. She felt amusement, joy, and love flow from the bird into her own body. A slow stream of electric liquid began to move from the bird and into her body through the contact, a trickle that grew into a powerful rush as it coursed through every inch of her body. She opened her mouth and laughed.

And then ...

"WHOAH!"

She recognized Thomas's voice calling out and frowned as the world of colour and sound shimmered and then faded away. She blinked and saw the outline of Thomas standing over her, the sky and tower forming a strange sort of halo behind him.

"Are you okay?" he asked.

"Yeah," her voice sounded raspy to her ears. "I'm fine. Great, actually."

"Are you dizzy?"

"I don't think so." She sat up. Thomas's hand remained on her shoulder, his eyes full of concern. "What happened?" she asked.

The technician shook his head. "I don't know. You touched the dish and then right away pitched straight back onto the platform as if you'd been hit with a big jolt of electricity." His eyes narrowed. "Were you?"

"No ..."

"Is your skin tingly? Any burning sensations, or do you feel like you're on fire from the inside out?"

Luna frowned. "That can happen?"

"Are you feeling anything like what I just described, Luna?"

"No."

He stared at her, eyes searching hers as the seconds

went by. Finally, he stood, one hand still gripping her shoulder. "Okay, then. Let's see if you can stand."

Luna rose to her feet and reached for the closest piece of metal framework.

"How ya feel?"

"I think I'm good."

"Dizzy?"

"Nope."

"Feel like throwing up?"

Luna frowned. "You're scaring me, Thomas."

He scowled and opened his mouth, but she answered him before could say anything else. "No. None of those horrible things are happening inside me. I really think I'm fine."

Thomas bent down and retrieved a thermos from his toolbox. He unscrewed the cap and poured a bit of yellow liquid into the lid and held it toward her. "Drink this, just in case you need a bit of sugar."

Luna accepted the lid and downed the lemonade in one pull. She handed him the lid back and he screwed it back into place.

"There were so many colours and sounds," she said.

"What?" Thomas frowned. "When?"

"When I touched the dish."

His eyes narrowed, and then he pointed to the platform beside the toolbox. "Come sit over here, Luna."

The girl did as instructed. He watched her for another few seconds and then knelt down to retrieve a tool from his box. His gaze met hers, and he leaned close so that she could hear him clearly over the wind. "You've had enough excitement for today, I think. Sit tight while I adjust the dish. It's a quick fix and I'll have it done in no time. Then we can head back down, okay?"

"Were there not supposed to be colours and sounds, Thomas?"

He frowned and then shook his head. "I have absolutely no clue what you're going on about. There aren't any colours to see up here, young lady." His brows furrowed and he bit the bottom of his lip—a sign that he was concerned. "I'm sure you're fine. Just sit tight and we'll get back to the ground before you know it."

10

"How is she?"

Mal felt sympathy for the young man standing on the doorstep, his face pale and haggard with worry.

"She's good. Sleeping." Mal stepped back and motioned him into the house. "Come inside. We can talk for a bit, then I'll let you go check on her."

Gage pursed his lips, nodded and stepped through the front door, moving to take a seat at the square wooden table.

Mal walked to the stove that was set in one corner of the room which served as kitchen, dining area, and living room. "I'll make some coffee and find a snack."

"Thanks," he said. "I'm sorta wired up on coffee already."

She turned to face him. "Does that mean you don't want one?"

"Nah, I'd still have another, I guess." He shrugged and then grinned. "And I'll never turn down a snack."

Mal chuckled and set the kettle on top of the flaming burner. Then she lifted the corner of a tea towel, cut a generous piece from the loaf of cinnamon bread, and placed it on a plate.

"Has she been sleeping much?" Gage asked.

"Not really." Mal slipped a dollop of butter onto the side of the plate for the bread. "She was a bit dizzy, though, and the rest has helped with that."

"Good."

Neither spoke while Mal finished making the coffee and poured two cups. She brought it all to the table and sat across from him. Then she raised her cup to her lips and blew lightly across the surface before taking a drink.

Gage used a dull knife to slather butter across the surface of the cinnamon bread. He took a bite and smiled, then reached for his cup of coffee and slurped. "Thomas said she saw something up there."

"Mhmm." Mal nodded.

"A blue bird."

Mal raised one eyebrow but said nothing.

"That's strange." He frowned. "Right?"

Mal considered him for a second and then shrugged. "Climbing the tower can be an awesome thing."

Gage shuddered. "That's not the word I'd use to describe it."

"No?"

The young man shook his head. "Terrifying sounds more accurate."

Mal smiled. "You're not afraid of heights are you?"

"No." He frowned, then shrugged. "I mean, standing on the hills, climbing houses, and going a short way up the towers hasn't bothered me. But the thought of going up as high as they did today ..." His frown deepened and then he shook his head. "I'd give it a go, but something tells me it's not for me."

"Extreme heights certainly aren't for everyone. There's no shame in knowing your limitations. Quite the opposite, in fact."

"I will try," Gage said. "If they let me."

Mal heard the determination in his voice and smiled. "You want to be a technician that badly?"

"No. Maybe. I don't know." He took another bite of cinnamon bread and stared at his plate.

Mal knew the truth of the matter. She'd known for years that the boy was smitten by Luna and would follow her wherever the girl ventured. Mal also knew that things would soon progress to the next level of intimacy, if they hadn't already. Taking another sip of coffee, she sighed, realizing that the next stage of parenting was soon to begin, and it would be filled with learning opportunities for all of them. "I don't think you need to worry about living in the top of towers."

"No?" He looked up. "What makes you say that?"

"Luna isn't going to become a technician."

"Really?" His cheeks flushed pink and he cleared his throat. "Thomas said she shows promise and that the technicians are interested in her joining them."

"Other groups want her as well."

"Sure, but ..."

Mal raised one eyebrow. "Do you think she will want to become a tower tech?"

"Well, when we talk about possible futures, being a tech seems to interest her most."

"It is one of the most interesting roles in the entire village. But that excitement can fade quickly."

"What do you mean?" Gage took another bite of bread and chewed.

"Climb those towers once, a dozen, even twenty or thirty times, and it's pretty fun. But what about after years have gone by? The whole experience can become mundane. And taxing on the body."

"I suppose." Gage didn't sound convinced.

"And in the middle of winter?" Mal shook her head. "It's horrible cold up there."

"You're right."

Mal watched him from the corner of her eye as she listed the same arguments to him that she'd shared with her daughter numerous times. Luna had always shrugged away the common-sense advice from her mother, but maybe if she began hearing it from Gage she would consider it more seriously.

"All of that makes sense," Gage agreed. "But if she sees blue birds and the towers talk to her ..." he shrugged. "Maybe those sorts of things make the climb worth it."

"I suppose it does." Mal furrowed her brows and stared at her coffee.

"You don't think she really saw a blue bird up there, do you?"

Mal met the young man's eyes. "I believe she thinks that she saw them."

"Them? I thought it was only one?"

Mal took another sip.

"Has anyone else ever had visions like that?" Gage asked.

"Not that I know of."

Gage frowned. Something in the village leader's tone didn't ring true. "It was a hallucination of some sort, right?"

"It had to have been."

"What would cause it?"

She pursed her lips and shook her head. "I don't know."

Gage nodded and took another sip of coffee, unaware that Mal did know what might have caused it, and that it worried her deeply.

11

"Hey there. How ya doing?"

Luna opened her eyes and smiled as Gage stepped onto the front porch. She was reclining on an outdoor chair with a blanket over her legs. Yawning loudly, she stretched her arms above her head before replying. "I'm fine, thanks. What time is it?"

"A little bit after five." Gage plopped onto the chair beside her.

"You should be home for dinner." Luna frowned. "What are you doing here?"

"Thought I'd come over and help your mom with the chores."

"Aren't you a sweetie?"

He laughed. "Sweeter than Mal's lazy daughter, who seems to have spent the day laying around doing nothing productive, that's for sure."

"Please." Luna snorted. "I did my chores."

"You did?"

"Of course."

"Then you're feeling a lot better?"

"Right as rain. Perfectly fine."

"I'm ..." The rest of the sentence caught in his throat and the best he could manage was to reach out and touch her knee. The contact made her smile, and he did too.

"Don't worry about me, Gage. I was only a little bit dizzy. Mom and Thomas confined me to rest just in case there was anything they couldn't see. But there wasn't. As of tomorrow morning, everything will be back to normal. Chores, school, the whole boring routine."

"Not all of it'll be boring." Gage leaned back in his chair and laced the fingers of his hands together behind his head. "You turn sixteen and become an adult."

"I turn sixteen." She shook her head. "Not sure I'm keen on becoming an adult."

Gage laughed. "Thankfully there are enough adults in the village who show us grownups can still have fun and act young."

"That is a relief."

Gage frowned.

"What's the matter?" Luna asked.

His shoulders shrugged and he looked down at his feet. "The trader hasn't arrived yet. I won't have a gift for you until then, and who knows when that will happen."

Luna made a *tsk* sound and her friend looked up with a frown. "It's a shame you didn't care enough about me to buy something last time he was here..."

Gage's brows furrowed and he opened his mouth to say something but then shut it and shrugged. "You're right." The corners of his lips twitched into a smile. "I wasn't sure how long-term the friendship would be, though. Why buy a gift that far ahead if we ended up being mortal enemies before the day arrived?"

A laugh of genuine amusement burst from Luna. Gage's smile widened and he joined in as her laughter continued.

When the moment passed, Gage shook his head. "I really do apologize. The only reason I waited so long was because I wanted the time to earn as much as I could. So your present would be as good as possible."

Luna dipped her chin and looked at him from hooded eyes. "Silly man. The money you spend isn't important. It's the thought that counts."

Gage blushed. No one but Luna referred to him as a man yet, and the sentiment meant something. "I feel the same."

"Good." Luna smirked. "Hold onto that feeling, because the odds are good I'll do something like buy you candy and not be able to resist eating it all before your day arrives."

Gage laughed. "I can picture it now. You hand me a fancy box filled with empty wrappers because you ate all the treats."

"That does sound like me, doesn't it?"

Gage raised one eyebrow and then joined Luna as she broke into laughter at the thought.

12

On the morning of her sixteenth birthday, Luna woke to the aromas of cooking bacon, fresh bread, and the sweet scent of pancakes.

With a grin and exclamation of delight, she jumped out of bed, got dressed, and skipped lightly down the stairs and into the kitchen.

"And there she is." Mal turned toward her daughter, a big smile on her face as she set the glass bowl of pancake batter onto the counter. "My baby girl, suddenly a grown woman."

Luna shook her head but smiled and walked into her mother's outstretched arms to accept a hug. Mal held her tight and for longer than Luna was used to.

"Come on, Mom." Luna giggled but did not break away as she held her mother back just as tight. "It feels like you're gonna try and hug me all day long."

"I'll let you go in a second." Mal spoke the words softly, her mouth close to Luna's ear. "But I wish you'd listened to my request about something else." She stepped back, holding her daughter by the shoulders.

"What's that?"

Mal smiled and shook her head. "I remember asking you—on many occasions, by the way—not to grow up so fast."

Luna laughed. "Mom—"

"I don't think I've asked for very much as your mother."

"Really?"

"Alright, maybe I asked for a few things." Mal shrugged. "But it would have been nice if you'd given me a few more years to prepare for this day—"

Luna laughed.

Mal raised one eyebrow and shook her head. "Yet here we are. I blink and you've gone from a baby to a beautiful young woman."

"I'm sorry?"

Mal laughed and pulled Luna in for another hug. A few seconds later she released her grip and smiled at her daughter. "I hope I say it enough, my dear girl, but in case you haven't heard it lately, I am extremely proud of you."

"Thanks, Mom." Luna nodded. "And you do. Say it enough."

"Good." Her mother turned back toward the counter. "Now sit down and I'll cook us some pancakes."

Luna took the final bite of breakfast and set her fork on the plate. "That was delicious as always, Mummy. Thank you."

Mal smiled. "I'm happy you enjoyed it."

"Well ..." Luna placed both hands on the table and made as if to push her seat back. "I suppose I'd better get those chores finished up before school."

Mal raised one eyebrow and shook her head. "You're funny."

"What?" Luna's eyes widened in mock surprise. "The chores must be done ... wait a minute." She cocked her head, eyes narrowing. "Did you do them?"

"I did."

"Yay!" Luna clapped her hands together. "Thanks, Mom. That really is one of the best gifts I can get, you know."

"Trust me, I do." Mal took a drink from her mug. "It's also a good way for me to stroll down memory lane. Until you got old enough to help out, the chores were all mine. Milking the cow and fighting with the hens for their eggs is good for me to do every once in a while."

"To make you appreciate not having to do them every day?"

"Exactly," Mal nodded. "But it also reminds me of simpler times. When all I had to worry about was a few chores and scrounging up enough food for us to survive."

"There was a lot more to worry about than that."

"True," her mother agreed. "But there was something meditative about the chores. It made the bigger problems fade away, if only for a short time."

"Hmm." Luna's brows furrowed as she considered her mother.

"What?"

"You make it sound as if doing my chores was a gift for you instead of me."

Mal scrutinized her daughter for a second and laughed. "Nooo."

"You don't sound convinced."

Another laugh. "I only need to do them once or twice a year."

"You sure?"

"Positive."

"'Cause I'd be willing to let you do them once or twice a week, if it helps keep you grounded."

Mal sniffed and shook her head.

"Or more." The girl shrugged. "My only concern at the moment is to help you, Mother."

There was a knock at the door, followed by Gage's voice loudly singing "Happy birthday to you" from outside.

Luna laughed and Mal smiled. "Get to school, old woman. I'll see you after, for cake and presents."

13

THE VILLAGE PROPER FEATURED A SINGLE WIDE MAIN street lined on each side by large and medium-sized buildings, which housed the artisan trades responsible for keeping the people of the village fed, clothed, and sheltered. A person standing at one end of the street could see the uniform design and exact building configurations on both sides, along the entire length. One large trade hall for each of the major professions was surrounded on each side by smaller buildings that served as living quarters for the most important artisans and their families.

The warehouse buildings where food and unused materials were stored were located at one end of the street, while the school and local government buildings were situated at the opposite end. In the very middle of the street was the wide town square, with three levels composed of fieldstone walls and flat paving stones. Some of the adults occasionally joked that the town square made it impossible to drive their cars down the street. The joke was funny because functioning cars no longer existed.

Mal's house was a ten-minute walk from Main Street,

on the end closest to the warehouse. That meant Luna entered Main Street at that end and walked its entire length every day on her way to and from school. She had complained about the extra walk from time to time, but she knew her mother's house was where it was for a reason. The village leader, Mal had told her daughter, must be up to date and informed at all times on the status of all citizens. By walking past every major building to and from work each day, Mal had the opportunity to observe the goings-on of the entire village. She was also accessible. If anyone needed to talk to the mayor, all they had to do was meet her on the street as she walked past. Their home was also closer to Main Street than other homes, except for the quarters of the professionals.

On the morning of Luna's sixteenth birthday, she and Gage walked down the street together, but the journey was much slower than usual.

"Happy birthday, Luna," Cataline Froza called out from where she sat on the steps of the Data Hall.

"Thank you, Cataline," Luna smiled.

"It would be delightful if you could stop by for a moment or two after school lets out. We have a special gift for you."

"That's very sweet," Luna shook her head. "But a gift isn't necessary."

"Nonsense." The woman stood and bent forward in a slight bow. "This is an important moment for all of us, young lady. You were the first child born in the village, and everyone has been eagerly waiting for this day to arrive. And then the sixteenth anniversary of the Beginning is tomorrow. ... It truly is a special time for all of us in the village."

"You're right." Luna smiled. "I would be grateful to

accept your gift. I'll come by after school."

Cataline's eyes brightened and her smile widened. "Excellent. I'll be here waiting when school lets out."

Luna and Gage walked on. They had gone less than twenty feet when Gage groaned. "This is gonna be a long walk to school, Lune."

Luna followed her friend's line of sight to a man sitting on the steps of the farmers' building. Seeing them, the man rose and raised a hand in greeting. Luna smiled and raised hers. Then her gaze drifted past him and she understood Gage's comment.

The elder of every major building was standing or sitting on the front steps, patiently watching her, with smiling faces, as she made her way down the street.

"Looks like you won't miss my gift after all," Gage said under his breath, laughing as Luna grunted and continued forward.

SEVEN LONG HOURS LATER, LUNA TRUDGED UP THE front steps of her house with Gage at her side.

"I feel drained." She moved to the swinging chair on the porch and plopped onto it, pushing against the floorboards to put the swing in motion.

"Me, too." Gage laughed and sat down in the wooden chair beside her, smiling as he looked out over the front yard. "Didn't you expect that sort of attention?"

"No way." Luna sighed, closed her eyes, and crossed her arms over her chest. "I mean, I thought I might get one little gift ... maybe two. But every profession hall gave me one, and they were all too expensive. Plus the invitations to join so many of the halls—it was way more than I could have imagined."

Gage chuckled and stood. "Thirsty?"

Luna opened one eye and looked his way. "Yes, please. Lemonade, if there's any in the fridge."

"It's your favourite drink, and your birthday." Gage smiled and opened the door. "I'm sure there will be."

Gage disappeared into the house and Luna glanced toward the barn. Her mom was walking toward the barn door, one hand carrying a pail and the other raised and waving toward the house in greeting. Luna smiled and waved back. A second later, her mother disappeared into the barn. "It is pretty nice not having to do the chores," she called out to Gage.

Her friend returned a minute later with two glasses of cold lemonade in his hands. "You're right. No chores is a treat." Luna accepted one glass and Gage sat back in his chair.

Luna took a long drink and smiled. "That's delicious."

Gage took a sip and sighed. "Do you taste honey in there?"

"I think I do, yes."

Gage nodded and set the glass on the small table beside him. "Honey is a bigger treat than the lemonade."

"Huh." Luna took another sip and nodded. "Yep. Totally honey in there."

They spent the next twenty minutes on the porch, sipping honeyed lemonade and chatting about the day. Luna finished her glass before Gage did. He noticed, downed the remaining bit with a gulp, then stood and collected her glass. "I'll put these in the sink. Then let's go for a walk."

"Sure." Luna stopped swinging. "Anywhere specific in mind?"

"Yep," Gage smiled and opened the front door. "But don't ask me where, because it's a surprise."

14

THE TWO FRIENDS SAT ON THE TALLEST HILL, THE ONE overlooking the western corner of the village.

A gentle breeze blew over them as both swung their legs back and forth over the edge of a bare stone outcropping. The hill sloped downward and away, such that the only thing between them and the wide silver line that warned of the village's edge was half a mile of knee-high grass, green-ish-brown at this time of year.

"I love this spot." Luna leaned back, her hands propped on the ground for support. Her head was tilted back, eyes closed, a contented smile on her face.

"It is a nice spot," Gage agreed.

"Was this the surprise?"

Laughter. "No."

Luna's smile became a frown, but her eyes remained shut. "Then what are we here for?"

"I'll tell you. When the time is right."

Luna opened her eyes and turned to face him. "Ooh. That sounds very cryptic, Mister."

Gage chuckled. "Have you figured out how to get all your presents home from the Town Hall?"

"You're changing the subject on me?" Gage shrugged, and she giggled. "I suppose I'll ask Mom to help me get them with the horse and wagon."

"I'll help."

"Thank you."

"Not like that's a surprise, is it?"

"Nooo." They helped each other, always and without asking. Neither was the kind who expected it, and both remained thankful for the constant offer of assistance.

"And what about the offers?" he asked. "Which profession do you think you'll end up choosing?"

Luna drew a deep breath and let out a long sigh as she looked out over the hills. "I don't really know. Many of them sound like fun."

"Not accounting or data?"

"Of course not," Luna snorted. "I mean, I can understand the processes and math, but counting grain stores and forecasting when we need more steel delivered isn't the kind of stuff I want to spend the rest of my days doing."

"I'm with you on that." He rolled his eyes. "Although I sort of feel the same about the tower technician position."

"Yeah, I could tell, the last time we were with Thomas."

"And that's the profession you're considering most, isn't it? Tower tech."

Luna shrugged.

"If that's your favourite one, you should go for it."

She frowned and turned her gaze to his. "But you hate it."

"That's not your fault. Or your problem."

"Still."

"Luna." Gage's brows furrowed. "You have to choose the profession that makes you happy."

"That's the thing. Without you joining me, I'm not sure it will."

Gage frowned but said nothing.

Luna sighed. "I've always thought we'd end up choosing the same profession."

"As a kid, so did I."

"As a kid? We're still kids."

"I am. You're an adult now."

Luna snorted. "One day as a sixteen-year-old doesn't make me an adult."

"Technically it does."

Luna laughed, but Gage's expression was serious as he stared down the hill, legs still swinging. "We've spent almost all our time together for as long back as I can remember."

"We have."

"I know we thought it made sense that we'd want to do the same as adults."

Luna frowned. "But now you don't?"

"Part of me does." He shrugged again. "But another—maybe the almost grown-up part—knows enough about how the village works to realize that was never going to happen, no matter what we wanted."

Luna wanted to disagree with him, to tell him he was wrong. But she knew enough about how the village worked, too. "You're right," she said. "There are more professions than there are kids to fill them. There's no way they'd allow even two of us to go to the same hall."

"Especially not at the start, which is where we come in. Some of the professional leaders are getting old," Gage reminded her. "I'm sure they'd feel better if a new trainee was under them. To continue the tradition and take up the majority of the workload."

"Yeah."

They sat quietly for a short time.

"It sucks, though," Luna said.

"It does."

She thought about not seeing her friend as much as they were used to. It saddened her, but she shook it off and leaned over to nudge him with her shoulder. "I guess we'll still be able to have lunch together. And see each other when our day is done."

"That's true."

"Oh, no." Luna's smile suddenly changed to a frown.

"What?"

"The chores."

"What about them?"

"I bet we'll still have to do them, won't we?"

Gage raised both eyebrows, eyes widening as he nodded with a deep sigh. "Yeah. I imagine we will."

Luna stared down at her feet and muttered a string of curses.

"Whoah!" Gage laughed. "That was an impressive bit of swearing."

She grinned. "I've been paying attention to Uncle Jack when he gets ticked off."

"Jack is very creative at his cussing." Gage laughed again. "But my dad and your mom aren't slouches at it. We've got the genes for quality swearing, that's for sure."

Luna smiled, closed her eyes, and rested her head against Gage's shoulder. "The adult's education has been comprehensive."

The warmth of the sun and comforting touch of her friend made Luna a bit drowsy. She felt herself begin to drift off to sleep, but Gage soon pulled her back from the edge of slumber with a gentle nudge.

"Hey, Luna?"

"Mhmm?" she murmured.

"I've got your first birthday present ready for you to see."

"Really?" She opened her eyes and turned to face him.

"Yep." He was smiling wide, with one hand pointed toward the village boundary. "Check it out."

Luna turned and her breath caught in her throat. "Oh, wow."

On the edge of the horizon, barely a dark blip in the distance, she spied a dark silhouette that both recognized, despite the lack of detail.

"The trader." A grin spread across her face.

Gage got to his feet and reached down to help her up. "I'd offer to race you down the hill, but you're getting up there in years. Maybe you'd best walk slow. And carefully."

Luna laughed and slapped him on the chest. Then she turned and the two began to jog down the hill to await the trader's arrival.

15

It took three more hours for the trader to arrive.

For the first half-hour or so, Luna and Gage waited alone, sitting on large rocks a few dozen feet back from the wide silver line of the village's boundary. One of the kids who lived nearby eventually walked past, looked across the open expanse, and then raced back toward the village. The same child returned a few minutes later, laughing and jostling with five other friends around the same age. They greeted Luna and Gage with a wave and then found another group of rocks to sit on, to wait for the trader.

Over the next two hours, small groups continued to amble into the area, greeting those already present and then moving to either join friends and family or form new little clumps of their own. At that point, most were young people. The adults always arrived closer to the trader's arrival, keeping busy until the moment was almost upon them.

THE SUN WAS ALMOST SETTING WHEN THE TRADER finally crested a hill and came into view, now only a few hundred yards from the line.

Children and young adults began to clap and cheer. The adults smiled and got to their feet in anticipation.

The trader continued moving toward them at a slow, measured pace. It was now possible to make out more detail. He walked with head down, face hidden by a wide-brimmed hat and form obscured by a faded black leather trench coat that was so long it almost swept the ground with each stride. One of the trader's hands rested on the back of his travelling companion, a dark grey donkey that moved at a slow yet steady pace, pulling an enclosed rectangular cart mounted to four large rubber tires.

"I can never get over that donkey," Gage said. "You'd think it would take three or four of them to pull a wagon that big, but it does the job all by itself like a champ. We have carts half that size and they are impossible for one person to lug around."

"Ours don't have rubber tires," Luna said.

"That makes it easier?"

"Mhmm."

"Huh." Gage rubbed at his chin.

Mal and Jack appeared and made their way to the front of the crowd, closer to the line than anyone else. Luna smiled after Mal turned, made eye contact, then grinned and winked.

Three minutes later, the crowd fell silent, all eyes trained on the trader and donkey as they approached the silver line.

Luna held her breath, eyes focused on the trader's hand, which now gripped the donkey's mane. A multicoloured stone bracelet encircling the trader's wrist began to glow, emitting a humming noise like no other she had ever heard. As they got closer to the line, the glow of the stones intensified, each colour becoming a single bright white light. Unbothered by the sudden brightness, the donkey strode forward.

Its muzzle touched the invisible barrier ...

Golden light shimmered over the surface of both the donkey and trader as they came in contact with the invisible energy of the barrier. Sharp cracks and startling pops sounded, while a constant hissing seemed to envelope them entirely as they made their way across the barrier and into the village. The light and sound show continued after both were inside the perimeter, transferring from their bodies to the large cart. But Luna kept her eyes trained on the star of the entire show: the trader's bracelet.

It continued to glow and pulse. She knew from asking that the light in it pulsed in time with the trader's heartbeat. She had also learned that the bracelet transferred its protective field to anything it touched. The trader touched the donkey, it touched the harness, and the harness touched the poles and then trailer. All three were connected, which allowed them to pass through the village's protective field of deadly energy. Luna wasn't sure how the rest of the villagers felt, watching this scene, but she was in awe of the small, colourful stones that encircled the trader's wrist.

Over the years, Luna had asked him as many questions about the bracelet as she could think of, adding one or two more new queries with each visit. Despite that, she had never been able to figure out how the stones worked. To her and to everyone else in the village, they were simply magic. A very important magic, because without the bracelet to let the trader come and go, everyone inside the village would eventually run out of essential supplies and die. As would the other villages the trader travelled to along his route.

The tail end of the wagon passed through the barrier. As suddenly as it had begun, the crackling and hissing ended. The glow from the bracelet flicked off, too, winking out as if it had never existed.

The crowd applauded, cheering and calling out to the trader.

The trader looked up, gazing first left and then right at the crowd, from beneath the wide brim of his floppy brown hat. He was smiling, bright blue eyes seeming to sparkle in contrast to the faint shadow cast from the hat's peak. He lifted his hand from the donkey and it stopped walking. Then he took two steps forward, removed his hat with a flourish, and bowed deeply, front leg bending while the rear one swept straight back in a smooth, polished motion. The crowd cheered louder, calling out welcomes. The trader held the bow for the count of two seconds, then stood and repositioned the hat with an agile twist of his wrist. He waved, turning around once in a complete circle. And then he raised one hand.

The crowd fell silent.

"Good day, good day, citizens of Sparrow village."

Scattered shouts of greeting sounded from the crowd.

"Where have you been, Trader?!" Someone shouted.

"Oh. You know." He grinned. "Here. There."

Laughter from the villagers.

"As always, I bring food, other goods, and news." His smile widened. "I also found enough room in my wagon to stow away a significant store of treats and even a few fireworks for tomorrow's party." His brows furrowed. "Unless I've arrived too late to celebrate the anniversary?"

The crowd broke out into cheers and applause once

more. Mal and Jack approached the trader. Jack said something and laughed as he pulled the trader close and embraced him, clapping him on the back before letting the man go and stepping back. Mal moved forward and hugged the trader next. She held the embrace much longer than Jack did, and Luna smiled.

When Mal and the trader finally finished their hug, the crowd became silent once more. Mal's smile was clear for all to see as she addressed the crowd. "We are fortunate and grateful that the Wild has allowed our trader to return to us. The Wilds are full of danger. We thank Aatun for bringing him back safe and sound."

There were shouts of agreement from the crowd, along with exclamations of "Blessings of Aatun!"

"Now that he is here," Malena continued, "the trading will commence after we feed the poor man and let him rest his weary feet for a bit."

There were groans from the people, but it was obvious from their tone that no one begrudged the man a short rest before opening for business.

"Give him an hour to eat, then you'll be able to find him in the village square." Mal turned toward the trader and the crowd began to disperse.

Gage and Luna remained on their rocks until most of the people had left. Finally they stood and made their way to where the two village leaders were standing with the trader.

He watched them approach, his smile widening into a grin. "Look at the two of you! All grown up into proper adults."

"God, I hope not," Gage laughed as he shook the trader's hand. "Welcome back, Will. It's really good to see you, sir."

"Sir?" He scowled. "So formal all of a sudden." Then he grinned and tousled the boy's hair. "Just like your dad." His gaze shifted to Luna. His smile widened as he held out his arms. "Come and give me a hug, girl."

Luna embraced him with a laugh, returning his tight squeeze with one of her own. They held each other for a long moment and then released their grip and stepped back in unison. "Happy birthday, Luna. I'm so glad I made it in time to celebrate this very special day with you."

"Thanks, Dad." Luna was beaming. "I'm glad you made it, too."

16

With one arm around his wife and the other around his daughter, Will made his way home for a fresh-cooked meal.

The three of them prepared the food together, falling with ease into the roles they had assumed in the small kitchen for as far back as Luna could remember. Luna sliced vegetables and put them in pots filled with boiling water, while Will prepared the mutton roast that he'd returned home with. Mal baked a fresh loaf of bread and prepared a pie filled with fresh peaches that Will had plucked from his cart as well.

The time spent apart seemed to disappear like smoke on the wind, as the three of them joked and laughed together while preparing their meal. They took turns sharing gossip and news, bringing each other up to speed on what had transpired while the family had been separated.

Luna paused with a peeler in one hand and a half-stripped turnip in the other as she watched Will sprinkle and rub a blend of spices onto the cut of mutton. "That looks good, Dad."

Will smiled. "Thank you, daughter. I think it'll taste delicious once it forms a nice crust. But I think it'll take more than an hour to cook."

"That's fine," Mal said. "We can make fresh sandwiches and eat some fruit, then come back later for the roast."

Will groaned and rolled his eyes, grinning as both women laughed.

"A light snack is better, anyway," Luna agreed. "It wouldn't do to fill up and get sleepy while you're trading goods with the neighbours."

"Everyone would like that, wouldn't they?" Will sighed and lifted the roast into the shallow cooking pan. "One time, I was so tired that the widow Baker got a new set of knives for free."

"She still brags about that deal," Luna said.

"I'll bet she does. Grab the door for me will ya, hun?" Will lifted the pan and waited for Luna to open the oven door. "Thanks." He slid the roast into the oven and stood as he closed the door and adjusted the dial. "Guess I'd best put it on a slow cook. I'm likely to be out there for longer than normal."

"Why?" Mal frowned.

Will smiled and put one arm around Luna, pulling her close. "Because it's my daughter's sixteenth birthday. And you're the first one born in the village to reach the age of adulthood."

"Adulthood," Mal sniffed. "Sixteen was too young for that designation."

"We agreed that it wasn't."

"Yes, but that was a long time ago." Mal shook her head and raised one eyebrow as she considered her daughter. "I've changed my mind. She should stay a kid for a few more years."

"Mommm," Luna groaned.

Will laughed and stretched his free arm toward his wife. She came closer and he pulled her toward him, kissing her gently on the cheek. "There's nothing we can do about it now, my sweet Malena. Our baby has grown into a woman. It's time to let her stretch her wings and experience a bit more of this game called life."

Mal scowled, disengaged herself from Will, and made her way to the fridge. Luna hugged her father with both arms and then went to join her mother, accepting the plate of cold sandwiches, which she took to the table.

Will and Mal joined her and took their seats.

"Fireworks." Will reached for a sandwich.

"What about them?" Mal asked as Luna's eyes widened.

Will saw his daughter's expression and grinned. "I brought fireworks. To celebrate Luna's big day."

"That's exciting!" Luna clapped her hands together and bounced up and down on her chair.

"Um." Mal reached for a sandwich.

"Yes?" Will took a bite of his and chewed while he waited for his wife to speak.

"I'm all for that. Fireworks for our daughter's sweet sixteen."

Luna squeaked, barely able to contain herself.

"But ..." Mal reached for the pitcher of lemonade and poured some into her husband's glass. "You already promised those for the big party."

Will sniffed.

"I'll admit it's not as important to us as Luna's birthday," She cast a conspiratorial wink toward her daughter.

"Thank you." Will dipped his head in a slight bow and took another bite.

"But it is to the rest of the village. Even more important, if I had to guess."

Will's eyes widened... "Go ahead."

"I'm thinking it might be a good idea to save the fireworks for the celebration tomorrow night."

"Politically speaking?" Will raised his eyebrows.

"That's right. Politically speaking."

Will frowned.

"You don't have to live with this bunch," Mal continued. "In a few days, you go off and leave the backlash for me to endure on my own."

"Not all on your own," Will said, shaking his head. "Jack must take a bit of the brunt of things, right?"

Mal laughed. "When did you ever see your brother shoulder the brunt of anything?"

Will laughed. "Always the golden boy, wasn't he?"

"I suppose."

"Did you know," Will turned to Luna and whispered. "That your mother almost married Uncle Jack instead of me?"

"Oh, please." Mal rolled her eyes, and Luna laughed. Will loved to pretend such was the case, but Luna had heard the story many times from all three of them, on various occasions. Jack might have been the popular one in school, but all seemed to agree that Malena had always only ever had eyes for Jack's younger brother, Will.

"How 'bout this?" Will brought the subject back on track. "We shoot off a few tonight. You know, use it to both commemorate Luna's birthday and tease for a bigger show tomorrow. Then we can blast the rest of them into the sky for the celebration tomorrow night."

Luna held her breath, watching her mother for the final decision.

Mal raised one eyebrow and considered each of them. Then she smiled and nodded once. "I think that's a plan I can get behind."

17

"Luna! Over here."

Luna turned her head toward the sound of Gage's voice, smiling and waving back at the young man, who was standing on the base of a street lamp, three feet off the ground, one arm wrapped around the dark metal pole and the other waving to get her attention.

"What are you doing?" she called out.

"I can't hear you," he shouted, motioning for her to join him.

Luna made her way through the throng of people crowding the main street. While evenings here were normally quiet, with families for the most part staying inside their homes after nightfall, the trader's return was always cause for a nighttime gathering in the centre of the village. Children got to stay up later than normal, and adults took the opportunity to gather with friends and neighbours, chatting about the weather and the transactions they had been able to make with the trader.

Luna finally made her way to Gage and smiled as he dropped down from the lamp post. "Heya," she said.

"Hi." He smiled.

"Been out here long?"

"Long enough." His grin widened.

"What is it?"

"Whatchya mean?"

"That smile says you're up to something that's likely gonna get both of us into trouble."

"Nope, not this time." Gage laughed and shook his head. "I'm just happy, is all."

Luna waited for him to say more but he continued standing there with a grin on his face. "Happy ..." she prompted. "About ...?"

"Will had it!"

She frowned.

"The present I was hoping to buy for you."

"Oh." She laughed. "Well, that's good, I guess."

Gage shook his head. "You're the worst sometimes, you know that?"

"Why do you say that?"

"You never get excited about gifts."

"Yeah."

"Why?"

"I don't know."

"You don't like them?"

She shrugged. "Sure I do."

Gage laughed again. "Well, you do a good job of hiding it."

"I don't know." Luna smiled. "I mean, I like giving gifts, but ... I guess I just hate to be a bother."

"Oh yes. That's you, alright." He raised one eyebrow. "Luna, the huge bother."

Laughter. "You know what I mean."

He shook his head. "I really don't. I love getting gifts. It's awesome."

"You don't find it stressful?"

Gage frowned. "How do you mean?"

"You know. Like ... pressure to show enough excitement to make the person who got you the gift happy—"

"You're kidding, right?"

She frowned. "No."

Gage chuckled. "I swear you're the best person I'll ever know, Luna."

"I doubt that."

"You care about people so much. Someone gives you a gift, and you're the one worried about hurting their feelings."

"Everyone's like that."

Gage laughed. "No. They aren't."

She frowned.

"Do me a favour."

"If I can."

Gage smiled. "When I give you your gift, don't stress out about how to react." She opened her mouth, but Gage shook his head and continued speaking. "Uh, uh, uh. Don't object, just listen, okay?"

She frowned but nodded.

"When I hand you the gift, open it and just ... enjoy the moment."

Her frown deepened. "Okay. I'll try."

"Good." He nodded. "Are you ready, then?"

"What? You mean right now?"

"Yep." Gage reached into his pocket and withdrew a small package. It was wrapped in white paper with red stripes and had a thin silver ribbon tied around it, finished with a neat bow.

Luna smiled and reached for the package. She held it in her hands, turning it over as she tried to guess what was inside.

"The present isn't the box, ya know. It's actually what's inside."

She laughed. "Oh. Well, good. I'm liking it more and more as we go." She turned it over once more and then tore the paper away to reveal a plain brown cardboard box. She opened the lid and her eyes widened.

"Oh, Gage," she whispered, reaching into the box to withdraw a black metal rectangle. It fit perfectly into the palm of her hand, the criss-crossed patterns on the outer handle improving her grip on it. She turned her wrist and observed the half-dozen grooves on the side. Using her thumb, she flipped one of the attachments outward to reveal a shiny metal blade. Luna held it up in front of her eyes. "It's beautiful."

"It contains five extensions," Gage said. "The knife, a screwdriver, saw, graphite rod, and tweezers."

Her gaze met his. "This is a tower technician's tool."

"It sure is. The one item no proper tower tech would be without."

Luna turned it over in her hand and felt tears form in her eyes as she spied the other side. Her name was engraved in flowing lettering into the matte black metal. She looked up at Gage. "You ordered this special?"

Gage's smile was wide, his own eyes glassy as he nodded. "A few months ago."

"But you said you were saving your money until ..."

"A little misdirection, to keep you from guessing."

She laughed, shaking her head as she folded the knife back and slid the multi-purpose tool into her front pocket.

"I'll have the holster for your tool tomorrow." He

grinned. "I have to get a bit of an advance from my dad early in the morning."

Luna shook her head. "There's no need for more, silly. You've already spent too much."

"Nah." Gage shrugged and looked at the ground.

Without thinking, Luna stepped closer and reached out, gently touching Gage's chin and lifting his face until he was looking into her eyes. His smile faltered. She felt a quaver in her stomach, a thrill of excitement.

Then she leaned forward and kissed him.

Gage's eyes widened and his lips tensed. Then he leaned in, his lips pressing a bit tighter against hers as one arm wrapped around Luna's waist.

She felt another thrill pass through her and she smiled while still maintaining contact. Her eyes met his and it was obvious that Gage was enjoying the moment as well.

When they parted, Luna blinked slowly, her eyes staring into Gage's.

"Wow." Gage breathed the word.

"That was amazing," Luna whispered, oblivious to the villagers staring at them as they walked past.

"I'm glad." Gage smiled, then added, "It was for me, too."

"Good."

Neither spoke for the space of a few heartbeats, both unsure what to say. Luna was the one to break the silence. "I guess we should go join the others?"

"That's not what I want to do."

Luna felt her cheeks flush with warmth. "No. Me neither. But we likely should?"

Gage nodded. "Yeah. I guess we should."

"It's almost time for the fireworks."

One corner of Gage's mouth twitched into a half-grin.

"As far as I'm concerned, the fireworks have already happened."

Luna shook her head and laughed, then slipped her arm through Gage's and began to lead the way toward the village square.

18

Luna looked at her watch and noted that the fireworks display had been going on for almost eight minutes.

She looked up and caught her mother's attention, raising both hands in a questioning manner. Mal shrugged and shook her head.

"What's wrong?" Gage asked, his head close to hers in an attempt to be heard over thunderous cracks.

"He was supposed to save most of the fireworks for tomorrow."

Gage laughed. "I'm sure he did."

"I hope so." She looked skyward once more and smiled as an explosion of bright blue, white, and orange blossomed to life from the darkness. As the streams of light trailed toward the ground, another explosion sounded from above. This time, missiles of pink and blue light fled each other and spiralled sideways before fading from sight.

After another half-dozen eruptions, the fireworks display came to an end and the villagers cheered and clapped to show their appreciation.

The street lights were turned on nearest to where Will stood, on a small stage in the village centre beside his wagon, illuminating him clearly to all. With a wide smile on his face, he bowed deeply, held the pose for a few seconds, and then straightened before turning and repeating the gesture. He completed the second bow and raised both hands in a soothing motion until the applause stopped.

"Thank you all for gathering tonight," he said. "I hope that everyone is pleased with the trades that they've made. I'm embarrassed to admit that far too many of you got the better of me during the transactions today."

There were loud guffaws and jibes, and Will grinned. He used the same line every time he came to town. "Okay," he admitted. "It's possible that I broke even on one, maybe two trades."

"You profit, we profit," someone shouted from the crowd.

Will smiled. "That is true, and we are all the better for such an arrangement. Everyone who traded managed to acquire some fine new things to use, eat, and entertain yourselves, while I have obtained fresh stock that the villagers at the next settlement will be grateful to see."

There was another smattering of applause.

"Thanks as well for sticking around to celebrate Luna's birthday. It's not news to anyone that her special day marks a milestone for all of us this year. There's an old adage that it takes a village to raise a child. Each and every one of you is proof that such is the case. It's incredible to see what can be accomplished when we not only accept such responsibilities but wholeheartedly embrace the task with open arms and love in our collective hearts."

People smiled, obviously proud of themselves and each

other as they patted shoulders and offered words of encouragement.

Will's expression became more serious as he looked out over the gathering. "For those of us who remember what it was like ... before ... this is a magical moment. I'm sure there were times you thought we'd never get this far. I know I felt that way. Too often to remember." He stood straighter and smiled. "But we have survived. And we've done it by sticking together."

"Together!" the crowd shouted as one.

Will raised one hand and pumped his fist into the air. "Never alone."

"Never alone!" The force of the declaration from the crowd echoed through the square with energy and passion that made Luna's skin tingle.

Will bent down and then stood, a glass of wine now in his hand. He looked at his daughter and raised the glass in toast. "Happy birthday, my darling daughter. We celebrate you this night."

Everyone turned toward Luna. Those who held glasses of ale or wine or juice raised them in toast. "Happy birthday, Luna. We celebrate you."

AFTER WILL'S SPEECH, THE CROWD DISPERSED AND THE villagers began to return to their homes. It wasn't late, but everyone knew that the festivities of the next day would begin early and last long into the night.

Gage walked Luna home. When they arrived, they stopped at the bottom of the porch stairs.

"Your parents aren't home yet," Gage said.

"Same as always. They're the last ones to leave the square." Luna smiled. "Along with your dad and cousins."

"Yeah." Gage nodded and then looked at the chairs on the porch. Luna noticed his expression and laughed.

"What?" He frowned as his eyes met hers.

"You're being strange."

"No, I'm not." She raised one eyebrow and he laughed. "Okay, maybe a little. But so are you."

"I am?"

"Mhmm."

They stood there, neither speaking.

"Nothing's different, Gage."

"It isn't?"

Luna shook her head.

"But—"

"We kissed."

"Exactly."

"That's it."

Gage frowned. "Oh."

Luna made a *tsking* sound. "No, not, 'oh.'"

"Um." Gage's frown deepened. "I'm confused."

"About what?"

"Well, we kissed." He shrugged. "I liked it."

"So did I."

"You did?"

She nodded.

Gage took a deep breath and let it out as if releasing a load of built-up tension. "That's a relief. I thought maybe you hadn't."

"I had the same thought about you."

More laughter. "How could you think that? It was amazing. I can't stop thinking about it."

"You can't?"

He shook his head.

"I don't think that's good."

"Why not?"

"I don't know. It just seems like we could ruin what happened by spending too much time thinking about it."

Gage's smile faded and he looked at the ground. "Yeah, I guess you're probably right. I am feeling a bit crazy already. Wondering about when it might happen again, what if it doesn't happen again, did you like it, will we like it next time, what happens after—"

"Exactly!" Luna laughed. Then she reached out and gripped Gage's shoulder. "You know I like you. You've known that for a long time."

"I had a hunch. You knew I've liked you too, right?"

"Yeah." Luna considered him for a moment. "I don't know why I did it."

Gage scowled. "What? Kissed me?"

She nodded.

Laughter. "I don't know, either, but I'm real glad you did."

"Me too. As long as it doesn't wreck it."

"Wreck what?"

Luna spread her hands to each side. "Everything."

"That's not possible."

"Really?"

"Really."

"I don't know. You remember the Starford family, right?"

"Yes."

"They got together, fell in love, got married."

Gage sighed. "Then they broke up and Ron got so depressed about it that he stepped over the line."

"Sheila did, too. A few days after Ron." Luna shook her

head. "They were both so happy, until they weren't. And now they're gone."

"Luna." Gage's tone was serious. She looked at him. "I'll never step over that line. I promise. If we ended up together, or apart, or never saw each other again, I'd never step out of the village."

"Promise me."

"I promise."

Luna nodded.

"You do the same."

"What?" She frowned.

"Promise me that you'll never cross the line."

She considered him for a long moment, then smiled and nodded. "I promise I will never cross the line."

19

EARLY THE NEXT MORNING, LUNA FINISHED HER chores and then joined her parents in the village square to help set up for the day's festivities.

They weren't alone in the task. Every citizen scrambled to finish whatever personal work they needed to do and then made their way to the square to lend a hand in setting up. Each new arrival brought along a tray or dish filled with food.

The tasks were split into two major parts. One group did the heavy lifting: positioning tables in the square, helping to move carts and direct traffic, and any other large-scale activity that needed doing. The other group tended to the finer details: setting the tables, stoking the fire pits, making sure each station was stocked with supplies. When the majority of the work had been completed, they all gathered and worked together to prepare the late morning breakfast, which was to consist of massive amounts of eggs, bacon, bread, and pancakes.

Although a spirit of happiness and joy filled the village square, there were sad emotions as well. After dropping off their food contributions, families visited the memorial located at the northern tip of the square. Luna would occasionally glance in that direction, watching people reach out and touch a name engraved into the stone monument, in remembrance of a loved one who was no longer with them. Someone who had lived in another, more different time, and perished in the transition.

That time, gone forever, was referred to as *the Before*. Those who had lived then chose the name to refer to a world that Luna would only know about from stories. An age before humanity had nearly been wiped from existence.

"Good morning."

"Geesh, Gage." Luna jerked and spun around to see her friend grinning at her.

"What?"

"You scared the heck outta me."

"Heck." Gage laughed. "You're an adult now. You could say *hell*, you know."

Luna raised one eyebrow. "Right, because we never said stuff like that when we were kids."

Gage's eyes widened and his head tilted to one side. "I'm not sure what you're going on about with this 'we' stuff." He grinned. "I'm still a kid."

Luna snorted.

"Three more months." He nodded. "So please, watch your language around the children. We are impressionable and innocent."

Luna shook her head from side to side and Gage laughed again. "Have I missed anything fun?" he asked.

"Oh, yes. An hour of setup. Most exciting."

"Oh, darn."

Luna smiled and her gaze returned to the memorial.

"Have you visited it today?"

She shook her head.

"Same here." He watched the families gathered in front of the wall in silence for a few seconds. "Kinda strange, don't you think?"

"What's that?" She asked.

"Someday there will be no one alive who remembers the people attached to those names written in stone."

"Yeah."

"I guess that won't happen any time soon, though."

Her gaze focused on Gage and she smiled. "Nope. The adults still have long lives ahead of them."

"Good." Gage turned toward the tables being set up. "'Cause while I might technically be of age—in a few months—to be involved in running this place, I'm in no rush for it to happen."

"Me neither."

"I'm gonna go help with setup. Looks like there's still lots of heavy lifting to do." Gage spied the basket of vegetables in Luna's hand. "You supposed to be with the cooks?"

"Oops." Luna laughed and turned on her heel. "Yes. I gotta go. See ya in a bit at breakfast."

"Save me a seat?"

"Of course." She began to walk away.

After half a dozen steps, she cast a quick look over her shoulder. Gage was walking away from her, toward the table setup crew.

Luna smiled. She'd been worried that their kiss would change things; make it awkward between them. But all seemed the same, which was good.

She frowned.

Or was it?

As always, the celebration day flew by for Luna.

The festivities provided an abundance of all the good things in life: food and drink, laughter and tears, dancing and singing. Everyone was in good spirits, making the most of the celebration and focusing on the positive. It was a time for relationships to be strengthened, tensions to be resolved, and everyone to commit once more to being a unified, supportive whole, as they delved forward into another twelve months together.

The people of the village spent the entire day at the party. There was much to do, and no one was bored. Everyone did their share to prepare, serve, and clean up for the three big meals that were eaten together in the village square.

Between those times, they spent moments mingling and touring the village, especially the profession halls. Normally closed, every hall was open to the public on this day.

This gave all the citizens a chance to speak with the professionals and engage them in discussions about the state of their trade, challenges encountered during the past cycle, and hopes for the upcoming year, with both sides offering their point of view.

Luna enjoyed her new popularity with the professionals, smiling politely and engaging them in conversation as each went out of their way to talk with her for as long as they could. She knew they saw this as their final opportunity to sway her toward choosing their hall. Luna was expected to announce her choice at the village's first selection ceremony, to be conducted the following afternoon.

This kept her busier than she usually was on celebration day. That's why Will and Mal had agreed to let Luna skip meal preparation duties to take full advantage of the day and spend as much time asking questions of the hall tradespeople as she wanted.

So she wasn't able to spend any time with Gage until dinner was over and everyone was gathering in the town square, waiting for dusk and the spectacular fireworks her father had promised.

"There she is." Gage sidled up to her, nudging her lightly in the ribs as he held out a thin stick of sweetened bread.

"Aren't you an angel." Luna smiled and accepted the treat, bumping the tip of it against his in a kind of toast before raising it to her mouth and taking a bite. "Mmm," she smiled. "I've barely had anything to eat today. I swear, there were moments when if one of the elders had offered food as a bribe I might have accepted a placement with them on the spot."

"Is that so?" Gage raised one eyebrow. "Then it's settled. By accepting the doughnut stick, you agree to become the first ever neophyte in Gage's profession hall. Welcome aboard."

"Oh?" Luna raised her eyebrows. "This is exciting news."

"Indeed." He raised the stick of sweet bread to his mouth and took a bite.

"Tell me more of this new profession hall. What function does it serve for the village?"

Gage smirked. "Comic relief."

"Interesting."

"Mhmm." He nodded, chewing and swallowing before he continued. "This village has been serious and sombre for too long. Time to add a bit of smiles and hilarity to the mix."

Luna laughed.

"See? Already it's working."

"I'm not sure I would be a good fit for your hall of fun and games."

"Well, that's a sad thing to hear." He shook his head. "Barely an adult and you've already lost your sense of humour." He turned to look at the people around him and then leaned back in close to whisper, "It looks like I got here just in time."

Luna tilted her head back and laughed. Gage joined her.

"Seriously, though," he said, "has the day been of any use? Did some other hall manage to make you consider them over the tower technicians?"

"Between you and me ..." Luna shook her head. "I'm happy with that decision, I think."

"Good." Gage nodded once, one corner of his mouth turning upward. "I'd hate to think my gift was doomed to remain tucked away in a drawer, unused, because you chose another profession at the last second."

"Nope." She shook her head. "That's not gonna happen."

The rest of the villagers were now moving toward the main stage, gathering around it as Luna's father appeared in the middle of the raised area to begin the night's final event.

"Come on," she said. "Dad's about to start his talk."

Gage turned toward the stage and grunted. "Then, let's go get a good seat."

"If there are any left."

The young man laughed. "If your mom somehow didn't save us one, we can always slum it with my family."

Luna smiled. The two families always found places close to the stage because of their positions in the village. "That would be almost as good," she admitted and led the way forward.

20

LUNA AND GAGE SLIPPED THROUGH THE CROWD AND came to stand at Mal's side. She smiled at the pair and reached out to rest one hand on her daughter's shoulder before looking back toward the stage.

Luna noted that Will was watching them with a big smile on his face, eyes glistening with unshed tears.

"He always gets emotional during this," Luna mumbled loud enough for her mother to hear.

"Because he's a big baby." Mal squeezed Luna's shoulder. "Who loves his family more than anything. They are happy tears, and it's one of the things I love about him. One of the infinite things."

Luna smiled and gave her father the thumbs-up. He nodded, wiped at his eyes with the back of his sleeve, then walked to the centre of the small stage and stood looking out over the assembled villagers.

A hush fell over the crowd.

Will began to speak.

"H1N1 dash j745. The jade plague."

He began to stride the length of the stage, looking out over the audience with an intense expression.

"Feels like only yesterday when those words meant nothing, doesn't it?" His eyes met those of one person in the crowd and then moved to another. And then another. After fifteen or so seconds, he resumed speaking. "Today marks one day longer than sixteen years since we first heard the name. Sixteen years. I'm sure all of you remember where you were that day. Driving the kids to school. Heading to work at the office. Planning a trip to Europe for the summer. All sorts of things made up our normal lives back then, didn't they? Things that we gave very little thought to. Boring, mundane decisions and actions that we took for granted. Sitting in front of our televisions, eating with friends at restaurants, riding the subways to or from a long day of work." He paused, nodding in response to the bobbing heads in the crowd. "Everything was right with the world, and it felt as if nothing could ever change that."

Will stared out at the villagers for the space of a breath or two. "And then it all did. Cell phone towers began to spew a green mist into the air. Mist that we would later learn contained the jade plague. Glowing green and sticky to the touch. Tens of thousands of towers began to pump it into the air, dousing the environment with molecules that no one could escape. We all had to breathe it in. The poison. Invisible particles that were created to kill us, or worse." He bowed his head for a few seconds, then looked up and continued. "Some went mad right away. They became violent, mindless animals with a single, terrible goal: to claw, bite, kick, and destroy any person they encountered."

There were murmurs from the crowd.

"From what we've been able to piece together, only

about one in ten thousand lost their minds and went feral. Most of you never encountered any of these poor souls, but for those who did, words can't describe the experience. I saw them. Too many times to keep track of." He shook his head. "I watched one kill over twenty people and injure another thirty before it was brought down. And then the wounded—all thirty—eventually turned into the same violent creature over the next few days, and started their own spree of madness and killing." He shook his head.

Will paused again and walked the length of the stage. "If that had been the worst it got, civilization might have been fine. Might have survived." He shook his head. "But the monsters were just a freak side-effect of the jade plague. Primarily, it was designed to be a super flu, fabricated and released into the world so that it could make people sick. Make them die. And that's exactly what it did."

Luna frowned and looked out over the crowd. This was the standard part of her father's speech, one he made every year. Despite its familiarity to the village, the reminder of what had happened—what had caused them to join together and form the village—brought sadness and pain to those old enough to remember. People wiped tears from their eyes, reached out to touch friends and family, and shook their heads in sadness.

"We have no clue who created the jade plague, or how far it has spread. After years of travelling between villages and speaking with the most knowledgeable people in each, we know that it covered at least this continent, which then had a combined population of a bit over 579 million people. Another thing we know for certain is that the mortality rate of H_1N_1-$j745$ was ninety-seven percent."

Will walked to the centre of the stage, his footfalls

sounding louder than they should as a strange, almost unnatural silence settled over the crowd.

"Four hundred million people infected by a disease designed to kill ninety-seven percent of the population. It's too terrible to comprehend. But then you do the math and realize that seventeen million people likely did survive." He waited for a few seconds, then shook his head and stared at the ground. "That's a big number of people still living. You think to yourself, maybe the human race isn't in danger of extinction after all, right?" He paused to let the thought hang. "But those seventeen million people were scattered across a large area, many of them in small groups when the infection appeared. In a small town of fifteen thousand, only four hundred and fifty may have lived. And that's only taking into account the mortality from the virus alone." Will sighed. "The reality was that even those who survived the plague were in danger. Mostly alone with no electricity, sanitation, or any of the other luxuries we'd come to rely on. Not getting sick was no guarantee of survival. In most cases, being left behind was a slower, more painful death sentence. And the ferals ..."

There were murmurs of recollection among the crowd. Will nodded his head and strolled back and forth across the stage twice before he stopped and faced them.

"Humanity should have died. I think that it would have —" He raised one arm to point at the giant structure off in the distance, to his right. "—if not for the towers."

"Praise be for Aatun," people called out.

"She is a miracle sent to us from heaven," others said.

"That's right." Will smiled. "It was towers that spewed death and destruction, but there was another network of towers that presented us with hope. A system possessing limited artificial intelligence. We don't know who created it, but we do know the name they attached to it."

Voices called out the name of Aatun, nodding their heads and smiling at one another as they began to softly chant.

"Aatun," Luna's voice joined the others, as did Mal's and everyone else.

Will nodded, walking back and forth on the stage for a few moments. Finally, he held his hand up and the crowd fell silent. "Yes. Aatun activated the tower matrix surrounding our village. *Aatun*, which means *the guardian*. One who teaches. She has guarded us since the beginning. Her field of energy keeps out deadly pathogens and ensures that our air is clean. She maintains a protective barrier around us to keep the wild things out. She gives us electricity to power the technology we were able to salvage. And it's not only us that she has saved. Thanks to Aatun, there are many such villages, each surrounded by its own ring of Deandria towers that form a protective circle around them."

Luna frowned, wondering, as she so often did, exactly how many villages lay scattered across this broken continent; how many people still existed in safe groups, like the one she called home. She had asked Will more than once, but he claimed not to know the answer. There was so much that no one seemed to know, and that vexed Luna.

"And so we gather," Will continued. "On the anniversary—not of humanity's greatest tragedy—but on the date commemorating the first day of our new lives together."

The crowd cheered, some wiping tears from their eyes, others smiling and nodding to each other with a gratefulness evident in their expressions.

A few minutes passed. When the crowd quieted, Will continued. "We have spent the day together, renewing bonds and celebrating our fortunes." He smiled. "And now we spend the evening with song, drink, and dancing."

"And fireworks," someone from the crowd called out.

"Yes." Will bowed his head. "And fireworks."

Will raised one hand toward the sky, and, just above his palm in the crowd's line of sight, a brilliant explosion of magenta, white, yellow and green filled the sky in a shower of fire.

The crowd cheered once again, and the fireworks display began.

21

It was long past midnight when Luna made her way up the path toward her house.

She saw her parents sitting on the front porch and smiled. "You two are up late."

Her mother chuckled, and the swinging chair she occupied moved back and forth in a gentle arc. "And you're home early. It's only 3 a.m."

Luna smiled as she joined them, sitting down in chair across from her father. "I must be getting old."

Will laughed.

"Did you have a good time?" Luna asked.

"It was an amazing day," Will said.

"Mhmm." Luna grinned, knowing that the couple had left the festivities just before midnight. She had stayed away from the house as long as she had in part to have fun with her friends, but also because she knew her parents would be taking advantage of having the house all to themselves for a few hours.

Mal noted her daughter's smile and rested a hand on Will's knee. "Thank you for the alone time, daughter."

Luna laughed and accepted a glass of iced tea from her father.

"Tomorrow is the day," Will said.

"Yes." Luna raised the glass to her lips.

"Biggest day of your life," Mal added.

"So far." Luna took a drink and noted the look that passed between her parents. "What is it?" she asked.

Mal shook her head and chuckled. "She doesn't miss much."

"Nope," Will agreed. "The girl's as clever as her momma."

"I don't get all the credit for that. Her father has some smarts, too." One corner of Mal's mouth turned upward. "He's just good at hiding it most of the time."

Luna and Will laughed. Mal smiled.

"Have you decided which profession you will choose?" Will asked.

Luna nodded. "I have."

Mal sighed and shook her head.

"What is it?" Luna asked.

"I can tell from your expression that you didn't choose *mayor*."

"I'm sorry."

Mal smiled. "That's fine."

"Are you sure?"

Mal nodded. "It's difficult to compete against the tower technicians. That is your choice, right?"

"Yes."

"It's a dangerous selection," Will said. "Those monkeys spend a lot of their time running up and down the towers, hanging from great heights and braving the elements as they go about their job."

"Those aspects don't scare me," Luna said.

Mal grunted. "A taste for danger. The fault comes from your genes in this regard, Will."

Luna laughed.

"What?" Mal frowned.

"Nothing." Luna had observed her mother's bravery in the face of danger as much or maybe even more than her father. She glanced at her father and knew he was thinking the same thing, judging from the set of his mouth and the glint in his eyes.

Mal furrowed her brows. "If not mayor, then how about data? Or perhaps accounting? " Luna groaned. Her mother laughed and shook her head. "No, I guess we all know those were never in the running."

"It would be terribly boring."

"Exactly." Mal nodded. "The protective side of me likes the choice for that reason. You would be safe." She shook her head. "But the other part of me knows you must follow your heart, and that leads you toward the same sort of excitement and adventure that pulled your father and I." She sighed and reached out to grip her daughter's hand. "You choosing to be a tower tech makes the most sense, based on the selections that you've been presented with so far."

"Thanks Mom, I'm glad you get it." Then she frowned. "Wait a minute. What's, 'based on the selections you've been presented with so far,' supposed to mean?"

Mal tilted her head toward Will. "Tell her."

Will sat forward in his seat, leaning his elbows on his knees. "One more profession has decided to invite you to join them, little Dove."

"Really?" Luna frowned, trying to think of one that

would entice her away from choosing to be a tower tech. "Which one?"

Will's eyes twinkled and his smile broadened. "You've been invited to become a trader."

22

Luna couldn't sleep.

She tossed and turned, lying on her side for a few minutes, flipping to her back for another few, and finally adjusting to the other side before repeating the entire rotation.

Choosing a profession was the biggest decision of her life, and she'd thought it had all been decided quite a while back. Tower tech. After careful consideration and weighing all the options, it had been the only choice that made sense.

But now there was a new option. One she'd never considered possible. One that tempted her.

"Trader." She whispered the word out loud, a smile forming on her face as she stared up at the ceiling in the dim glow cast by the light of a full moon streaming through her thin curtains.

Luna had asked her father why he'd waited so long to extend the offer. He had exchanged a glance with Mal and then said: "There are a few reasons. I'm sure you can guess at most of them, so I'll leave it for you to do so."

And that's what she'd been doing ever since. Asking questions and trying to come up with answers.

She was a thinker. Everyone knew this about her. Luna realized that she would have driven herself crazy if she'd had months to dwell on this offer and guessed that was one reason her father had waited.

Then there was the timing of the revelation. Late at night, with only a few hours before she must announce her choice to the village ...

"I wish I could talk to Gage about this," she muttered out loud.

A thought flashed through her mind and she smiled. "Yep," she said. "I'll bet they didn't want to give anyone the opportunity to talk me out of it." Her mind tumbled with visions of certain villagers attempting to do that very thing. Shaking their heads and warning her of the dangers that came with being a trader. Well-meaning citizens doing their best to cajole her into selecting a profession inside the village instead of leaving it behind.

Gage would have been the most adamant of all. Especially after ... the kiss.

Could she do it, she wondered. Leave everything she'd ever known behind and venture out into the unknown?

The thought both thrilled and terrified her. Her father didn't speak much about what happened when he was travelling. Whenever he had, it was almost always about what was going on in other villages. Luna realized that she knew little to nothing about the spaces between.

"They wouldn't put me in danger, though," she stated out loud. "They're my parents. It's their job to make sure I stay safe."

Luna completed one more rotation of tossing, then kicked the covers off with a sigh and got out of bed. The clock on her night table said it was 5:17 a.m.. She draped a blanket around her shoulders and walked downstairs, filled a glass of water from the sink tap, and noticed a light coming from the front porch. Luna peered out the front window and then went to open the door.

Will looked up at her and smiled. "Heya."

"Hi." She came out and seated herself across from him.

"Couldn't sleep?"

Luna snorted. "That can't surprise you."

"It doesn't."

"I thought you'd be sleeping."

"Yeah." He crossed both arms and stretched his feet out in front of him.

"You know, you're not really playing fair with this offer, Dad."

Will smiled. "Life isn't fair, Dove."

"I guess."

"I know this comes as a shock," Will said, "But your mother and I thought that waiting until now would be the least stressful way to handle things."

Luna nodded. "That's what I've spent the last little bit coming to realize."

He smiled. "I figured you would. Tell me why else you think we might have done it this way."

"With little notice, I can't overthink the decision."

"That's right," he agreed. "There's not enough time. You'll have to listen to your gut, which is the best way to decide on things."

"For me, at least."

Will nodded.

"Plus, none of my friends or the other professionals can try and talk me out of it."

"That's right," he nodded. "Because they won't know about the offer until the decision has been announced."

"And," she said, grinning, "you've actually managed to present me with a choice that might be more exciting than being a tower tech."

One corner of Will's mouth twitched upward. "Being a trader is way more exciting than tower tech, that's for certain."

They sat together in silence for a few minutes.

"I stayed awake down here in case you decided there were questions you wanted answered."

"I appreciate that."

"Do you have any?"

Luna frowned and then shook her head.

Will's eyebrows rose. "Really?"

"Really."

"Wow." He pulled his legs up and sat straighter in his chair. "I never thought I'd see the day when you couldn't think of a question to ask."

Luna smiled. "Oh, I can come up with a ton. I just don't think there's any point in asking them."

He considered her for a moment. "Huh."

"Does that disappoint you?"

Will shook his head.

"It's because the answers to any and all questions are obvious."

"I see."

Luna shrugged. "It's a difficult job."

Will nodded.

"Challenging."

"No doubt about it."

"And dangerous."

His lips pursed, but he nodded once more.

"You and mom have obviously given this a lot of consideration, and if either of you felt for any reason that I wasn't the best choice, then you wouldn't have made the offer."

Will laughed softly and reached out to pat his daughter on the knee. "You're right on all counts, sweet girl. Which is no surprise. No surprise at all."

Luna took a long drink of water and stared out into the darkness.

"So?" Will asked. "Are you going to accept the offer?"

Luna's eyes slid to meet his and she grinned. "I guess you'll have to wait until tomorrow and see."

23

Luna climbed the final few rungs of the tower ladder and stood on the platform, enjoying the feel of the wind blasting her face and twisting her hair as she stared down at the land below.

She'd realized this was a dream halfway up the climb, but these lucid events were always a delight when they involved being near or on top of towers, so she didn't try to wake herself up. Instead, she'd made the final steps of the climb and stood with arms wide and eyes closed, enjoying the warmth of the sun on her face.

"It's beautiful up here, isn't it?"

Luna opened her eyes, brows furrowing as she turned her head and saw a woman at her side. She was a few inches taller than Luna and had long, straight, jet-black hair that extended well past her waist. Her skin was pale and smooth. It reminded Luna of the few times her mother had put on makeup for a special village event. Dark shading encircled the woman's almond-shaped eyes, accentuating the bright amethyst colour of her irises.

"That's strange," Luna muttered.

"What is?" The woman smiled, the expression making her eyes appear even more vibrant.

"I've never met someone I don't know in these dreams before."

"This dream is different."

"Interesting."

"Indeed."

Luna waited for the woman to say more, but she only smiled, obviously comfortable with remaining silent.

"I'm Luna."

The woman extended her hand. "It's my great pleasure to meet you, Luna."

Luna reached out and clasped the woman's hand. As she made contact, she felt a heat, accompanied by a faint tingling sensation that rushed into her body, enveloping her like a warm embrace. Her hand jerked, but she didn't pull away or break contact. Luna frowned.

"Is something wrong?" the woman asked.

"Not at all." She shook her head. "Quite the opposite, in fact. I suddenly have this overwhelming feeling that I already know you."

"You do know me."

"Really?"

The woman nodded. "You've known me your entire life, Luna. Since before you were born, I have sung to you, and you have always been able to hear me."

"Sung to me? Before I was born?"

"That's right." The woman released her grip and let her hand fall back to her side. After a moment she reached out and grabbed a steel girder of the tower. As she did, a pleasant song began to fill the air, subtle and beautiful.

Something inside of Luna recognized the song. Her eyes widened. "You are the tower."

The woman smiled again. "You are almost correct. The towers are my children. This particular one is a son. He asked to be present for this meeting, but I decided to appear alone to keep things simple. For this first encounter, at least."

"Your children?"

"Yes, Luna. I am the one responsible for all of the towers. I make certain that all remains safe, both for us and the villagers."

Luna's eyes widened. "You are Aatun?"

"Indeed." The woman performed an intricate and graceful bow, her right arm sweeping in front of her torso as she half-lowered herself toward the ground and then straightened once more. "I am Aatun."

"I had—" Luna paused, finding herself breathless all of a sudden.

Aatun smiled.

"I had no idea," Luna continued, "that you were an actual person."

"An actual person?" Aatun spoke the words as if tasting an exotic food for the first time. She nodded and then smiled. "I suppose I am. Although I possess no physical human body."

Luna frowned. "You're standing here, right now, in one."

The tower incarnation shook her head. "This is merely a projection of myself."

"Isn't that all a body is? A physical projection of one's self?"

The woman's smile widened and she broke into melodious laughter composed of chimes and sing-song hums all woven together in a way that caused shivers of pleasure to run up and down Luna's spine. "I suppose your description is an apt one."

Luna smiled, pleased at the compliment.

Aatun removed her hand from the tower and laughed again; the sound was louder this time, and filled with happiness. It sent a thrill through Luna that she had never imagined could be experienced.

"You are a treat, dear girl," Aatun said. "I am happy to be able to spend this time with you."

"Me, too." A thought occurred to Luna, and her smile faded.

"Do you wish to ask me a question?"

Luna grinned. "I'd love to ask you a million questions!"

Aatun laughed once more.

"I don't know where to start, though."

"I can imagine."

"Really?"

"Of course. There are those I would feel the same way about, were I able to meet them."

"That's interesting to hear." Luna's brows furrowed. "Who would you meet that would make you starstruck in their presence?"

The guardian raised one eyebrow. "And of course your first query is one that I should not answer."

Luna laughed and continued to stare at Aatun, basking in her presence.

"I sense that you have decided to leave the village."

Luna's smile faltered.

"It is how I imagined the scenario would play out." One corner of Aatun's mouth twitched upward. "Will is nothing if not predictable."

"You know my father?"

A silent nod.

"Do you speak to him as well?"

"I speak to many. How each individual chooses—or is able—to hear me is up to them."

"Would it upset you? If I left the village and became a trader?"

Aatun smiled again. It was the sort of smile her mother would give when Luna had said or done something silly. "Of course not. The choice brings a specific set of challenges, but this surprises no one."

"Challenges for whom?"

"Another question with infinite answers."

"It seems I'm much better at asking questions than you are at answering them."

"You're right," Aatun laughed. "We do appear to be off to a rocky start, don't we?"

Luna nodded.

Aatun's eyes narrowed and she looked off into the distance. "Our time together grows short. Soon you will wake."

"Will we see each other again?" Luna asked.

"Of course. But for now I want you to know something before you make your final decision to leave the village." She reached out and cupped Luna's cheek with her hand. Again, there was a small tingling of energy that passed from Aatun into the girl. "Once you step beyond the line, I can no longer protect you."

The words caused a sudden churning in Luna's stomach. Her brows furrowed and she opened her mouth to speak, but Aatun continued to deliver her message. "Should you leave, look to your father for protection. And if you ever become separated from him, immediately make your way to the closest village. Do not stop to sleep. Don't veer from the roads to look for help, even if it seems that might be a better option. Run as fast as you can for the closest village and get across the line. Do you understand?"

Luna nodded.

"Good." Aatun smiled and lowered her hand. "Then I wish you luck." She began to shimmer and fade from sight. "Till we meet again, dear girl."

Luna raised one hand in farewell.

Seconds later, Aatun was gone.

24

LUNA WAS AWAKE AND DRESSED EARLY THE NEXT morning, before the sun rose.

She moved about her room quietly so as not to wake her parents but smiled and gave up the effort when she heard sounds of movement and hushed voices coming from their room below.

She made her way down the stairs ten minutes later and smiled at the sight of both of them sitting at the dining table.

"Well, good morning." Will raised a steaming cup of coffee to his mouth. "We were starting to get worried that you meant to sleep through the day."

"Please." Luna snorted as she came to his side and kissed him on the cheek. "I can't remember ever being up this early."

"Are you hungry?" Mal asked from where she stood at the kitchen counter. "I figured something light to get us all started. Toast and fruit?"

"That sounds good, Mom." Luna made her way to the coffee pot and kissed her mother on the cheek before reaching for a cup and pouring. "I'll drink this quick and get to the chores."

"No need for that." Will raised his cup in a saluting gesture. "They've already been done."

Luna laughed. "This week has been one of my best runs of luck when it comes to avoiding chores."

"If you choose a profession in the village and stay," Mal's voice was quieter than usual, "I'll do half the chores from now on."

Luna turned toward her mother, pursing her lips as she felt a wave of emotion wash over her. In all the excitement she hadn't stopped to consider things from Mal's point of view. "Oh, Mom." She reached out and gripped Mal's hand. "If I leave, it won't be to avoid chores. Or to get away from my amazing mother."

Mal smiled but continued to stare at the cutting board in front of her. "I know you wouldn't base such an important decision on the desire to avoid work, daughter." She raised her eyes and smiled. "I'm just trying to sweeten the pot a bit to keep you here."

"You don't want me to go?"

Mal's eyes flitted to Will and then back to Luna. "I want you to do what feels right."

"I'm not sure what that is."

"Yes, you are." Mal's expression returned to normal as she straightened, the strong and confident woman who ran the village once more present, instead of the concerned mother. "Your heart sang the first moment the correct option presented itself. It still does, when you weigh the choices and consider which is best for you." She reached out and gripped Luna's hand. "You are no longer a child, as much as that saddens me. Now is the time for you to select the next part of your path to walk."

"What if I choose wrong?"

Mal grinned. "You can always change your mind."

"Really?"

"Of course," Will said. "The choosing ceremony is only the first step of your journey, Dove. The village wants—needs—for a new professional to be happy in their role. There will be many moments along the path to mastery when you can back out; switch from one profession to another. Should you ever feel that the wrong decision has been made."

"I didn't realize that."

"There's too much about this process to cover all at once." Mal placed a cut-up orange on a plate of other fruits and handed it to Luna. Then the two women joined Will at the table.

"You'll continue to learn about how it works as you go." Mal dished a portion of the fruit onto a plate, which she set on her placemat. "And we are all prepared to be as flexible as we can. This is a key step toward the village surviving and thriving. One that all of us have been eagerly waiting for."

"It's key for all the villages," Will said.

A sudden thought occurred to Luna. "Am I the first child born in *any* of the villages?"

"Yes, you are." Will plucked a piece of fruit from his wife's plate and popped it into his mouth, drawing a *tsk* from Mal. Will smiled and chewed as he continued speaking. "You're the canary in our network of mines."

"Canary in our mine?" Luna's brows furrowed. "What's that mean?"

"It means," Mal said, "that you will be the indicator of how well we made our plans. A test case for measuring the validity of our ideas as we move forward."

"That's a bit of pressure." Luna selected some fruit from the big bowl in the middle of the table and added a piece of toast to her plate as well.

"Don't worry too much." Mal shook her head. "Being first is actually a bonus for you. Everyone will be much more open to changing and adapting to things as they happen on this first go-round. You're helping us set policy and procedure."

"That's right." Will smiled. "The kids who follow in your path may grumble with how it all turns out, but they'll be your generation's children and grandchildren, so you can take the blame and explain why you messed things up for them. If that's how it all turns out."

"Oh, I'm not worried about that," Luna raised one eyebrow. "I'll blame my crazy parents and the addle-brained villagers who were in charge at the time."

Will shrugged. "That's what I'd do."

The three of them laughed and then spent the next few minutes eating quietly.

Mal broke the silence by reaching out and holding her daughter's hand. "We are very proud of you, Luna."

Luna smiled. "Thanks, Mom."

Will set his cup on the table and reached out to grip her other hand. "We love you, baby girl. Always and forever."

Luna felt her vision blur and she nodded, blinking back tears. "I love you, too. Both of you. And I'm not worried about the future, because my amazing parents have done their best to prepare me for whatever comes."

Mal glanced at her husband. He smiled at her and nodded his head, eyes glassy as well.

The three held hands for another few seconds, then Will released his grip and pushed back against his chair.

"Well," he stood. "I guess it's time to get this show on the road. Who's with me?"

Luna smiled and got to her feet as well.

"Hold on there a second, lazy bones." Mal reached for the plates and handed them to Will. "Let's clean the dishes and tidy up first."

"Oh." He frowned and then accepted the plates. "Yeah. That's probably a good idea."

"Traders." Mal looked at her daughter and rolled her eyes. "Always heading out before cleanup begins."

"Never having to clean up?" Luna grinned. "Looks like you've given me another tick in the plus column for choosing that profession, Mom."

Will laughed and Mal shook her head in mock disappointment before smiling a second later.

25

"I THOUGHT GAGE WOULD HAVE BEEN HERE TO WALK with us into the village."

Will rested his hand on Luna's shoulder as they walked. "He was."

Luna turned and gave her father a questioning look.

"I found him sitting on the front porch when I came out to do the chores." Will shrugged. "But it was too early, so I sent him home. Told him that you'd see him at the ceremony."

"Oh."

Will chuckled. "Don't worry, Dove. He'll be there. Everyone will."

Luna walked in silence, wondering if she would have told Gage about her decision if she'd spent time with him this morning. Part of her said she would. They'd always told each other everything, as far back as she could remember. But this was different. "I don't think he'll be happy about this."

"Likely not," Will said. "But he'll come around."

"Maybe."

"Gage and you are like brother and sister." Will paused and exchanged a look with Malena. "I'm certain that he'll be happy for you instead of sad for himself."

Luna nodded.

"Besides," Mal said, "in a couple of months he'll have his own Choosing ceremony and become immersed in whatever profession he decides to pursue."

"That's true."

"And you'll always come back home to visit."

Luna turned toward her mother. "I've not decided for sure to become a trader, Mom."

Mal raised one eyebrow and reached out to grab her husband's hand. "Sure you haven't."

Will chuckled and gripped Mal's hand, swinging it gently back and forth as they walked.

LUNA HAD ATTENDED MANY CELEBRATIONS IN HER life, and all had been conducted in the main area of the village.

Most events involved at least a few fireworks and many booths filled with wonderful things—treats and candy and crafts. A few citizens ran an acting troupe and had given performances of some of the classics that had been written from the Before. Every autumn, they had a great gathering of food and fun to celebrate a successful harvest, complete with games and dancing. There were even certain birthdays that were marked by partying, especially new births and milestone birthdays, not only for children but also adults.

Despite the numerous grand-scale events she'd experienced, nothing had been as spectacular as the sight that filled her eyes as she turned onto Main Street with her parents for today's Choosing ceremony.

Every profession hall was open and decorated in a grand manner. The Agriculture Hall had its double-sized doors open wide, with all the most exciting tools and machines of the trade displayed on each side of their great building. The men and women who made up the professionals stood before it in their finest clothes, smiling at Luna with genuine warmth and encouragement in their eyes. Beside them, the Smithy also had its doors open; a mockup of the forge was set up to one side, with a working fire and the youngest smith standing at the anvil, complete with heavy apron and hammer in hand.

"Wow," Luna breathed as she stared down the street and saw that every profession house was similarly decked out, each with doors opened wide and decorations hanging from roof to side houses, with each displaying their capabilities, working professionals, and the finest machinery they could safely position in the available spaces.

"Looks like everyone's brought out their finest," Will said beside her. "Many want you to choose them, and they are going all-out to get that to happen."

"If you don't feel special and wanted today," Mal whispered so only the three of them could hear, "Then you never will."

Luna stood in the middle of Main Street for another few minutes, eyes wide as she took in the scene before her. Finally she looked toward the far end of the street. It was clear from the size of the crowd gathered that everyone not manning a station at a profession hall was there in front of the stage that she would stand on to declare her choice. Luna raised her hand and waved.

Many raised their arms in reply, cheering loudly and smiling to show their support.

"This is ..." Luna shook her head. "Too much."

"Nonsense." Mal rested a hand on her daughter's shoulder. "Were it possible, we'd make it a million times better. That's how big a deal this is."

Luna turned to smile at her mother and shook her head. "It's perfect exactly as it is, Mom."

Mal nodded, her eyes moist with tears.

Will laughed and motioned the way forward with his hand. "When you are ready, young adult. Lead us in."

Luna smiled and then began to walk slowly forward.

26

It took a little over an hour for Luna to make her way to the stage at the end of Main Street.

There were twelve major profession halls to visit along the way. She spent a few minutes at each, purposefully viewing the intricate displays and smiling at the professionals who watched her with eager, hopeful eyes. She spent extra time at each of the professions she had been seriously considering, making small talk with the professionals and elders, nodding as they exchanged encouraging remarks with her about how they couldn't wait for her to select them today. Luna engaged them playfully, nodding and laughing, but was careful not to reveal anything about her ultimate choice.

After each visit, she thanked the elder—the leader of each hall—for their interest in her and the work they had gone to simply to entice her to select their profession.

It was clear that the elders were each proud of their people, and they were pleased about their efforts to recruit the girl. Each took a few moments to engage with Will and Malena, expressing how impressed they were with Luna as a young person and how grateful they felt for her kindness and gracious words.

The final hall was that of the tower technicians. It was no secret in the village that this had been Luna's favoured profession. Most people expected her to choose the technicians, despite the hopes of a few other halls who felt they might still be in the running.

When Luna entered the tower technician area, the entire crew of techs gathered around her, some patting her on the shoulder and others calling out that they already had her quarters prepared and couldn't wait to make things official.

Luna laughed and smiled, sharing the banter with a familiarity that revealed her comfort with this group of people, more than any of the others. She caught the worried expression on her father's face and smiled inwardly, glad to cause him at least a tiny bit of concern before the ceremony began.

Thomas was the final technician to approach her. He smiled and placed a hand on her shoulder. "Nervous?" he asked.

Luna pursed her lips and nodded.

"Good." He grinned. "Never a bad thing to have a bit of nerves, right?"

Luna smiled, remembering the lesson he had taught her long ago and continued to bring up whenever it applied. "Nerves wake the body up and make you more aware of the world."

"And it's always good when one can be ..."

"More present in the world," she finished the thought with a grin.

"Exactly." Thomas's smile widened. "Enjoy the day, Luna. You've certainly earned it."

"Thanks, Thomas." She paused. "For everything you've done to help me become a better adult."

The tower tech's eyebrows furrowed slightly, but his smile remained as he gave her another quick nod. "You've taught me as much as I have you, Luna. And we're only just getting started."

She felt her eyes fill with tears. She'd been looking forward to joining the tower technicians for years now, and the realization that it wouldn't be happening moved her. She reached up to wipe a tear from her eye and then reached out to grip Thomas's arm before turning and walking back to the street.

"Well, that was harder than I thought it'd be," Luna mumbled to her parents.

Will chuckled and placed an arm around her shoulder. "The hard stuff is just getting started. Being an adult comes with some crappy stuff."

"Maybe, but you and Mom seem to have turned out okay."

Will laughed. "Yeah, 'cause we've worked hard to remember a secret that most adults forget."

"Oh yeah? What's that?"

Will jostled her shoulder in a playful manner. "You only have to act like an adult when absolutely necessary. The rest of the time, you should do your best to have fun, laugh, and love."

Luna considered her father's words and frowned. "That's a secret?"

Mal laughed. "Thankfully it isn't for anyone in this family."

Will nodded. "There will be times when these points may be tough to remember, though."

"Which is when it is most important to do so," Mal said.

"Thank you," Luna said. "I'll do my best to keep that in mind."

———

THEY MADE THEIR WAY TO THE END OF THE STREET near the Town Hall and school. A raised dais had been erected, large enough to accommodate all of the elders plus another five or six people.

Luna looked at the assembled crowd. She was used to seeing everyone gather for celebrations and festivities, but this was different. They were all here to see her; to watch as she choose the profession that would shape her for the rest of her life. That would contribute to the continued existence of the village.

The significance of what she was about to do loomed before her like a bank of storm clouds approaching. She looked to her left and right. The faces of the villagers seemed suddenly strange to her, blended and fuzzy, as if they weren't faces that she'd known for her entire lifetime.

"You okay, hun?" her mother's voice came from beside her, but it sounded odd to her ears as well.

Luna became aware of her pulse, blood pounding in her temples like a hammer beating out a rhythm inside her body. She frowned and shook her head, eyes scanning the crowd in confusion ...

And then she saw Gage.

He stood near the front of the group, and his was the only face she could clearly make out. He watched her, wearing a smile, eyes intent as his gaze locked onto hers. His smile faltered, replaced by a frown, as if sensing that she was struggling. A second later, the grin she had come to know so well returned. He nodded once, then turned and pointed toward the stage.

The muffled sounds of the crowd became clear once more, and the sudden confusion melted away. The pounding inside her head dissipated, as if it had never been there.

"Yeah," she gave a single nod, answering her mother's question. "I'm totally fine."

27

Luna and her parents climbed the steps to the stage and stood in front of the empty chairs that had been designated for them.

Luna and her mother were to sit in the centre, while Will's chair was located at the far end of the dais.

Malena motioned for her daughter to sit. When she had done so, everyone else on the stage took their seats and waited for the crowd to become silent.

Less than a minute later, a hush settled over the crowd.

Malena stood. She reached down and gripped Luna's hand, squeezed once, and shot her a reassuring smile before letting go and turning to face the audience.

"Today is a momentous occasion for all of us," Malena spoke the words with practiced ease, her expression calm and assured. "The first child born since the Before has finally reached the agreed-upon age of adulthood." She turned to look at her daughter. "Sixteen might seem too young to be considered so, but we settled on the number by remembering that it used to be the age when teenagers gained their first responsibility in the old days—that of being able to drive."

Adults throughout the audience nodded in agreement.

"With this in mind, and by unanimous consensus, sixteen is this and every other community's age of both adulthood and consent." Malena smiled. "And, although driving isn't an option in this new world that we find ourselves living in, it is a perfect time for our offspring to select a profession. A good age for them to take the next step in the cycle of life that we now find ourselves. An appropriate time to begin passing critical knowledge and skills from one generation to the next."

Malena paused to let the words to sink in. She looked past the crowd, surveying the village they had built. As her gaze took in the houses and profession halls, she nodded. "We have accomplished much as a unified people. And now, sixteen years after beginning a new way of life, we welcome our first child into adulthood. This is a solemn occasion and the next crucial step to ensure that we may continue to prosper and thrive in this new age of mankind. To survive catastrophe and rise from the ashes of the terrible death and destruction that nearly wiped humanity from the face of the planet forever."

The crowd applauded and cheered, some calling out words of encouragement to Luna while others shouted phrases such as *We survive!* and *To prosper and thrive!*

Malena allowed the cheering to go on for a few seconds and then raised one hand for silence. When the crowd was quiet, she continued. "You all know that I'm not good at long, drawn-out ordeals."

Laughter and nods of agreement came from the audience. Malena's desire for action and timely decision-making were traits that endeared her to the village.

"And so, without further ado, let us begin the Choosing."

The crowd expressed its agreement with another round of cheering and applause. As the noise died down, Malena turned and motioned for Luna to stand.

Luna rose from her chair and came to stand at her mother's side.

"We all know this young woman," Malena said. "She is the first adult among us who has spent her entire life inside the protective walls of the village. Each and every one of you have had a hand in her upbringing." Malena reached out and placed a hand on Luna's shoulder. "The professions have considered her for years, as she has likewise considered them. Many have expressed a desire for her to join their halls. Now it is time for Luna to make her decision as to which profession she will join. It is time for her to choose."

Malena and Luna turned to face the elders. The profession leaders rose from their seats as one, hands clasped together in front of them as they waited behind the small tables that held the common tools of their office.

Malena led Luna to the far end of the stage, stopping in front of the agriculture elder. Luna met the elder's gaze and bowed. The elder bowed back. Then Luna moved to consider the small leather pouch that rested on the table between them. Strapped to a belt, it would hold some of the precious seeds which, buried in the ground, would grow into the grains that were the staple food of the village. Luna counted to ten in her head, then nodded and moved to the next elder and repeated the process.

Behind her, the villagers watched in silence, waiting as she gave her final consideration to each profession.

Luna considered the final profession, smiling at the tower technician's tool resting on the table. With a smile and nod at the elder, she turned to make her way back to the centre of the stage.

As she did, Will cleared his throat. "Excuse me?" he said.

Luna turned back toward her father, who occupied a seat at the end of the stage. There was no table in front of him. Only Will, Malena, and Luna knew what was about to unfold.

"You have not considered all of the offers, dear daughter."

The crowd murmured but then quieted, to hear what was transpiring.

"I haven't?" Her brows furrowed.

Will shook his head and reached into an inner pocket of his black trench coat.

"Which profession did I miss?" Luna asked.

"That of trader." Will withdrew his hand and opened it. Luna's eyes widened and the crowd gasped audibly behind her. Resting on the trader's palm was a bracelet of multi-coloured stones, identical to the one he wore around his wrist except a bit smaller in diameter. Luna stared in wonder at the bracelet, which allowed a person to pass through the protective barriers of the villages and roam the lands between.

Luna took a step toward Will, her eyes locked on the bracelet with awe. In the short time she'd had to consider the offer to become a trader, she hadn't stopped to realize that getting her own bracelet would be part of the deal. Of course it made sense, now that she saw it glittering in her father's palm ... she laughed and shook her head.

Will grinned and drew his hand back a few inches. "Not interested?"

Luna laughed again, her eyes dancing up to meet his. He winked and extended the bracelet forward.

Luna waited, not wanting to insult the other elders by abandoning their offers so quickly. She looked to the tower technician elder. The man's lips were pursed, his brows furrowed to convey his displeasure with this new development. Luna opened her mouth to say something, but the elder shook his head and raised one hand. "I know, dear," he said. "Choose how you must."

"You truly were my first choice," Luna said.

"Until now."

"I'm sorry."

The elder frowned. "Never be sorry, Luna. Choose a path and follow it." One corner of the man's mouth twitched upward. "If someone offered me that bracelet I'd likely accept it, too. And that's saying something, considering that—unlike you—I understand and can better appreciate the dangers that lie beyond the protection of Aatun and her towers ..."

"Dangers?" Luna heard the fear in the man's voice, and it caused something in her mind to snap to attention. "What dangers?"

Will chuckled. "You're making a nasty final play for her, Desmond."

The elder met the trader's eyes with a blank expression. "What do you mean, Will?"

"You're trying to scare Luna into declining my offer."

"Am I mistaken?" The man's eyes widened. "Is it now safe out there in the Wilds?"

Will's smile faded and he shook his head.

"Let her remain with us," Desmond said. "She will be a powerful tower technician. I expect she'll have my job before she turns thirty."

"No," Luna said and both looked to her. "The choice is not my father's. It's mine."

"Of course." The elder dipped his head in acknowledgement.

Luna reached out and took the bracelet from her father, smiling at the coolness of the stones against her fingertips. Then she turned toward the crowd and held the bracelet into the air.

Seconds passed in dead silence. With a frown, Luna took her eyes from the bracelet and scanned the crowd.

Everyone stared back. She saw blank expressions on their faces.

"Looks like they aren't sure how to take your choice," Will muttered from beside her.

"No," Luna sighed. "I guess they aren't."

28

With her choice made, the crowd began to disperse and return to their homes. Aside from a few smiles and personal congratulations, most of the villagers were quiet and subdued. It was a significant contrast to the cheering and applause that had flavoured the day earlier, and it clearly conveyed a sense of disappointment.

Luna glanced at her wristwatch and noted the time was 10:22 a.m.

"The ceremony is over a bit earlier than we scheduled for," Malena noted.

"What happens now?" Luna asked. "I know the original plan was to go to the hall with the professionals that I chose to join. But the traders don't have a hall."

Will chuckled. "Sure they do. It's a little place I like to call home."

Luna frowned. "So then we go home and sit around until noon?"

Her father laughed. "You make it sound like a bad thing."

Luna sighed and her mother nodded. "Going home is a

144

good idea. It's likely best to remove ourselves from everyone's sight and let them cool down a bit."

"I don't understand why everyone seems so upset," Luna said. "The ceremony was about choosing a profession, and that's what I did."

"Your mother's right," Will said. "Let's go home for now. On the way there, you can think about why the villagers might be less than impressed by how things turned out."

"Okay." Luna followed her parents from the stage, glancing at the few villagers still milling about. Each time she met someone's gaze, the woman or man would look away. Luna opened her mouth to speak with one of the women nearby but froze when she noticed Gage standing in the back of the area.

"You okay?" Will asked. He turned to follow the direction of her stare. "Ahh. Do you want to go and talk with him now?"

Luna began to nod, but Gage turned and strode away.

"I guess not," she said.

"Come on." Malena put an arm around her daughter. "You'll see him later."

Luna watched Gage until he turned the corner and disappeared from sight. Then she walked down the steps to catch up with her parents.

⸻

"Anyone hungry?" Malena said as they stepped onto the front porch.

"Maybe a sandwich to tide us over until the feast?" Will said. "That sound good to you, Luna?"

"Sure."

"I'll bring them out to the porch," Malena said.

Luna sat in a chair and stared at her hands.

Will selected a seat across from her. "You're okay, right?" he asked.

"I think so."

"Do you feel sick?"

"No."

"Dizzy?"

She shook her head.

"Good."

The sat quietly for a few minutes.

"Have you managed to come up with any guesses as to why the rest of the village is less than pleased by your selection?" Will asked.

She raised one eyebrow and looked up to meet his eyes. "Because they think my choice does them no good?"

"That's likely a good part of it," Will said. "They expected you to choose a profession in the village. As far as they're concerned, they're in worse shape than they were yesterday."

"I get that."

"Do you agree with them?"

She considered her father's question for a few seconds, then shook her head. "I don't."

"Why not?"

"Because traders are important to the villages, too. Maybe more important than any other profession."

Will chuckled. "That sounds a bit arrogant."

"Am I wrong?"

"Not at all." Will spread his hands to the sides. "Without traders, no village could survive very long."

"Some could?"

"Nope."

Luna frowned. "But I thought ... our village seems to be pretty self-sufficient. Sure, there are a few items we get from others, but we would find a way to do without. If we had to."

"Our village could survive longer than most if it was cut off from the rest, but in the end it would die. Same as all the others."

"Then, it's a good thing. For a new trader to apprentice."

"Yes, it is," Will nodded. "And the elders understand that already. But the rest of the village will take a while to see this as a good thing."

The screen door opened and Malena appeared with a tray that held a plate of sandwiches, a pitcher of lemonade, and three glasses. She set the tray on the table between them and took a seat beside Will. "Everyone will come around," she said. "Eventually."

Luna snorted.

Malena smiled. "Today's ceremony surprised them, is all."

Will reached for the pitcher and began to fill the glasses. "You're right."

"Still think it was the best way to get it done?" Mal raised one eyebrow as she asked her husband the question.

"Without a doubt." He handed a glass to Luna and then another to Mal. "The longer they had to consider the idea, the worse they'd have gotten about it."

Malena took a drink from her glass, eyes watching her daughter.

"Do you disagree?" Will asked.

Mal shook her head.

"They will come around," Will repeated. "No one likes change."

"I should make you stick around until they do," Mal said.

Will laughed. "You don't have the power as mayor to make me stay that long."

"How about as your wife?"

Will's smile melted. "Uh, yeah, I suppose so."

Mal laughed and nudged him with her shoulder. "Don't be so dramatic. I doubt I could make you stay as your wife, either. You've never been very good at listening to—or following—orders of any sort."

Will shrugged and reached for a half of a sandwich.

"Do we have to go to the lunch?" Luna asked.

Malena frowned. "Of course we do. It's in your honour."

"I don't want to."

Will took a bite of sandwich. "Why not?"

Luna shook her head.

"They aren't angry with you," Will said. "And I don't care if they're mad at me. They'll get over it."

"I doubt many of them will even show up to eat," Luna said.

"Wanna bet?" Mal asked. When Luna frowned, her mother laughed and leaned across the table to pat her daughter's leg. "They were surprised and shocked, sweetheart. Don't fret about it. Today is still the important day it was before you made your choice. And your father's right. They are getting their heads around things now. Most will be over it by the time lunch hour hits, and be there to eat and celebrate."

"Okay." Luna took a drink of lemonade and stared at the table.

Will exchanged a look with Malena. She nodded and he

rolled his eyes. "Fine," he said. "Go ahead and do that now, then."

Luna looked up and gave them a puzzled expression. "Who are you talking to?"

"You."

"Go do what now?"

Will raised one eyebrow. "Go talk to Gage."

Luna shook her head. "I doubt he'll want to talk with me."

"Maybe not." Will took another bite of sandwich and continued speaking while he chewed. "But there's some free time at the moment, and I suggest taking advantage of it. If you don't give it a shot you might not be able to talk with him alone for a while."

"I could do it tomorrow."

"Nope." Will shook his head.

"Why not?"

"Because we'll be busy tomorrow."

"Doing what?"

There was a twinkle in her father's eyes as he grinned at her. "Taking your first trip outside of the village."

29

"Sorry, Luna." Gage's father, a tall, broad-shouldered man with thinning brown hair shook his head. "He woke up early and struck out to do some errands around the village for me."

"Oh." Luna frowned. It wasn't like Gage to get up and start working early. "Okay. Can you tell him I stopped by, please?"

"Of course."

"And that I'd like to talk to him. Today, if that can work."

The man smiled. "Sure thing."

"Thanks, Mr. Lee." She turned and began to walk away.

"Congratulations, by the way."

Luna turned back and smiled at the village's elder of security and protection. "Thanks."

"I thought for sure that you were gonna pick the tower techs."

"Yeah."

"Lost some money on the whole ordeal, actually."

Luna frowned. Betting was discouraged in the village. It

was strange to hear the man responsible for enforcing rules like that admit that he'd broken one.

Mr. Lee noted her expression and laughed. "It was only a little bet. Something to add excitement to the day."

"I see."

"Are you certain?" His brows furrowed. "About becoming a trader, I mean?"

"Like my dad? Yeah, I'm sure."

"It can be dangerous out there ..."

"That's okay." Luna pursed her lips, then smiled. "If it turns out to be too unpleasant, I heard I can exit the training and make another choice."

The statement seemed to please the elder. He smiled. "That's true."

"Thanks again, Mr. Lee." Luna turned and began walking toward the street.

As she did, something in the corner of her vision caught her attention. She froze mid-step and whipped her head to the right to catch a better look.

A man dressed in a long black trench coat disappeared around the corner of the tower technician's building.

"Everything okay?" Mr. Lee called out.

"What?" Luna frowned, then waved a hand. "Yes, everything's fine."

She walked to the end of the Lees' laneway and turned toward home, her mind fixed on what she'd seen. The man had been far away, and she'd only managed to glimpse him for a second, but a couple of things bothered her immediately.

The first was that she didn't recognize him. Living in an enclosed village meant knowing everyone who lived there. No one besides a trader could travel between villages, and Luna had never heard of a trader sneaking into a village without the entire population knowing about their arrival.

The second thing was the man's long black trench coat. She had only seen one person wear a coat like that.

Her father.

LUNA CRESTED THE SMALL HILL AND SAW HER PARENTS sitting on the front porch.

Will raised his hand in greeting, and Luna returned the gesture. Will looked back to Malena and gestured wildly, as he often did when telling a story. A few seconds later, Malena tilted her head back and laughed loud enough that Luna could hear her across the distance between them.

A few minutes later, Luna was close enough to hear them speaking.

"—and the smith promised the agriculture elder that she'd never do that again." Will sat back with a smile as Malena clapped her hands together and rewarded her husband with another delighted laugh.

"That is too much," Malena shook her head. "I can't wait to tell Sally when I see her."

Will chuckled and jutted his chin in Luna's direction. "So how did it go? Is he still sulking?"

Malena held a hand up and Luna slapped it in greeting and then sat on the swinging chair beside her mother. "He wasn't home," Luna said. "I waited for a half hour, but ..." she shrugged.

"I'm sorry to hear that, Dove," Malena said. "I'm sure once the two of you talk it over, things will be fine."

"I guess."

Will leaned back in his chair and laced the fingers of his

hands together behind his head. "If he's anything like his dad—"

"Oh, he is," Mal offered.

Will raised an eyebrow and smiled. "Then he'll need a bit of time to stamp his feet, huffing and puffing like a big ol' ogre to let off steam. But when that phase is over ..."

"He'll be all 'I'm sorry, Luna,'" Mal said in a deeper voice, to mimic Gage's, "and 'I wish I hadn't behaved like that, please forgive me.'"

Will chuckled and Luna smiled. "That does sound a bit like him," Luna admitted. "I hope he does it sooner than later, though." She frowned and looked at her father. "When do we leave?"

"No set plan for that yet."

"I thought we were going out tomorrow."

"Thought we'd start today, actually."

"Really?"

"Sure." Will sat forward, one arm stretching out to rest on the back of the chair. "A quick jaunt over the line to see what's beyond."

Luna smiled and looked at her mother with excitement. The frown on Malena's face made her smile to fade. "Is something wrong, Mom?"

Malena shook her head and smiled. "Everything's fine."

Luna's eyebrows furrowed.

"She's an adult now, Mal," Will said. "No point in hiding things that are important. Especially when those things concern her."

Mal sighed and shook her head. "Fine." Her gaze slid to meet Luna's. "I'm getting pushback from the village about your choice to become a trader."

"I don't see why," Will snorted. "It should come as a surprise to no one; either that she was offered the role or that she accepted it. She's my girl. A trader from the day she was born."

Mal raised one eyebrow but didn't disagree.

"Like Dad said," Luna smiled. "They'll have to get used to it and move on, right?"

"That's what I said, yes," Mal said.

Luna heard the hesitation in her mother's voice. "But?"

Mal shook her head. "There's no but." Her gaze hardened. "You're the first to formally choose a profession. If we can't agree from the start of this process that we all spent years debating over and developing, it doesn't bode well for the future of our system."

"I agree," Luna said with a nod.

"I wish everyone did." Mal looked out over the front yard, the muscles in her jaw clenching. "Here's hoping we can make the majority agree. If it's put to a vote."

"A vote? It's that serious?" Luna felt a pit form in her stomach.

Mal smiled and patted Luna on the leg. "I doubt it will end up like that. Not if I have my way. And I usually do."

"Amen to that." Will grinned. Mal flashed him a feigned look of annoyance and then smiled too.

Malena stood. "Let's not allow this to interfere with the fun of today. We can have a quick lunch, then you two can abandon me and head out into the big wide world."

Will laughed, and Luna stood to join her mother.

30

LUNA FOLLOWED HER FATHER UP THE LARGEST HILL ON the west side of the village and then down into a small valley that was remote and uninhabited, isolated by the natural terrain.

"Do I get a trench coat like yours?" she asked as they walked.

Will smiled. "No."

Luna frowned. "That's not part of the uniform?"

He cast a quick glance at her over his shoulder before looking forward once more. "Other traders have visited from time to time," he said. "Have you ever seen one wearing a trench coat?"

"No."

He nodded as if that answered her question and turned forward once more.

"Where'd you get yours?"

He shrugged. "I don't remember."

Luna laughed.

"What?"

"Nothing."

Will stopped walking and turned to face her once more. "That wasn't a 'nothing' laugh."

"I can't recall the last time you didn't remember something. It's not something you say."

"Sure it is. There's lots of things I don't remember."

"Really?"

"Yep." He nodded and then smirked. "Here's a grown-up secret that I can share with you. Now that you're an adult." He leaned forward and lowered the volume of his voice. "Adults don't know as much as they would have you think."

Luna laughed. "Is that so?"

"Absolutely."

"They all seem to do a very good job hiding it."

"We sure do."

"This is a pretty big revelation, Dad."

He grinned. "The first of many, dear girl. The next few months are going to be filled with a ton of things that'll surprise you."

"Does anyone in the village have a trench coat? Like yours?"

"More trench coat questions?" Will scowled. "This is a strange topic to grill me on, even for you, my overly curious daughter."

She waited with a pleasant expression on her face.

"Have you seen someone else in the village with a trench coat like mine?"

"Oh, no, you don't."

Will's eyes widened. "Oh no I don't what?"

"We're not playing that game." Will stared at her, a blank expression on his face.

She laughed. "The game where you answer my questions with questions of your own ... to stop me from asking you any more questions ..."

Will frowned. "I know of no such game."

"Oh, please."

He watched her for a long moment and then winked. "So? Did you? See someone else wearing a trench coat like mine?"

Luna slapped him gently on the shoulder and shook her head. "No. It's just that I've always thought your jacket was pretty awesome and it occurred to me that maybe it was part of the trader uniform. You're right; I've never seen another trader wearing one, but like you keep saying, I'm kinda special."

"That you are."

"I wondered if maybe you'd get me one."

He considered her for a few seconds and then chuckled. "Fair enough. I'm sorry, Dove, the coat isn't part of the uniform, nor do I have an extra one to give you."

"Bummer."

"What I do have." He smiled and reached into his pocket. "Is this." He opened his fist to reveal the bracelet he'd presented to her on the day of Choosing. After the ceremony he'd collected it back, telling her that she'd be allowed to keep it on her person only after she'd passed the appropriate phase of training. "This is part of the trader uniform. It's the only part, actually." He held it up and shook it gently. "And it's yours."

Luna held out her palm and grinned as Will dropped the bracelet into her hand.

She held it up to her face, turning it slowly through her fingers as she marvelled at the bright stones, noting that each was a different colour. Red, blue, green, yellow—and many streaked with blends of different colours, such as orange with black and amber with silver shooting through it like lightning. She examined each stone carefully, noting the difference in texture and markings, before turning it again to consider the next. "The stones are so cool to the touch," she said.

"They warm up when you wear the bracelet," Will said.

"Really?"

"Yep. Your body heat soaks into them and they become warm."

"Huh."

"It's how you can tell if the stones are real or not."

She looked past the stones to her father. "What do you mean?"

"If you see a bracelet and the stones don't warm up, that means they're fake and won't work."

"Fake bracelets?"

"That's right."

"Where would I encounter that?"

"Sometimes a bracelet will appear for sale in a village."

"For regular people to buy?"

Will nodded. "If they can afford it."

"I can't imagine why someone would want to buy one."

"Living in the same village for a lifetime is natural to you. It's all you know. But it feels like an unbearable prison to some who were free to come and go wherever they wanted. Before."

"Is that why some people cross the line?"

"It is. Some people can't take the confinement and would rather die than be contained. Or ... if a chance to purchase a bracelet presented itself—even if the odds were good that it was a fake—many would take the chance and risk it. And almost all of them are fakes. Plastic or glass strung together to look real enough for someone to make a quick profit. I've heard of three people buying such bracelets." He shook his head. "It only turns out well for the person who sold it. Unless they get caught."

"Have you ever heard of someone being sold a bracelet that isn't a fake?"

"Once or twice. But we got them back."

Luna considered this information and returned to examining the remaining stones. When she was finished, she looked at Will. "Can I put it on?"

"Of course."

Luna slid the bracelet over her right hand and smiled, holding it up for her father to see.

"Put it on your other hand."

"Why?"

"You're right-handed, which means you use that hand more. If you wear the bracelet on your right hand, you increase the odds of damaging it in your day-to-day activities."

She nodded and slid the bracelet off her wrist. "That makes sense."

"Good."

She slid it over her left hand and nodded. "Feels a bit strange on this side."

"It'll feel natural in no time." Will motioned toward the wide silver line twenty feet in front of them. "Shall we?"

Luna looked toward the barrier, and a sudden weight formed in her stomach. She pursed her lips and continued to stare, her feet unmoving.

"It is scary, the first couple times."

"Especially knowing what happens if you cross the line," she said. "If you've seen someone do it before ..."

Will rested his hand on her shoulder and gave a reassuring squeeze. "It's time to take the leap, dear girl. Don't worry, you'll be safe."

She met her father's eyes and nodded.

"Follow me," he grinned. "I'll lead us across."

31

HOLDING HER BREATH AND FOCUSING HER FULL attention on her father's back, Luna followed Will toward the silver line, the warning that signalled instant death to those who stepped over it.

Will walked toward it with confidence and then stopped about five feet away. Then he turned and slowly continued moving backward. "There's nothing to be scared about, Dove. You've seen me do this so many times. There are no special motions or words required. You can walk, run, slide, or move across the line any way you like."

"The bracelet doesn't have to cross the barrier first?"

Will snickered. "If that were the case, I'd be missing a hand or two, wouldn't I?"

Luna felt her cheeks warm in embarrassment. "Yes. Right. That makes sense."

Will came to the line and stopped, arms spread in the dramatic pose he liked to use when standing in front of crowds. "You don't even need to be wearing the bracelet to cross."

"I don't?"

Her father shook his head. "As long as it's on you—in your pocket or backpack or something—you're safe to cross the barriers."

"Huh." Luna's brows furrowed slightly as she considered this new piece of information.

"I know what you want to ask," Will said. "Why wear it, then?"

Luna nodded.

"A few reasons. One, it's the badge of office and people should see it. Two, being a trader provides one with a certain measure of safety, in the villages and in some areas between."

Luna nodded. Traders were the only means of communication with the outside world. No one would risk harming a trader and cutting themselves off from the other villages and the precious resources that resulted from the cross-barrier trade. Will's second point made her pause. "Safety in the between areas?"

Will nodded.

"I'm not sure what you mean by that."

"Don't worry about that for the moment." He made a waving motion with one hand.

"But—"

Will laughed. "We'll get to that in time, dear curious daughter." He jabbed a thumb over his shoulder. "Let's focus on the activity at hand, shall we?"

Luna's frown remained, but she pursed her lips and nodded once.

"So, like I was saying. Have the bracelet on your person and then just step across the line." He turned and took two steps. Luna felt an uncontrollable twinge in her stomach, the way she always did when her father stepped over the line. She was old enough to know that this was a conditioned response, one she'd experienced since childhood—her inner instinct for self-preservation activating in response to an action that she knew, deep inside, should lead to instant death. The feeling of dread passed when Will did not explode in a crackling flash of brilliant light. It was replaced by sudden joy and exhilaration that her father was still alive, despite the insanity of what he'd just done.

Will took another few steps away from the line and then turned, allowing one hand to sweep toward the ground as he bowed from the waist theatrically. When he straightened, there was a mischievous smile on his face. "And that, my darling girl, is all there is to it."

Luna nodded tersely, her stomach roiling once more as she realized her turn to do the insane was fast approaching.

"The best way to do it," Will said, noting the doubt and fear in her body language, "is to not think about it at all."

"Too late."

Will laughed. "Then stop thinking about it."

"You make that sound easy, Dad."

"Because it is, daughter."

Luna's eyebrows furrowed deeper.

"I would never allow you to do something that would hurt you."

The words touched Luna in her core. She felt the twisting in her stomach pause. "I know that's true."

"What do we say about fear?" he prompted.

"Fear is the mind killer," she recited without pause or hesitation. It was part of the opening soliloquy from an old science-fiction book she and her parents loved. One that they had read over and over, incorporating many of the principles and ideas into their family philosophy of the world and how to deal with it.

"That's right," Will nodded. "So ignore it and do your thing."

Luna took a deep breath, banished the fear, and began to walk forward.

32

THE LINE.

That's what everyone in the village—and every other village, according to the traders she had spoken with —called it.

Her mind raced as she strode toward it, one foot moving in front of the other with purpose and measure. Created and maintained by the same source of power that kept the protective barrier functioning around the village, the line never appeared scuffed or faded. Silent and subtle, it encircled the village and performed its solemn role of declaring to all that they were close to the invisible barrier that protected them from the dangers of the world beyond.

It was the only visible clue that the barrier existed. Simple but effective, it represented both fierce protection and complete destruction, should one try to cross it.

A memory from her childhood flashed through Luna's mind: her father standing on the ledge of the rock quarry–turned–swimming hole. There were flat areas along the cliff edges that people used as platforms to jump and dive into the water. The shortest jump was from a ledge fifteen feet above the water's surface. Luna remembered the first time she had jumped from that ledge. She also recalled at this instant how, to her seven-year-old eyes, it had felt a hundred times taller. She'd walked to the edge and then frozen in place, staring in fear at the water below, unable to jump.

The day she'd jumped was not the first, or even the tenth, time that she had stood on that ledge and looked down at that water below. There had been many climbs before, and she had always turned back.

Her parents had never judged or teased her about it.

On the day she finally jumped, her father had said something that now came flooding back to her mind.

"It's not the height or the fear stopping you, sweetheart. It's all you. Only you."

It had made so much sense at that moment. With a smile and a nod, Luna stepped off the edge, excitement coursing through her as she plunged toward the water.

The same excitement was pulsing through her body now, the same exhilaration broadening her smile, as Luna's foot rose over the line and she stepped off another sort of cliff into a new life.

Popping and tingling sensations began to dance across her skin. She was tempted to stop, to stand at the barrier and bask in the energy. It was like stepping into a hot shower on an icy cold morning. But she didn't. Instead, she did her best to be in the moment, to feel what was happening as her next step took her through the invisible field and into a world she'd hardly dreamt of entering.

The sensations ended as quickly as they'd begun. She took four more steps, and then she was standing in front of her father.

"Well?" he asked.

"That was," she breathed, "amazing."

"You did it!" Will drew her into his arms and hugged her tight. "You actually did it."

Luna laughed and returned the hug, then stepped back. "You sound surprised."

"Nope." Will shook his head. "Not surprised at all. I remember a young girl standing high above the water at the quarry. It took her a few tries to get up the courage to jump, but she did it. I knew this would be similar."

"That's strange. I was thinking about that same moment as I crossed over just now."

"And on your first attempt." He smiled. "I'm very proud of you."

"Thanks."

"Your Mom thought it wouldn't happen today."

Luna laughed. "Really?"

"Yep. She guessed it would take three or four tries." Luna scowled and Will laughed. "She wasn't selling you short. It often takes a new trader more than a dozen attempts to get up the courage to make the first crossing."

"Is that so?"

He nodded. "And that's with people who were alive before the barriers were created. Three was a very aggressive expectation. She believes in you."

The knowledge made Luna smile. "And what about you? How many tries did you think I'd need?"

Will laughed. "Like I said, I remember standing beside that little girl high above the water." His eyes were glassy, his smile filled with pride as he reached up to wipe away a tear. "You're my girl. I knew you'd do it today."

Luna felt a sense of deep satisfaction, thankful both her parents felt so confident in her. Also grateful that they always had. "I'm glad you were here to see it, Dad."

"Me too, Dove." He jutted his chin toward the barrier. "And so are they."

Luna turned and felt a wave of emotion wash over her.

Standing on the other side of the barrier were her mother and Gage, both smiling.

Luna raised a hand in greeting, tears of happiness in her eyes.

"Way to go, Dove!" Mal cheered.

Luna laughed and gave a tiny curtsey. Then her eyes met Gage's.

He nodded once and smiled as he began clapping his hands.

33

"So? What do you think so far?"

Luna considered the question as she strolled at her father's side, walking parallel to the village barrier through the tall, unkempt grass. "It feels different, but I'm not certain if that's real or just because I'm excited at the newness of this all."

"It's—" Will began, but Luna held up one hand to stop him from saying more.

"Don't tell me. Let me try and figure it out."

They walked in silence for the next few minutes, Will setting a leisurely pace that Luna matched without thinking. Will looked over his shoulder and waved to his wife. Malena smiled and returned the gesture.

"It is different," Luna finally declared. Long seconds passed without comment from Will. "Isn't it?" she asked.

"What makes you think so?"

She smiled. Her father often responded to questions with probing queries of his own. That was one of the things that made him a good teacher, she reflected. "The sounds, smells ... even the colours and the way things look. They all seem the same, except,"—she shook her head—"a tiny bit off."

Will chuckled.

"Am I wrong?"

"Nope. You're exactly right."

Luna grinned at the praise in her father's voice.

"Most don't detect the subtle differences until they've crossed back and forth dozens of times. You're a natural at this stuff, kiddo."

"At what?" Luna snorted. "Stepping across a silver line?"

"No," Will shook his head. "That's the easy part."

"You know, I feel sort of embarrassed."

"Why's that?"

Luna met her father's gaze. "You've been a trader for my entire life, and I know almost nothing about the job."

A bark of laughter escaped Will's lips. "That's more to my credit than your lack of interest. Ever since you've been able to talk, deflecting your questions about being a trader has been almost a tougher job than actually being a trader."

One corner of Luna's mouth curved upward into a grin. "I *have* tried to know more."

Another laugh. "That you have. And now, after all these years, I can finally begin to share the secrets that I've had to keep from you." He nodded. "It will be good to teach you all about this stuff, Dove. Hiding it from you over the years has been one of my greatest struggles."

"Is that why you offered me the job? To finally share the secrets?"

Will shook his head. "I'd like to say yes, but the truth is, if I didn't feel you were qualified to do this, I wouldn't have made the offer. But I'm certainly glad things turned out this way."

"Me, too."

Will stopped walking, and Luna did as well. He looked around and then turned so that his back was to the village. "Let's head this way. It's time for your first lesson."

"I thought we were only going for a short walk today."

"Yes." He nodded. "And a short lesson. This way." He began to walk and Luna fell into step beside him.

***

THEY CRESTED A HILL AND WALKED DOWN INTO A small valley. Luna noted types of trees and plants that she'd never seen inside the village. She stopped at a squat, wide shrub with blue berries scattered through its branches. One hand reached toward a berry and paused before touching it. She looked toward her father, eyebrows rising.

"Go ahead." He said.

Luna plucked the berry, examined it for signs of small bugs, and then popped it into her mouth and chewed. "Oh, wow," she mumbled, her eyes closing and a smile appearing on her face.

"Tasty, right?"

Her eyes popped open. "Way better than the ones that grow inside the village."

"Yeah."

"How come you've never brought any home with you?" she asked.

"Didn't want to ruin it for you."

"The surprise of tasting them now?"

"No." He shook his head. "The taste of the ones that you've been used to eating."

"Ahh." Luna nodded. "I suppose that makes sense." She plucked another berry and popped it into her mouth. "It's definitely ruined now, though. The ones I grew up eating aren't half as sweet. They'll taste horrible next time I eat one."

"You'll survive without these in a bowl beside the others to compare." He smiled. "And when they are in season out here, you can enjoy the treat."

"Wait a minute." Luna's eyes widened. "Oh, no."

"What is it?"

She paused and then laughed. "Never mind."

"No, tell me."

"I had a sudden thought these might be poisonous. You know, because we're outside of the barrier."

Will raised one eyebrow. "But then you remembered I'm your father and wouldn't let you eat something that could hurt you?"

She felt her cheeks flush with warmth and smiled. "Yeah."

"I know this is a lot for you to process and take in. Don't worry, I'm keeping an eye out."

"Thanks."

"But you make a good point. As a rule of thumb, don't eat anything out here unless I've taught you it is safe."

"That makes perfect sense." Luna stood and they continued to walk toward the middle of the clearing. As they did, Luna noted that the grass was bent to the ground, as if the space had been walked upon often. Then she saw a small table, old and cracked, with faded brown paint. The table had a single drawer with a round, white knob in its centre.

"Check it out." Will stopped beside the table and jutted his chin toward the far hill they were facing.

Luna noted various kinds of debris, scattered at intervals across the area. A rectangular door was propped up twenty or so feet away, while a big metal can two feet square rested twice as far from them. There was a stack of rubber tires, two bales of hay half-covered by a tattered beige tarp, and other large items. "What's with all those things?" she asked.

"They are targets."

"What do you use them for?"

Will reached for the drawer and pulled it open. Luna leaned closer and saw it was empty.

"There are many things to learn before you get to make trips between villages on your own," Will said. "Some are more important than others, but all are vital in their own way."

"Okay."

"The things you will learn out here ..." Will's eyes locked onto hers with an intense gaze. "Are not to be shared with villagers."

Luna frowned.

"I'm serious, Luna. No one can know what we do or talk about."

"Okay."

"Not even Gage."

Luna pursed her lips.

"Do you agree to keep these secrets?"

She nodded. "I do."

"Good." Will jutted his chin toward the targets. "I'm about to show you something that will take a bit of time to process."

"I understand."

"Not at first, you won't." His smile looked sad. "But it'll make sense soon enough."

She frowned and Will reached behind him, pushing his trench coat out of the way. Luna noticed some sort of harness wrapped around her father's shoulders, which held an object hanging under his left arm. Will's fingers wrapped around it, withdrawing it from the black leather holding it in place.

It was a length of shiny silver metal. A third of it—the part farthest from his hand—was thin, with sharp angles that melded toward the middle portion, which was wider and then turned at a sudden right angle to form a grip, which rested in his hand. He placed the item on the table and let his coat fall back into place. The metal thing thunked as it touched the wood.

Luna frowned and stepped closer to examine it. She would have reached for it, but something in her mind said not to touch this thing and she let her hands hang loosely.

She considered the device for half a dozen breaths. Then she looked up at her father, noting his serious expression.

He reached down and picked it up, holding it with the long narrow portion pointing skyward between them. "This is called—"

"A gun," Luna whispered.

Will paused, a frown darkening his face. "How do you know that?"

She shook her head.

"We've been very careful to keep items such as this out of the villages, especially away from the children," Will muttered. "There must have been a story or magazine that snuck through with mention of them."

"No," Luna said.

"Then how—"

"A dream." She looked up and met her father's eyes. "I saw one in a dream. A few nights ago."

Will's confusion deepened. "That's not possible."

"I know it sounds crazy, but it's the truth."

He considered her for a long moment. "Do you know what it is capable of?"

"Yes."

"In the dream—" He paused, as if not wanting to ask. "Who was holding the gun?"

Luna closed her eyes for a moment and then opened them. "I was."

34

Will stared at Luna, eyes narrowed as thoughts tumbled through his mind. "I know you've had strange dreams every so often." He shook his head. "But this is ..." He shook his head. "It's a bit much to process."

Luna nodded. "I know. But it's the truth."

Will's other hand moved to the side of the gun. He pressed a small button and a piece of metal slid from the bottom of the handle in his grip. Will set the black metallic piece onto the table, then placed the main part down beside it. He met Luna's eyes and nodded toward the weapon. "Tell me what you know about it."

"Not much." Her eyes slid toward the gun. "I didn't know it broke apart into two pieces. In my dream, I was older ... a couple of years, maybe. And I had a gun. Not this one. Mine was a little smaller."

Will slid his arm beneath his coat, behind his back. He withdrew a smaller gun that looked similar but not identical to the one on the table. It was dull black, shorter overall, and had a smaller hand grip. He set it down beside the first and looked at his daughter. "Did it look more like this?"

"Yeah." Luna stared at the second gun. "I think this was the one."

"Pick it up."

She frowned.

"Go ahead."

Luna reached down and let her fingertips brush across the grip. Then she took a deep breath, exhaled, and picked it up.

Will noted her expression and chuckled. "Heavier than you thought it would be, right?"

"No." Luna grinned. "It feels ... perfect." She turned and raised the gun, putting both hands on the grip as she looked down the barrel toward the targets in the distance. "Is it loaded and ready to shoot?"

"Yes." His expression darkened. "And here's your first lesson. Guns are extremely dangerous. Never—and I do mean that...never—allow the barrel to point at you or someone else. Never holster the weapon without making sure that it can't shoot accidentally. We will talk about safety constantly, and you will never roll your eyes. You'll not say, 'I know, Dad'. Safety is key. Do you understand?"

"I do."

Will stared at her for a long moment and then motioned with his hand. "Okay, then. Let's see what you can do with it."

Luna felt a sense of calm as her eyes narrowed to focus on her target: a cracked wooden door propped against the steep hillside in the distance. Her right index finger slid up and covered the trigger, slowly applying pressure that increased until—

BAM!

The gun kicked upward and back at the same instant as the boom thundered from the weapon's muzzle. Luna's eyes widened in surprise; the sound and recoil much stronger than she remembered from the dream. Despite the shock, she kept her eyes on the door and noted the puff of wood as the bullet exploded into its target.

"Damn," Will said. "You actually hit something, girl."

"Wide and high," Luna murmured. "I was aiming for the top right window pane."

Will laughed. "Well, you only missed it by a couple inches. Well done. You're a natural at this."

Luna lowered the gun so that it was pointing toward the ground and smiled as she met her father's gaze. Then her brows furrowed.

"What's wrong?" Will's smile faded as he noted Luna's concern.

"I shouldn't know what a gun is, or how to use it."

"Are you sure you never saw mention of such a thing in the village? In books or magazines?"

"I can't remember ever seeing it. You just said you tried to make sure none of us learned about them."

"That's right."

"Why?"

"A few reasons, but mostly because there's no need for children to know about such things. Guns—or violence at the hands of others," he shook his head. "Those are things from the old days. Before the towers were raised to protect everyone from stuff like that."

"Aren't such things important to know about?"

"Not in this new world. Not for the average person who will spend their entire lifetime inside a village."

"Which isn't us."

Will's smile faded.

"In my dream, I used a gun to kill someone."

"Aw, Dove," Will groaned, "I sincerely hope that it never comes to that."

"What else are guns used for, Dad? Besides killing?"

"Well ... protection—" He paused.

Luna waited for him to say more.

"That's all guns are for, Luna. Using deadly force to protect yourself from things that can hurt you if you don't stop them."

Luna's gaze swept outward, scanning the limits her vision. "What sort of things can I expect to run into out here?"

"I'll teach you as we go on," Will said. "For now, let's just focus on practicing with the gun."

35

Luna smiled as they crested the hill.

Her mother sat on the rocks, waiting for them to return. Gage was there, too, gesturing as he spoke to Malena, a wide smile on his face. He stopped speaking when he noticed Luna and Will, and his expression became more serious as he swivelled to face them.

They came close to the line and Will motioned toward it. "After you."

She nodded.

"Same as before. A simple step over and you're back inside the safety of the towers."

"So simple," she said.

He raised one eyebrow. "As long as you have a bracelet."

Luna's right hand moved toward her left wrist, her fingertips brushing against the now warm stones of her bracelet.

"Off ya go." Will smiled.

Luna nodded and walked toward the line, feeling the tingle of energy sweep over her as she stepped into and then past the invisible barrier for the second time that day. She turned and watched her father enter, remembering the sense of awe and wonder she'd always felt at seeing him cross the line. It felt much less mysterious now that she could do the same thing herself.

"Look at the new trader!" Gage stood and applauded, his eyes sparkling as they met Luna's. She felt her cheeks flush with sudden warmth and smiled as Gage and Malena made their way toward them.

"Well?" Mal's eyes were wide. "Was it as exciting as you expected it to be?"

Luna laughed and looked over her shoulder at the space beyond the line. "The world on the other side of the barrier looks pretty much the same as it does on this side. At least," she raised an eyebrow and glanced at her father, "the tiny bit of it that Dad allowed me to see."

"Pretty much the same," Gage said, "isn't exactly the same, is it?"

Luna grinned, pleased that he'd picked up on the distinction. She opened her mouth to say more, but her father cleared his throat and shook his head. She nodded and Gage chuckled. "Trader secrets already, I see."

"Not for traders only." Mal smiled and batted her eyelashes. "I know them, too."

Gage laughed. "Well, I'm glad I was here to see you make your first trip over the line, Luna. It was incredible."

"I'm glad you were here too, Gage."

There was a moment of silence.

"Let's give the kids some space," Mal suggested, stepping close and twining her arm through her husband's. "I want to discuss a few pieces of village business with you on the way home."

Will sighed. "Trader and mayor business. I suppose I've put that stuff off as long as possible." He smiled at

Luna. "Great job out there today, Luna. See you at dinner."

"Thanks, Dad." Luna nodded, giving him a look that assured him she wouldn't share any of the information she'd learned during their session over the line. She watched her parents make their way over the hill and then turned back to Gage.

"Hi," he said.

"Hi."

Silence hung between them for long seconds.

"I'm sorry," both said in unison. Then their eyes widened and they laughed at the same instant as well.

"Let me go first," Gage said.

"Okay."

"I've been an idiot."

"No—"

"Uh-uh." He held up a hand. "Let me finish." She smiled and nodded. "When your dad spoke up and offered you a position as trader it sort of blew my mind—"

"Mine, too."

Gage continued, shaking his head with a confused expression. "And before I could even process the thought ... you were saying yes." His eyebrows furrowed. "My whole world kinda melted in front of my eyes." He looked at the ground. "I know we've both spent a lot of time thinking about our lives and where things would go once we become adults. There've been so many possibilities to consider and think about." He shrugged and looked up, sadness in his eyes as they met hers. "But never in a million years did it occur to me that I'd have to spend the rest of my life without you living in the village."

Luna opened her mouth to speak but pursed her lips and remained silent.

"I'm not mad." Another pause. Gage raised one eyebrow. "Okay. I am mad."

She laughed.

He grinned. "But not at you. Now that I've had a bit of time to think about the whole thing, it makes perfect sense, you becoming a trader."

"It does?"

"Sure. You've always been a strong and smart kid. Your mom is the mayor and your dad is a trader. You were bound to follow in one of their footsteps. I know you had zero desire to be mayor, so ..." He shrugged.

"It never occurred to me that becoming a trader might be an option," Luna admitted.

Gage laughed. "Yeah, me neither."

Luna grabbed Gage's hand and led him to the rocks, where they sat down together. "I'm glad you're not mad," she said. "When I went to see you and you weren't around ..."

"I'm not mad *now*." He smiled. "I was less than thrilled for the first little bit."

"Gage," Luna sighed.

"I know. My temper." He shrugged. "In my defence, I figured it was best to avoid you until it cooled down. Plus, it gave me time to adjust to the news. I didn't want to say something that I'd regret. Something that wasn't true and only came from a place of hurt."

Luna nodded. "I'm sorry if this has hurt you. I never wanted that."

"It's fine." He shook his head. "I know you didn't mean to hurt me. And you didn't." He saw her expression and quickly continued. "Honest, Luna. You didn't. I guess I was mostly sad to know that you're leaving me behind. When we kissed ... well, I thought there might be more to that. But now that you're leaving—" He shook his head. "Seems like only a few days ago everything was so good. And now it feels as if it's all gone, before it ever got a chance to start."

Luna wanted to tell him that things were fine, that nothing had changed. To assure him that the future still held them together, as at least friends, and maybe more. But she realized she had no idea what becoming a trader would lead to. She had barely learned anything about her new role, but she'd already discovered it was dangerous. In her mind's eye, she saw herself firing the gun at the targets.

Then she had another flash. Of the dream where she had killed the beast that was the boy sitting next to her right now.

Gage sat silently, waiting for her to say something. To reassure him. She thought long and hard for a few seconds, then reached out and patted his knee. "Don't worry. I'm sure life will be fine for both of us. And that we will always be friends, at least."

His laugh was filled with bitterness.

Luna frowned.

"I know, you're probably right," he sighed. "But I was hoping you'd say something more positive."

"Oh. Well. Maybe we—"

"Yeah," he held up a hand and stood. "Maybe." He leaned down and kissed her gently on the cheek, then straightened and began to walk away. "I've gotta get the chores done before dinner. I'll call on you tomorrow?"

"I'd like that." Luna felt a pang of sadness as he nodded and continued walking.

36

As Luna was getting ready to do chores the next morning, Will announced that he had business to attend to in the village. Mal would be gone all day, too, and Luna would be free to spend the day on her own.

At first, the prospect seemed exciting and she smiled through the morning chores so hard it almost made her cheeks sore. But afterward, the allure of her freedom quickly faded.

Luna walked up the front porch steps and sat down on the swing to think. She'd never had an entire day free to herself before. After a few minutes of considering how to fill that time, her excitement dimmed.

With a sigh, she realized that everything she enjoyed doing involved spending time with friends, reading, or hiking.

"Well," she said to herself as she got to her feet. "Since everyone's in school, I guess I'll read for a bit."

THREE HOURS LATER, LUNA SET DOWN HER BOOK AND decided to have lunch. She made a sandwich from leftovers and reclined on the couch once more to eat it.

Sandwich finished, she sighed loudly and looked around.

"Maybe a walk into town," she said to herself, dropping the book on the end table as she stood. She took her plate to the sink, donned a light jacket, and glanced at the clock on the wall as she opened the door to leave: 11:30 a.m.

Chuckling to herself, Luna shut the door behind her, pushing once to make sure the lock was engaged.

Then she headed into town.

IT DIDN'T TAKE LONG FOR LUNA TO SPOT THE MAN IN the long black trench coat once more.

She'd been walking down Main Street for a few minutes, greeting people she passed. She'd spent a few minutes speaking with a tower tech, and as the woman walked away, Luna stared up at the Tower Technology Hall, her thoughts focused on what life might have been like had she chosen that as her profession.

Continuing on toward the Town Hall, she cast a quick glance over her shoulder to look at the tower tech building again. And that's when she saw him, walking toward her from less than a block away.

The man was tanned, with angular facial features beneath black stubble. His black hair was short and tousled. He was too far away to discern the colour of his eyes, but close enough that she could tell he was watching her.

Her pulse quickened, and she felt a tightness in her

throat that she recognized as fear. She opened her mouth, wondering if it might be best to scream.

And then the man abruptly turned left into a side street.

Luna stood in place, questions flooding her mind. Was he really following her, or had it been a coincidence they were on the same street, walking the same direction? If he was following her, where should she go? He had numerous options now: he could circle around and get in front of her, or he could hide and keep following from a safer distance.

Luna shook her head and laughed nervously. "He's not following you, dummy," she chided herself in a soft whisper. *But who is he?* She wondered silently. *And why didn't any of the villagers who were near him on the street stop to ask the same question?*

There were never strangers in the village. The tower barrier made sure of that. That a stranger was here could mean only one of two things: Either the man was someone that everyone knew and she had somehow never seen before. Or he was a vision that only Luna could see.

Most of her visions occurred in dreams, but there had been a few times when she'd experienced waking visions similar to this, seen things others couldn't. It had never felt this real, but she couldn't rule out the possibility.

Luna turned on her heel and began to make her way to the Town Hall. The best thing might be to meet up with her parents and have lunch—another lunch—with them.

She decided to worry about the mysterious man in the black trench coat when—if—she saw him again.

37

Luna saw the man in the black trench coat four more times over the next three days.

The sightings were never close up, nor did they last for more than a few seconds, which both frustrated her and continued to pique her curiosity. She had never kept secrets from her parents, but something told her not to say anything to anyone about this.

Sighting number five occurred as Luna was walking to meet her mother for lunch. It was the most fleeting glimpse of all—a portion of black trench coat disappearing around a corner. Not entirely certain if the sight was real or her imagination, she continued walking and turned onto Main Street near the Town Hall.

Spotting her mother standing in front of the main building, talking with a villager, Luna raised her hand in greeting. Mal returned the gesture. As she got closer, the villager walked away and Mal turned to greet her daughter.

"Good morning."

"Uh-oh," Luna said.

"What?"

"You don't sound like you're in a good mood."

"I'm not." Mal's eyes slid toward the retreating figure of the villager and she shook her head.

"Is it something Emma said?" Luna watched the woman turning up the sidewalk toward the main building of the Smith Hall.

"Her and others."

"I'm sorry to hear that your morning hasn't gone well."

Mal took a deep breath, sighed and shook her head. When she met her daughter's eyes, a smile replaced the frown. "There has been too much whining and complaining from the citizens lately. I know that listening to and dealing with stuff like this is part of my job, but ..." She reached out and touched Luna's shoulder. "Come on. Let's go get lunch and forget all about the trials of politics, shall we?"

"Sure."

As they entered Malena's office, Luna smiled to see her dad sitting in a chair across from the mayor's desk, feet propped on the edge of it with one leg crossed over the other. He looked up from reading a sheet of paper and jutted his chin toward them in greeting.

"There you are." Luna gave him a kiss on the cheek.

"Yes, here I am. And look at you!" Will accepted the kiss and let the page rest on his lap. "Finally awake and walking around with the rest of us."

"Please," Luna snorted. "I was awake long before you were, dear Daddy. The chores didn't do themselves, you know."

Will snorted.

"Wait a minute." Luna furrowed her brows and gave

each parent a look. "Is that why we're still in the village and not out teaching me how to be a trader? So that I can keep doing the chores?"

Will chuckled and removed his feet from the desk, sitting up and leaning forward to place the paper he'd been reading on top of a small pile of others. "I told you she was clever, Mal. Our master plan has been discovered."

Luna laughed but stopped when she noticed that her mother didn't appear to find the joke funny. "Mom?"

"Hmm?" Mal, now seated at her desk, was reading the page Will had set down.

"Where are you right now?"

Mal sighed and held the paper toward Luna. "Read this."

Luna read, feeling a sense of dread set in as she was halfway through.

"Yeah," Will said. "Not the best of news."

Luna finished reading and looked at her mother. "The council wants to negate my choice to become a trader?"

"And they've begun formal procedures to do so," Mal said.

"Can they do that?"

"No," Will said.

Luna waited for her mother to agree, but she didn't. "Mom? Can they do that?"

"Not specifically."

Luna shook her head. "What's that mean?"

Mal leaned back in her chair, lacing fingers together behind her head. "There are provisions in the constitution that might allow it."

Will huffed. "If they warp and twist the words to their limit." He shook his head. "This is disgusting."

"Will—" Mal said.

"No." He made a swiping gesture. "This is exactly the sort of thing we've worked so hard to avoid, Mal. Corruption and manipulation for personal gain and power."

"I don't think it's as bad as that," Malena said.

"Maybe not yet, but this is how it starts."

Mal opened her mouth to say something, then nodded. "Yes. You're right."

There was silence for a few seconds.

"I'm sorry," Luna said.

"For what, Dove?" Will asked.

"I didn't mean to cause so much trouble. Not with the villagers, and definitely not between you and Mom."

"There's no trouble between your father and I," Mal smiled. "As always, we agree and are as one."

"That's right," Will said. "We discuss things and sometimes disagree for a bit behind closed doors, but our minds are more alike than any two people on the planet." He smiled at Malena. "And we knew this would happen someday, even though both of us hoped it wouldn't."

"People hate change," Malena said. "They all thought you would choose a profession and remain in the village."

"But new traders are vital to our existence as well," Luna said. "They must realize that."

"Many do," Will said. "But some are too dim—"

"Or too selfish," Mal added.

"Or too selfish," Will agreed, "to allow this to go without being challenged." He stood, stretched his arms over his head, and groaned loudly before continuing. "But it looks as if that's how things are gonna be."

"What do we do, then?" Luna asked. "Do I change my selection and agree to choose a profession inside the village?"

"Is that what you'd like to do?" Mal asked.

"No ..."

"Then there's your answer," Will said. He placed one arm around Luna's shoulder and leaned in to kiss her on the cheek. "Don't worry, daughter. We'll stand up to the frightened bullies and fight. And win."

"Good." Luna smiled and looked to her mother for encouragement. When she saw the expression on Mal's face, her smile faded. "We will win, right, Mom?"

Mal nodded, a look of grim determination on her face. "That's right, Luna. We will."

38

"And ..." Will's voice. "Begin."

Eyes closed, Luna reached out and felt for the pistol and ammo magazine that had been placed on the table before her father blindfolded her. In an instant, she realized that he'd switched the placement of the components before telling her to start.

"Tricky," she mumbled, switching the pieces so that the magazine was in her left hand and gun in right. With a quick flick of her thumb, she made sure the bullets were pointing up and away from her, then positioned the magazine into the butt of the pistol grip and pushed upwards until she heard the audible click that told her it was secure and in place. Next, she used her left hand to pull back the slide and load a bullet into the firing chamber. Her body turned half a step to the right—away from where her father's voice had sounded—and she raised the weapon to shoulder height with both hands on the grip. Her thumb touched the safety button to make sure that it was engaged. "Ready to fire," she announced, holding the pose.

"I didn't move the targets," Will said. "Aim for the top right window pane of the big door and take a shot."

Luna pressed her lips together and nodded. Her thumb flipped the safety off as the weapon moved to where she pictured the target in her mind's eye. As the gun stopped moving, she fired, and a single, loud explosion erupted from the weapon, followed by silence. Luna remained frozen in the ready position, pistol aimed and finger on the trigger to fire again if her father commanded her to do so.

"At ease," Will said.

Luna engaged the safety and lowered the gun while her other hand came up and slid the blindfold from her eyes. She squinted, looking off into the distance. "I didn't hear the bullet strike wood."

"It didn't."

"Damn." She ejected the magazine, used the slide to remove the chambered bullet, and set the weapon onto the table, shaking her head in disappointment. "I thought for sure I had the right line on the target."

"Oh, you did."

"Then how could I have missed? Unless ..." She paused for a second and then a smile appeared on her face. "There was no sound 'cause the bullet went straight through the small window pane."

Will laughed. "That's exactly what happened. I saw the puff of dirt behind the spot."

Luna laughed, too. "There was no glass to break because I shot it out days ago."

"Great job." Will patted her on the shoulder. "Next time, I think I'll make you shoot three or four targets from memory and see how you do."

"Okay." She began to pull the blindfold up toward her eyes.

"Not now," Will said. "There will be no more shooting today."

"Time's up already?"

"Yeah." He reached for her gun, slid the magazine into place, and tucked it into the back of his belt.

"Boo."

"We have a few more hours this side of the line," he said, "but that time should be used to teach you things you need to improve on." He grinned. "You shoot as if you've been doing it your whole life."

"Thank you."

"I'm not certain that's a compliment."

Luna laughed. "Must be in the genes."

Will considered her words and nodded. "Your mother is a good shot."

"And you."

"Oh, yeah." He grinned. "I am too."

"What are we gonna spend the rest of our time doing then?" she asked. Will's sudden grin conveyed an eagerness that made Luna groan. "Not foraging?"

"Yes. Foraging." Will's eyes widened as he said the word.

"I hate foraging."

"Because you're no good at it."

"Exactly."

"Which is why we need to spend more time practicing."

"But it's boring."

"Maybe, but the skill is way more important than knowing how to use a weapon."

Luna scowled. "I don't believe that."

"Well," he said, shrugging, "maybe not *more* important, but at least as. Out there in the Wild, I've found it necessary to forage for food and water way more often than fire my weapon."

"I don't see why you'd need to forage. A trader has supplies. More than enough to get you from one village to the other." She frowned. "Right?"

"Yes. But getting stuck in the Wild longer than expected is always a very real possibility. I want you as prepared as possible for when it eventually does happen."

"I guess you're right."

"Of course I am." Will looked at his wristwatch. "But let's eat lunch before we begin. How's that sound?"

"Perfect."

Luna retrieved a nylon backpack from beside the table and the two moved to a grassy area away from the shooting range. She unzipped the bag and reached in to retrieve a plastic container that held two sandwiches. She peeled the lid away and held the container toward her father.

"Thanks." He grabbed half of a sandwich and waited to eat until she took a bite of hers.

Luna paused before taking a second bite. "How do you think the council session will go?"

"When it finally happens?" Will took another bite and chewed slowly. "No idea why they put it off until next week instead of dealing with it right away." He shrugged and smiled. "I expect that it'll turn out smooth as silk. Same as always."

"I sure hope you're right."

"Your mom has been in discussions with each of the council members, and every elder she's spoken with has assured her they are voting on our side."

"If that's true, then why the need to vote at all?"

He sighed. "Because apparently the council wanted a few extra days to consider the idea before formally accepting. We do expect some of the members to use this as an excuse to add some modifications to the village constitution regarding the Choosing procedure and rules. Small things that sound as if they will help over time."

"So that the next time a Choosing happens there are no surprises?"

"*Fewer surprises* is how your mom is selling it, but yes." Will smiled and took another bite. "If you ask me, I think it's silly to try and anticipate every detail down to the smallest thing. It's impossible to completely control an event. Something always seems to happen that no one thought of."

Luna nodded in agreement. They had discussed this often over the years. At first she'd disagreed, but experience had taught her that Will's words on the subject contained truth and wisdom.

"Have you thought about the future?" Will asked. "Where you see yourself in three years, or ten?"

"I always think about the future."

"See it, you mean."

She smiled. Her declarations more often than not came true.

"Foretelling the future might be more difficult than you're used to. At least for the next little bit."

"Why do you say that?"

Will popped the last bit of the sandwich into his mouth. "Life choices for the average villager are simple, but now you have more options as a trader. And that could make it more of a challenge for you to say how it will all end up."

"I doubt it. Things might be a bit different from how I'd expected, but life is life. I've always imagined that I'd grow up, work, have a family, raise kids, get old, and die. I expect that's how it will end up turning out still. Traders have lives too, right?"

"They do," Will chuckled. "And you're right, in the broad scheme of it all. But I think that, when you look at it a bit closer, it could have some twists and turns you hadn't anticipated. Your general assessment sounds accurate and factual, but it seems to have removed all of the fun and excitement from life."

"I suppose it does sound dull, yeah."

"Try not to let it be. Life is in the little stuff, Dove. The smallest detail—something that might appear to be trivial in the moment—can be the very thing that gives your experiences a distinct flavour when you remember them years later. That's not always true, but sometimes it can be."

Luna nodded, considering her father's words.

"Being a trader will probably add a bit more zest to your experiences than regular people end up getting."

She smiled. "I'm sure it will. Thank you for that."

Will snorted. "There will be times you won't be so thankful. The life of a trader isn't as fun as most think, but I'm sure you'll be awesome at it."

Luna reached for a second half of sandwich. "What sort of extra things do I have to consider then? That a normal villager wouldn't?"

"Where you will end up living is one."

She paused mid-bite, her eyes narrowing. "Won't I just live here in this village?"

"Sure, but you could also live in another village. Any of them, actually."

"Really?"

Will nodded.

"Wow." She let the sandwich rest on her lap. "I hadn't thought of that."

"Because it wasn't an option before now."

"You're right. I guess I'll have to give it some thought."

Luna stared at her sandwich. "I mean, when I think of home, this is it. And of course, I'd want to be close to you and Mom. And ..."

"And maybe you decide there's a boy here to settle down with?"

"Maybe." Luna frowned as a thought occurred to her. "Hey, can I ask you a question?"

"Fire away."

"Did you tell anyone the exact day that you would return to the village on this last trip home?"

"The exact day?" Will frowned and shook his head. "No. I couldn't have, because I wasn't sure myself. Unknown complications can always pop up in the Wild. I often give your mother and a few villagers a range of dates that I hope to return by, but no, I didn't tell anyone the exact day I'd be back."

"That's what I thought." Luna frowned, continuing to stare at the sandwich in her hand.

"Why do you ask?"

She shrugged and looked up at Will with a smile. "I thought maybe you had a more accurate way of doing things. Something that you'd reveal, now that I'm training for the job."

"Nope. No secret there." Will brushed the crumbs from his lap and stood. "Okay, let's get to learning more about foraging now, shall we?"

39

"Looks like you've got company." Will jutted his chin toward the line and Luna followed his gaze.

Gage sat on a broad, flat stone with legs swinging as he watched them approach. He smiled and raised a hand in greeting.

"Ugh, not now." Luna grumbled under her breath but smiled and waved back.

Will chuckled. "I never thought I'd hear you say such a thing about your pal. At least, not so soon into your relationship."

Luna's brows furrowed, eyes narrowing as she looked toward her father. "What do you mean, relationship?"

Will raised a hand and made a calming gesture. "I simply meant that this whole trader issue has to be causing a bit of tension between the two of you."

"I suppose it is."

"At least the boy doesn't appear to be jealous of you, so that's something."

Luna frowned. "Why would he be?"

Laughter. "You've been offered a chance to do something the rest can't. To come and go as you like between villages. To step through the barrier around your home and explore beyond. I'm sure every kid dreams of doing that at some point or another."

Luna thought about what her father was saying and nodded. "Yeah, you are right about that." She could quickly think of at least three kids who'd spoken often about getting away, safely stepping over the deadly barrier to see more of the world. "Now that I think about it, I can definitely remember Tina Johnson saying on more than one occasion how fun and interesting the life of a trader must be. I never guessed she was wishing she could be one, but now that I look back on it ..."

"Exactly," Will said. "And that's what I mean about Gage. He's never seemed the type to want that."

"You're right. He's never once thought about it, except when I might have brought it up."

"You haven't had much time to talk with him since your Choosing, have you?"

She shook her head.

"But you don't want to now?"

"I guess I do." Luna glanced in the direction of her friend and then back at the ground as she continued to walk. "What I'd really like is some time alone to process everything."

"You mean some time to worry?"

She inhaled and started to shake her head, then smiled and cast a sideways glance at her dad.

Will smiled back. "I know you."

"Yes, you do."

"Sometimes it's easy to guess what's on your mind, because we tend to think the same way."

"Great."

Will laughed again. "Not always, Dove. Don't worry, most of the thoughts in your head are all yours."

"It's okay," she smiled. "I don't mind having similar thoughts to yours."

"No?"

She shook her head. "You've managed to turn out okay, as far as I can tell."

A loud laugh escaped Will. "I'm glad you think so."

"Same with Mom. I know I take after her as well."

"The better parts are from her," Will agreed.

"And you, too." Luna adjusted the pack on her back with the roll of a shoulder. "I understand that I've got strengths and talents that come from the both of you, and I'm grateful for them."

"Good."

They walked the rest of the way to the barrier without speaking. As they approached the line, Will leaned toward her and spoke softly. "Want me to give you something to occupy your time when we get in there? An excuse to avoid having to hang out with Gage?"

Luna considered the offer and then shook her head. "Nah. You're right. We haven't had much time to spend together since the Choosing. I guess now's as good a time as any to hang out and talk."

"Talk?" Her father's eyes twinkled.

Luna raised one eyebrow. "Yes. Talk."

"Good." Will nodded. "Then I'll allow it."

Luna laughed, and after a second her father's stern expression became a smile.

Luna and Will stepped across the barrier and into the village. They continued walking toward Gage, Luna slipping the bracelet from her wrist and returning it to her father as they made their way to the foot of the small hill. Gage stood and came down to join them.

"How are ya, Gage?" Will reached out to shake hands with the young man.

"I'm pretty good, Will." Gage shook the trader's hand and then took a step back.

"You're next, right?" Will nodded toward Luna. "Choosing your profession in ..."

"A month and three days." Gage smiled.

"Choosing, but who knows how long before you actually get to start training."

Gage frowned. "What do you mean?"

"I mean," Will raised one eyebrow and shook his head. "That if your Choosing goes like Luna's, then the council will cry and moan and complain that you shouldn't get to do the profession you end up selecting, either."

"Ahh." Gage smiled. "I hope it doesn't go that way." He paused. "Unless I choose to be a trader as well." He laughed at his comment and the other two joined in. When they stopped, Gage's brows furrowed a tiny bit. "I'm not sure if I'm joking about that or not."

Will's expression conveyed amusement. "I never pegged you for the sort that would want to be a trader."

"I never pegged Luna for that, either," Gage said.

Will snorted. "*You* didn't, no."

There was an awkward silence as a look of understanding appeared on Gage's face. "You're right. What does a dumb kid like me know about anything?"

"I didn't say that, lad."

"You didn't *say* it, no."

Will pursed his lips, paused, then smiled and turned toward his daughter. "I'll leave you two alone. Be home for dinner?"

"I will." Luna nodded. "Thanks, Dad."

"Good work out there today, Dove." His gaze flicked to Gage and then back. "You're a natural, that's for sure."

Will walked past them and Luna looked at Gage, raising both eyebrows and shrugging. Then they began to walking, silently matching each other's pace as they headed toward their favourite spot to sit and talk.

"He doesn't think I'm serious," Gage said.

"About being a trader?" Luna watched the scenery in the distance as they walked. "I think he got the hint that you are."

"Well if he didn't, he will at my ceremony."

Luna's eyes slid to consider her friend. "If you want to be a trader, you'd better not wait until the ceremony to let the adults know."

"You waited."

She laughed. "Because I had no idea the profession was even an option." A thought occurred to her. "Are you saying you did?"

"No," he answered quickly, scowling as he did so.

Luna's eyes narrowed. "Well, now that you do, I don't think it's a good idea to wait and hope that my father will offer you a bracelet for no reason. Treat it like a normal profession and begin to show your interest to those who can get you an invitation to join."

"I've never liked that rule," Gage said. "That the professionals have to make an offer in order for us to be able to choose it."

"Why not?"

"Because. It's called the *Choosing*. We should be able to

choose from any of the professions, not just those who allow it."

"I used to think that way, too," Luna said.

"But not anymore?"

"Nope." Gage flashed her a look and she raised a hand. "Don't be mad at me for saying that."

"I'm not—"

"It actually makes sense," she continued. "If they don't think you'll do well in the profession, then why should you be able to choose it?"

"Because maybe it's what you want more than anything else."

Luna smiled. "If that's true, then you'll show them before the day of Choosing. Think about the professions that offered spots to me. I spent a lot of time with them, learned from more than one of their professionals, and expressed both interest and aptitude. Over the years it became clear which ones I was most interested in, by the amount of time and work that I put into them."

"Yeah, that's true. Everyone knew you were selecting the tower technician profession by the time your Choosing day arrived."

"Exactly."

"And yet." He raised one eyebrow. "You chose trader instead."

Luna laughed. "Dad kept that a secret, right until the moment he offered it."

"Maybe he will do that for me as well."

"After hearing him talk a few minutes ago, do you believe that?"

Gage sighed. "No."

Luna stopped walking and turned to face her friend. "Is that what you really want, Gage? To be a trader?"

He met her gaze and then nodded. "I've always dreamed about seeing what's out there. We talked about it so many times."

"Yes." She raised one arm and placed a hand on his shoulder. "But being a trader is more than crossing the line to see what is happening out there."

"I'm sure it is."

She stared at him silently, wondering if he had what it took to be a trader. Wondering if she had what it took.

"What?" he asked.

Luna let her hand return to her side. "Nothing."

"You wanted to say something."

"No."

He watched her for the space of three heartbeats, then began walking once more.

"Gage."

He kept walking.

She considered her friend for another few seconds. Then she took a deep breath, sighed, and followed him.

40

LUNA EASED HERSELF ONTO THE EDGE OF THE LARGE flat rock and let her legs dangle over the edge. Gage sat down beside her, so close that their legs touched.

Luna turned toward him, one eyebrow raised.

"Oh." He scooted over so they were close but separate. "Sorry."

"Nothing to be sorry about." She shook her head and looked out over the fields below.

"Yeah." He paused. "I just thought. After the kiss ..."

Gage paused again. Luna got the sense he was waiting for her to say something, but she didn't know what to say and so remained silent.

"Yeah." He said the word again, his tone conveying his confusion.

They stared off into the distance for a few seconds.

"So ..." Gage began. "How cool is it to be out there? Past the line?"

"Dunno." She shrugged. "I haven't been that far out yet."

"Still," his voice became more animated. "Even a foot beyond the line has to be pretty exciting."

She smiled. "It is kinda cool."

"We haven't had any time together since you've started going out." He turned toward her, tucking one leg under the other, his eyes wide. "Tell me all about it. What did actually stepping through the barrier feel like? And how about—" He paused, then laughed and nudged her shoulder with one hand. "Sorry. I'm rambling."

Luna laughed, worries dissipating as she became caught up in her friend's genuine enthusiasm. She turned to face him, crossing one leg over the other in her most comfortable sitting position. "It felt strange," she began. "Tingling, like static from when you rub your socks across fur or a piece of carpet, but stronger. It danced all over my skin as I stepped across. And that was only the beginning of the fun."

Gage stared back at her, eyes wide with interest as she began to tell him about the experiences she'd had so far.

———

"Wow." Gage leaned back with his hands behind him for support. "That all sounds insanely cool."

Luna laughed. "Now that I say it out loud, it doesn't actually sound like that much."

"Are you kidding me?" His eyes widened. "Just the experience of stepping over the line and not exploding into a cloud of ash—" he laughed. "You do remember that no one can survive crossing the line without a bracelet, right?"

"Yes."

"And then looking back and seeing the line. From the other side." He turned to stare at the line in the distance. "Okay, so it's not anything that would fill an action story."

He turned back to her. "But to us, all of us who are stuck living in the village for the rest of our lives ..." He smiled. "I'm so happy for you, Luna."

Luna heard the change in his tone as he spoke the last sentence. No. More than heard. She could feel it. A flush of emotion tickled her as she stared at Gage.

Gage must have felt something similar, or at least sensed it in her. He reached out and rested one hand on her knee. A second passed, and then another. Emboldened by the silence, he leaned in, closing his eyes as his lips moved toward hers. Luna began to lean forward as well. And then, an instant before their lips touched ...

"No." Her eyes popped open and she jerked her head back, watching as Gage's eyes slowly opened and he frowned in confusion.

"No?" he asked.

"I'm sorry, Gage."

His brows furrowed and he leaned back so that he was sitting straight once more. "Did I do something wrong?"

"Not at all."

"It felt right. Like the other night."

"Yeah." Luna's head nodded. "I felt it, too."

"Then why didn't—"

"Because it's not—" she interrupted him, "like the other night."

He stared at her for a long moment. "I don't understand."

"Everything is different now."

"I don't think that's true."

"It is." She shook her head and waited for him to agree. When he didn't, she continued, "I'm going to be a trader now. I'll be out there." She turned her face toward the village border. "And it can be dangerous. It wouldn't be fair to ask you to—"

"Dangerous?" Gage's brows furrowed. "What do you mean?"

Luna pursed her lips. She had only shared the basics of her experiences so far. Her father had told her to keep all mention of danger, guns, and violence secret, and that's what she'd done.

Until now.

"Nothing." She shook her head from side to side. "Forget I said that."

"I can't. You're telling me there are dangers—"

"Gage." She snapped, narrowing her eyes to convey a commanding expression. "Forget that I said that."

Gage watched her for the space of a few heartbeats, then shrugged. "Okay."

"I mean it. I wasn't supposed to say that. If my dad finds out, I'll be in trouble."

"Don't worry, I won't say anything." She watched him. He smiled. "I promise."

Luna nodded and then closed her eyes. "I'm sorry. I liked the kiss. The other night."

"Me too."

"But now, with things changing in our lives—"

"It's okay. I understand."

"I think it's better to wait for a bit—"

"Sure." He held up a hand to cut her off from saying more. "Of course. I get it. Don't worry, I won't try anything like that again."

Luna could hear the disappointment and pain in his voice. She wanted to reassure him, to tell him he was taking it the wrong way. But she knew that the more she said, the worse it would end up sounding. "Thank you."

"Sure." He stared off into the distance.

"I don't want to lose my friend," she said. "Over this."

"Oh, Luna," Gage sighed and then reached over to pat her knee. "You're not going to lose me. Over this."

She frowned. He had repeated the phrase to mirror the way she had said it, but something in his tone made her think he'd meant the words in a different way than she had.

And then a memory struck her like a lightning bolt.

"How did you know?" she asked.

Gage's brows dipped downward. "How did I know what?"

"The last time my dad returned to the village. On my birthday." She saw the emotion disappear from Gage's face, replaced by a blank, unreadable mask. "You took me to the border and we watched him appear."

Gage stared at her.

"How did you know he was coming home that day? And that he would be coming from that direction?"

Gage laughed and shook his head. "I don't think that's how it went, Luna."

"It is."

More laughter. "I guess from where you were sitting it might have looked that way, but you're wrong."

"How so?"

He chuckled again and then his eyes met hers. "He'd been away for a long time. And it was your birthday. I knew he'd come home in time, just like you did."

She frowned. That did make sense.

"As for which direction, I borrowed my dad's binoculars."

"Ahh." She nodded, remembering the last time Gage had 'borrowed' his father's precious binoculars. The two of them had come to this very spot and used them to look out at the world, seeing much further through the strange device than they could with their naked eyes. She also remembered getting caught with them. Gage's father had been so furious that they'd never dared take them again.

"And I had to come looking for him a lot. Yes, I brought you to where your dad was on the day he appeared, but that wasn't the first day I started sneaking out to search."

"Really?"

"Not even close." Gage snorted and shook his head. "I started climbing up here to look for him thirteen days before he arrived."

"Oh, wow."

"Yep," Gage nodded. "Every morning and every night, before the sun went down."

Luna frowned, then realized why he'd done it. "To add to the surprise for me?"

"Exactly." He smiled. "I knew you were worried about him." His smile softened. "And I wanted to make that worry go away."

Luna pictured her friend getting up early and staying out late to come here and search for signs of her father on the horizon. Using a precious piece of equipment that he wasn't allowed to have to do so. Taking risks and spending his time ... all to make her feel better. "That was sweet of you, Gage."

He shrugged but gave her a shy smile.

"Why didn't you tell me?"

"There was never a good time to slip it into the conversation."

Luna laughed. He wasn't the sort of person to brag. That was part of what she liked about him. "Well, I'm glad I asked about it."

"Me, too."

A brief moment of silence passed between them. Then Gage leaned close and nudged his shoulder lightly against hers. "So," he changed the subject. "Tell me more about your adventures in the Wild. Anything else exciting happen out there yet?"

"Oh, yes," she nodded. "There's a range set up for—" she caught herself and clamped her mouth shut.

"A range?" Gage frowned. "What's a range?"

"No. I can't." Luna shook her head again, silently berating herself for saying too much again. She stood and brushed off her hands on the front of her pants. "I'd better go."

"Did I do something wrong again?"

"No." She turned and took a step back from the edge of the flat rock. "Dad gave me a reading assignment and I should get to it."

"You sure?"

She smiled down at him. "Totally."

Gage stood. "Let me walk down the path with you at least?"

Luna shook her head but then reconsidered and nodded. "Sure."

41

Luna entered the Town Hall with her parents. She wished them luck, then turned toward the stairs that led to the viewing gallery on the second floor, while they made their way to the main doors to the council chamber.

Luna reached the top of the stairs and was surprised to find the spectator area already filled. She managed to find a spot in a corner of the front row. As she shuffled past the others to claim her spot, she nodded and smiled politely. Some returned the gesture, but none spoke to her, which she found unsettling.

She lowered herself into the empty seat, getting comfortable while looking out over the assembled crowd. She spied Gage sitting on the opposite side of the gallery.

Seeing him surrounded by so many relatives reminded her just how big the Lee family was. Gage's father, Tasker, was the eldest of four brothers and two sisters, all of whom had settled in this village when the happening had struck. Each had at least one child and many had two or three, which meant Gage's family was larger than any other in the village.

Luna waited for Gage to look her way, but he didn't. One of his cousins noticed her and leaned forward to whisper into his ear. He nodded but continued to stare down at the council floor.

Luna frowned, unable to shake the feeling that her best friend was purposely avoiding looking her way. She considered why that might be, letting various explanations drift through her mind as she turned her attention to the ground floor and the assembled council members below.

The area was furnished with large rectangular tables, one for each profession. Each was occupied by at least two and as many as half a dozen men and women. Every table except for her father's; he was the sole occupant at his table, placed at the outer edge of the assembly. Luna had asked if she could sit with him—such was her right, as an apprentice —but Will had thought it best for her to watch from the balcony, seeing as how this gathering would address concerns about her and the role she had chosen. "No sense adding fuel to the fire," he'd said, and her mother and uncle had agreed.

A door opened on one side of the assembly area and a man dressed in a long black robe emerged. He paused, head turning from side to side as he surveyed the assembly before him. Then he strode toward a high-backed wooden chair placed against the far wall of the room, which all the other tables faced. He was the Speaker, the person in charge of maintaining order and decorum during council proceedings. He paused in front of the Speaker's chair and turned to face the assembled crowd.

"All rise." The Speaker's voice was loud and powerful, filling the room so that everyone could hear it. Conversation died down, whispers and muted voices becoming silent as those on both the ground floor and the balcony stood and focused their attention on the Speaker.

"Be advised," the Speaker continued, "that all who have business in this village should now come forward to assemble and be heard. Let council come to session." The Speaker stared out at the councillors for the span of two breaths and then looked up toward the gallery for an equal length of time. Satisfied with what he saw, the man nodded once, gathered a handful of his robe in each hand, and sat down in the large wooden chair. "You may be seated."

There was a faint murmuring of voices and scuffing of chairs against hard wood floors on the main level as the council members and the audience above took their seats.

The Speaker waited for silence to return, then looked toward Malena and nodded his head once. "Madam Mayor, please announce the day's business as described in the previously agreed-upon agenda."

Luna looked to where her mother sat at the middle table. Malena stood, one hand reaching out to accept a piece of paper from Uncle Jack, who sat at the mayor's side in his capacity as deputy mayor. Her eyes scanned the page for a second, and then she began to read aloud.

"If it please the council, this being a specially created meeting, we have gathered to discuss only one subject today." She raised one eyebrow and looked up from the page. "That of Luna Reymont and her choosing to become a trader."

Malena set the piece of paper on the table and sat down again, nodding once toward the Speaker.

He returned the gesture and looked out over the council. "Are there any here who would speak to the laws previously agreed upon regarding this matter?"

No one spoke, and the Speaker raised one eyebrow. "Then why are we here?"

Gage's father, Tasker Lee, rose from his seat. He was a large man with broad, muscular shoulders, broader than those of the other four muscular men who sat with him. He made a small quarter-turn and faced the Speaker. "If I may, Mr. Speaker?"

The Speaker motioned toward the security elder with one hand. "The floor is yours, Tasker."

"Mr. Speaker, to the best of my knowledge, there is no issue with the current laws." He raised one eyebrow and sniffed. "And if Luna Reymont had chosen properly, we would not be gathered here today."

"What's that supposed to mean?" Malena asked.

"It means," Tasker Lee continued to speak in the direction of the Speaker, conveying a lack of respect in his refusal to face Malena, "that Miss Reymont choose to become a trader instead of selecting one of the recognized professions outlined in our village constitution."

The crowd in the gallery began to buzz, neighbours turning to mutter at this revelation.

Luna frowned in confusion. What was Gage's dad talking about?

The Speaker stood, a scowl on his face, as he raised one hand. "Order." His deep voice boomed the word, cutting over the rest of the noise like a clap of thunder. "Order, people!" his voice commanded once more, and the crowd quieted.

Luna watched Tasker Lee, a smile of self-satisfaction spreading across his features as his gaze flicked toward her father's table.

Will pursed his lips, head shaking slowly. Even from where she sat, Luna could tell that her father was angry.

"Mr. Speaker," Malena said. "There is no one—in this village or any other—who would deny that the role of trader is a profession. For Tasker Lee to do so now is ridiculous."

"I'm not denying that it's a profession, Madam Mayor." Tasker shook his head. "Only that it was not included on the list of professions that our children could choose from when the time came for them to make their selection."

Jack stood, his face blank and expression calm. He trained a dead stare on the security elder and glared at him for the space of two or three heartbeats.

Tasker Lee smirked while the men gathered around him snorted with quiet amusement, obviously not intimidated by the attention.

"You would have us lose our connection to the other villages, Tasker?" Jack asked. "Or are you stupid enough that such a thought has never occurred to you?"

The man beside Tasker, his brother James, stood suddenly, his chair scraping loudly as it slid away from him. "Watch your mouth, Reymont," he growled, "or I'll come over there and fix it so the doc hasta wire it shut for a few weeks so it can heal proper after I break it."

One corner of Jack's mouth twitched upward in amusement. It was known that Luna's uncle could handle himself in a fight, and that he never backed down from a challenge. "I'm right here, Jimmy boy. Don't trip on the way over to visit."

Tasker reached out and placed a hand on his brother's shoulder. He spoke a few soft words and James sat down, the anger in his eyes changing to amusement as the other man seated beside him said something and jabbed the man lightly in the ribs.

The crowd remained silent, riveted on the drama unfolding before them.

"I know the importance of the traders, Madam Mayor," Tasker said. "And it's for precisely that reason that this must be addressed at this juncture. I would also like to add that this is our village's first Choosing. We all knew that small hiccups would occur during the first few; things that we had not considered." He smiled as he looked toward the Speaker. "If the mayor, deputy mayor, and their trader family member want to try and keep the vocation in the family, and thereby keep the rest of us under their thumb, ensuring our continued obedience for another generation ..." He shrugged. "Well I suppose there isn't likely anything a single person like me could do to stop that from happening."

The balcony spectators began to speak amongst themselves once more. Luna frowned as dissent bubbled up from people around her. She had never considered what Tasker Lee was suggesting, but it was obvious from the talk around her that most in the village had, and that they weren't happy at the thought.

The Speaker scowled and stood to his feet, calling for order once more. It took longer to restore quiet to the hall, but it eventually happened and the Speaker took his seat again, while motioning for Tasker Lee to continue.

"The fact is, Mr. Speaker, that this point deserves further consideration—and perhaps even debate—before finally deciding as a community to either add the role of trader as an accepted profession or to deny it from being so. And if it does turn out that way, then we will have to instruct our newest adult to choose again." He raised one eyebrow. "And choose properly this time."

Luna watched as her mother looked first to Jack, and then toward Will. Will gave a small nod and Malena returned the gesture. Then she turned back toward the

Speaker, arms spread out and a smile on her face as she spoke. "If this is something that concerns the majority, then I agree, Mr. Speaker. I highly doubt it does—"

"Then let's vote on the matter," Tasker said.

Malena met the man's gaze. "Absolutely. I suggest we convene in seven days' time to vote on whether this is worth further debate and discussion. Should that be the case, then we will arrange for—"

"No." Tasker made a chopping motion with one hand. "We vote now, before you can make visits to strong-arm or pressure anyone to vote how you want them to."

"How dare you suggest that I've ever done such a thing," Malena said.

"Please." Tasker chuckled. "This isn't my first council session." He turned to face the Speaker. "Voting on whether we give this matter further consideration is simple, Mr. Speaker, and it should be done now."

The Speaker considered the arguments in front of him. "If three others will back you on this, security elder, then I will agree to your motion."

There was no need for Tasker to say anything further as the hands of five elders shot into the air, each signifying their support for an immediate vote.

The Speaker raised one eyebrow and glanced at Malena. "It seems I must call for a vote now."

Malena sat down and crossed her arms.

"Council members," the Speaker said, "you have heard the argument before us. The profession of trader is not on our village's accepted list of professions for new adults to choose during their ceremony. Tasker Lee feels further consideration is required before deciding to add it to the list or leave it off. If you agree with him, stand in support and be counted."

Luna watched as elders from over three-quarters of the tables stood in support. The Speaker counted them and then asked for those opposed to stand. Malena and Jack stood, as did Will.

And that was it.

Luna felt a heavy weight in the pit of her stomach as the Speaker reached for a hammer and rapped it once against the edge of his wooden chair.

"The issue is settled," the Speaker declared. "Further sessions are required to determine if Luna Reymont will be allowed to remain a trader."

42

THE SPEAKER'S WORDS STRUCK LUNA LIKE A HAMMER between the eyes.

She felt a numbness envelop the top of her skull and slowly seep into her body, while all around her the villagers began speaking to one another in hushed voices.

She couldn't be sure how much time had passed, but eventually people began to stand and make their way toward the exits on each side of the gallery. Luna turned toward Gage, hopeful that he would look her way, that he would see her distress and come over to make sure that she was okay.

But Gage didn't turn. Instead, he stood with his cousins and followed them to the exit.

Luna felt a sinking sensation in her chest as she watched him disappear. Hot tears blurred her vision. She closed her eyes and bowed her head, letting her chin droop against her collarbone as the muffled sounds of villagers gossiping and commenting about her life and future continued around her.

"Luna?"

She felt a hand gently touch her knee, grasping it firmly for a moment to convey the concern she'd heard so clearly in her father's voice.

"It's gonna be alright, Dove." He sounded calm, confident.

The energy of his conviction flowed into Luna and she opened her eyes, looking up into his. "It didn't sound that way to me, Dad."

One corner of his mouth twitched upward into a grin. "Politicians. They always make everything sound so grim."

A small bark of laughter escaped her, followed by a choking sob as fresh tears formed in her eyes.

"Aw, don't cry, Luna."

She shook her head, lips pressed together tightly as the tears came—tears not of sadness or frustration, but anger.

"I know." He sat down beside her. "It's maddening that a bunch of frightened old people have a say in your future, in how you will live the rest of your life."

"It is," she agreed. "I wish ..." She shook her head. "I wish that I'd lived in the time before all this. Then I'd have been in control of my future. I'd have had the ultimate say in my life and how I live it."

Will grinned and chuckled.

"What?"

"It wasn't any better back then, darling."

"But ..." She frowned. "It wasn't?"

"I'm afraid not." Her father shrugged. "It seems that the struggle to be accepted as an adult and the frustration of being treated like a child is as ageless as parents and children."

She smiled. After a few minutes, Luna took a deep breath, wiped the tears from her eyes with both hands, stood.

"Ready to get out of here?" Will asked.

"I am."

"Good." Will stood as well and draped one arm around her shoulder. "Your mom and uncle will be waiting for us at home. When we get there, we can talk about what happens next."

WILL OPENED THE DOOR AND STEPPED INTO THE house. Luna sat down with her mother and uncle at the dining room table. Malena held a pitcher of iced tea over an empty glass and began to pour when Luna acknowledged her silent query with a nod.

"Well," Will sighed as he settled into the empty chair at the head of the table. "That was interesting."

Jack snorted and Malena shook her head.

Luna raised the glass to her lips. "You two don't seem as upset as I thought you'd be."

"Oh, we are." Malena took a deep breath and exhaled slowly. "But rage accomplishes nothing. At least not right now."

"Here's what's going through my mind, Dove." Will leaned back in his chair. "I'm considering how all of this affects the four people sitting in this room." He placed both hands behind his head and laced his fingers together. "And the truth is that no matter what happens, it isn't the end of the world for any of us. We are all healthy and safe. We have this house for shelter, and food to feed us. The barrier created by the towers around the village continues to function, which means we are safe from all outside threats." His eyebrows rose and his eyes widened. "Which means we're fine, in the grand scheme of things."

"Yeah, I guess that's true." Luna frowned. She'd heard her parents tick off these things to be thankful for on more than one occasion but never realized until now that considering the bigger picture did help calm the nerves. "I might not be able to become a trader, though."

Will smirked and Jack snorted. Mal raised one eyebrow but said nothing.

Luna compared the idea of that against the certainties her father had listed and smiled. "You're right. I guess it's not the end of the world. Still, I really want to be a trader."

"Yes," Will said. "But if for some reason it turns out you can't, will that ruin the future for you?"

"I suppose not."

"And it's not as if you'll be doomed to do something you detest, right?" he continued. "You've spent the last ... how long, wanting to be a tower technician?"

"At least four years," she admitted.

"See? There you go." Will flung out his hands and smiled. "No matter what happens, that profession will remain available for you."

"Your father's right," Mal said. "But that doesn't mean we're giving up on you becoming a trader, Luna. It's much too early in the game to throw in the towel and let the opposition win."

"About that," Jack said. "I'm not the only one sitting here surprised at the amount of pushback this subject has raised, am I?"

"You're not," Will said. "I think all of us were caught on our heels today."

"And Tasker Lee as the leader of such resistance?"

Mal's eyes narrowed and she bit lightly at the corner of her lip.

"He's aggressive," Will said. "Always has been."

"Yes, but he's also always been loyal to the village." Mal shook her head. "Now I'm no longer certain that's the case."

"That might not be a fair assessment," Luna said.

Jack frowned. "What do you mean?"

"From his point of view, he might feel ambushed. Like he said in council, the rules have been clear and defined for the past sixteen years." Luna shrugged. "And now—to him and many others—this could look as if the rules have suddenly changed for no good reason. I can see that upsetting people. It would upset me too, I guess, if I wasn't the one benefitting."

Will sighed. "I suppose that could be the case." He looked at Malena and nodded. "I guess that if someone had pulled this sort of thing on us, we'd be up in arms, too."

Jack stared at the table and Malena took a sip of iced tea from her glass. "I agree."

"What if you apologized to him?" Luna suggested. "Explain why it was necessary and reassure him that it won't happen again."

"Or if it does, we will do a better job of communicating it with the rest of the village," Jack said.

Malena watched her husband for a few seconds. "What would you do if the situation was reversed, Will? If Tasker had done something of this sort and then came to talk about it after the fact?"

"That's easy." Will smiled. "I'd pretend to accept the apology, make it seem like I was on board to work together again ..."

"And then at the first possible opportunity rip all of his

power away, to make sure he could never double-cross us again?" Mal guessed.

"Yup," Will smiled. "That's exactly what I'd do."

The four sat without speaking for the next few minutes.

Finally, Luna took a long drink of tea and set the glass on the table. "I think I've got an idea that might work to get him back on your side."

Will looked to Malena. She shrugged and his gaze swivelled back to Luna. "Let's hear it."

43

Luna dreamt of being older.

Of being married to Gage.

She woke up, got out of bed, and went downstairs to prepare dinner. As she turned the burner on and retrieved eggs and milk from the fridge, a sense of deep nostalgia came over her. She remembered the kitchen of her parents' house and how they had spent so many hours preparing breakfast together. Laughing and loving while they cooked.

The front door opened and she turned, smiling, as Gage entered. His hair was greying at the edges and thinning on top. He smiled and removed his jacket, hanging it on the rack near the door and stepping out of his boots before coming to stand beside her in the small kitchen area.

She leaned toward him and smiled as he kissed her cheek.

"Good morning, beautiful," he whispered, nibbling playfully on her ear lobe before stepping back and looking at the eggs on the counter. "What's for breakfast?"

"I was thinking pancakes."

"Yum." He knelt down, opened a cupboard door, and reached in to retrieve a container of flour. "We still have vanilla extract?"

"A tiny bit." She nodded toward the cupboard on her left. "I'll have to buy more from the trader next time they come to the village."

Gage stood and found the vanilla, plucking the small brown glass bottle from the bottom shelf of the cupboard that she'd indicated. "That should be soon, right?"

"Mhmm." Luna cracked an egg and let the contents plop into the large mixing bowl.

"I think it's gonna snow today."

"Really?"

Gage unscrewed the cap and held the little bottle over the bowl. "Yep. In a couple hours or so. The clouds are dark and full."

She watched him shake three dashes of dark brown liquid into the bowl. The vanilla hit the eggs and swirled with the yolks. "I still don't know if I like it."

"Like what? Snow?"

"Yes. It never snowed when we were kids. It's a pain in the arse."

Gage laughed. "There's not much we can do about it, love. Unless you know how to travel back in time."

"I wouldn't, even if I could."

"Me neither." He paused. "At least not to avoid the snow. It would be fun to visit with your mom, though."

Luna pursed her lips and nodded. "Yes. That would be good."

They spent the rest of their preparation time working in silence. Luna finished the pancake batter while Gage heated the pan and got plates and cutlery out and on the table. *We work so well together,* she thought to herself, then smiled. That should be no surprise, considering all their years of practice.

Luna prepared the pancakes, stacking them one atop another while Gage stood beside her, leaning against the counter and talking about little things, as married couples did.

Finally the last pancake had been made and they moved to the table. She carried the syrup, Gage the plate of pancakes.

Luna sat down and reached for a pancake, stabbing it with her fork and placing it on her plate. Gage walked to the bottom of the stairs.

Luna watched him and frowned.

"Kids!" he shouted. "Time for breakfast." He looked at Luna and winked, smiling as he yelled up once more. "We're having pancakes."

"Kids?" She mumbled ... and then ...

LUNA SAT UP IN BED, GASPING FOR BREATH AS IF HER body had forgotten to draw air while she slept.

Her pulse was racing and she took deep breaths to feed her starving lungs. She looked around and frowned. The room seemed both familiar and strange at the same time.

"I'm a kid," she whispered. Then she smiled and tears filled her eyes. Tears of happiness, because she knew that her parents were downstairs, sleeping soundly. Mixed with tears of sadness for a life suddenly taken away.

"It was all a dream," she whispered, her mind frantically grasping to hold onto what she'd experienced. Memories of being married to Gage, of having children, and having a life with him.

"Just a dream," she whispered once more, the dream fading slowly as she lay back in bed and stared up at the ceiling.

44

"Heyo, Luna."

Luna smiled as she turned in the direction of the familiar voice. Thomas raised a hand in greeting, a smile on his face as he strode toward her with a harness slung over his left shoulder and a toolbox gripped in his right hand. She waved back and waited for him to get closer before calling a greeting back to him.

He stopped a few feet away and looked up to where she sat on the stone ledge, raising his left hand to shield his eyes from the sun. "Whatcha doing up there?"

"Not much. Sitting. Thinking."

"All alone?"

"Yeah," she said.

"I'm going to check out a tower."

"Good stuff."

"I happen to know that there's an extra harness in the storage closet there. Would you care to join me?"

"Ooh," Luna's smile widened. "I haven't climbed a tower since before my Choosing."

"What?" Thomas's eyes widened. "That's terrible."

One corner of his mouth rose in a grin. "Guess you'd better come along then," he beckoned with his free hand. "Let's go."

Luna scrambled to her feet and made her way down the hill. Thomas waited for her to join him, then the pair set off.

Luna smiled, eyes closed and face tilted toward the sun. A gentle breeze played against the loose curls of her hair. "Thank you for this, Thomas," she said. "I really do love it up here."

Thomas chuckled beside her. "Always happy to have you along."

She opened her eyes and turned to face him. She could see something in his eyes ... regret, or maybe sadness. "What's wrong?" she asked.

"It doesn't make sense to me, is all."

"What doesn't?"

He looked out over the fields and sighed. "That you didn't choose this."

"Oh."

"You're such a natural. At all of it. You aren't afraid of heights. You climb like you were born to it. Your fingers are nimble and handle all the tools with ease." He shook his head. "And you could hear the towers. Such a gift, and yet ..."

"I know."

Thomas snorted.

"Seriously," she said. "I understand your disappointment. I'd feel the same way if I were in your place. You spent a lot of time with me. Teaching and showing me how it all works. I'm sorry I let you down, Thomas."

The tall man frowned. "Let me down?" His head shook from side to side. "No, no, dear girl. Don't think that you've let me down." He paused for a second, a smile appearing on his face. "I mean, technically, I suppose you did—"

She laughed.

"But it's your life," he continued. "If you feel that being a trader is more to your liking, then it's good that you chose that instead." He shrugged. "Still, it is a bit of a bummer for us in the tower profession."

"I get that."

Thomas sat on the edge of the platform and Luna joined him. They looked down, legs swinging in the breeze.

"Looks like my choice might not matter," Luna said. "Who knows, in a few days or weeks I might end up having to be a tower tech anyway."

"*Having to be.*" He made a sour face. "I can hear the disappointment in those words, that's for sure." He squinted as he looked out over the bright field. "You're learning one of those crappy but unavoidable lessons in life, I see."

"What lesson is that?"

"That none of us are ever truly free to do everything that we want."

Luna snorted. "Yeah, I guess I am."

"It sucks, right?"

"It does." She leaned back. "My whole life, I've had to do what my parents say. Wake up, go to sleep, eat this, don't eat that. Do the chores. Go to school." She shook her head. "I thought that would all change once I came of age. That I'd be able to decide what I did and when I did it."

Thomas chuckled.

"I think that's what was so exciting about the actual Choosing ceremony. The decision—what I could choose to be—was all mine. No one else could tell me I was wrong or override what I choose." She rubbed at her face with one hand. "But then they did."

"You know," Thomas sighed, "I'm thirty-eight years old, and being told what to do by other people still grates on my nerves. At least once or twice a day. Every day."

"That's comforting." Luna grimaced. "Knowing it never gets any better."

Thomas laughed. "For some—most, I would bet—being told what to do isn't an issue at all."

"You think so?"

He nodded. "Seems like most people actually enjoy having others make the decisions for them."

"That's crazy."

"I agree. For people like you and me, it's never a fun thing."

Luna nodded in agreement.

The next few minutes passed in silence.

"I guess it could be worse," she sighed. Then a thought occurred to her and she sat up straighter. "Oh no."

"What's wrong?"

"I just had a terrible thought. What if I have to choose again and the tower techs won't take me this time?"

Thomas considered her for a moment. Then he reared back his head and laughed. Luna frowned and then smiled as he continued laughing.

"That was funny," he said when he finally stopped laughing, wiping a tear from one eye. "Thanks for that."

"Why is it so funny? Because I'm right?"

Thomas laughed again. "No, you're not right." He shook his head. "Not even a bit. You have always been—and will continue to always be—welcome in the tower technician profession."

Luna felt a tightness in the muscles of her back that she

hadn't realized was there loosen as relief swept over her. "Thank Aatun for that."

"Indeed."

"Thank Aatun ..." she mumbled the words again. "Huh. I'd forgotten about that."

"Forgotten what?"

Luna's brows furrowed as she recalled her encounter with the goddess of the towers. "Maybe this will all turn out for the best after all."

"What makes you say that?"

Luna smiled and turned to face Thomas, tucking one leg comfortably under the other. "When I spoke to her, she said I'd be leaving the village. She wouldn't have said such a thing unless it was going to happen, right?"

"When you spoke to her?"

"Yes."

"You lost me, Luna. Who were you speaking to?"

Luna paused. Then she decided it was okay to reveal the truth and continued speaking. "I spoke to Aatun, and she told me that I would be going outside the village. She didn't say 'if.' It was definitely when, like she knew for sure I would be going out."

Thomas frowned as he stared at her.

"That must mean everything will turn out fine," she continued, "and I'll be allowed to become a trader."

"Hold on a sec." Thomas held up a hand, eyebrows furrowing. "You prayed to Aatun. I get that. Many do. But what makes you think she told you something specific, like you would be travelling outside of the village?"

"Because that's what happened," Luna laughed. "I didn't just pray; I actually spoke with her. And she spoke to me."

A long pause.

"When did this happen?" Thomas asked.

"A few days ago."

"And ... where did you see her?"

"I was standing on a tower."

"But you sai—" He paused again; then his eyebrows rose and he nodded. "Ahh. Are you saying you saw Aatun in a dream and she spoke to you?"

Luna laughed. "Yes. What? Did you think I was saying I saw her in real life?"

"I wasn't sure."

"Well, that would be crazy. To claim I was able to see her in real life."

"Right," Thomas said. "But talking to her in a dream is fine?"

Luna stared at her friend. She'd never told him about her dreams. How real they could be sometimes. Or her visions. "You know what?" She shook her head. "Never mind. You're right. It's crazy to give any thoughts to silly dreams."

"Dreams?" he asked. "You've had more than one dream about Aatun?"

Something in the tone of his voice made her pause. "No," she lied, shaking her head again. "Forget I said anything. It was stupid."

Thomas watched her, eyes narrowing as he did so.

She laughed. "Stop it. I'm fine."

His serious expression melted away and a smile spread across his face. He stood and reached down to offer her a hand up. "I'm sure you are. Let's get this repair finished and head down."

Luna plucked a tool from Thomas's toolbox and accepted his hand. He helped pull her to a standing position and then began to make his way to the control panel.

Then he held out a hand and Luna placed the tool in his palm.

He began to adjust a screw inside the panel. "It does sound kind of cool, though," he said, attention focused on his work.

"What does?" Luna asked.

"Having dreams like that."

Luna didn't reply.

Thomas paused and looked at her out of the corner of his eye. "I'm sorry if my reaction freaked you out."

"It didn't." She watched him, hoping he didn't realize she was lying again.

Thomas considered her for a moment. Then he nodded and went back to working on the panel.

45

Desmond Baker stared at Thomas and considered the information in silence for the space of a few heartbeats. Then he nodded and reached out to grip the tower technician's elbow, giving it a gentle squeeze as he did so. "This is interesting information, Thomas." He began leading the technician toward the door of his office. "Very interesting, indeed."

"I thought you would appreciate me bringing it to you right away, Elder."

"Absolutely." Desmond turned the doorknob and gave the door a light push. It swung outward in a slow, lazy arc, the air cylinders that controlled its motion making it stop just shy of hitting the outside wall as it fully opened.

"This means that Luna could be the one, right?" Thomas turned toward the older man, eyes wide with excitement. "As it was foretold in the sacred texts?"

"This revelation does sound interesting," the tower elder acknowledged.

"I know more must be done before we can say for sure,"

Thomas said. "But I never imagined that I'd be alive when the prophesy came true."

Desmond tightened his grip and came to a stop, prompting the other man do to the same. Thomas frowned, glancing down at his elbow and then to the elder.

Desmond released Thomas and made a placating motion with the flat of his hand. "Until we can explore this matter further, it is extremely important to keep this information to yourself."

"Sure." Thomas's eyebrows furrowed and then returned to normal as he nodded. "Of course. That does makes sense, Elder. If others knew, they would be jealous."

"I think their main response would be one of disbelief." The elder raised one eyebrow, a wry expression on his face. "Quickly followed by ridicule."

"Do you really think so?"

"What would you say if another hall proclaimed that a child of the village was able to directly communicate with the goddess of the towers? A goddess that many still refuse to admit exists, by the way."

"You're right," Thomas sighed. "I forget there are villagers who don't believe in her. Or that they think she is nothing more than an A.I., capable of little more than maintaining the protective barrier around our village."

"It's not their fault." Desmond smiled. "We are the only ones who get to directly communicate with her."

"I do wish others would take the time to learn her language," Thomas said.

"Everyone is busy within their own vocation. Beeps and clicks are of no interest to them."

Thomas pursed his lips and stood straighter. "Don't worry, Elder. I will keep this information to myself until you say otherwise."

"Thank you."

The tower tech nodded and began to walk down the hallway. Desmond watched the man for a few seconds, then closed the door and returned to his seat behind the large wooden desk near the far wall of his office. "Well? What do you think of that?"

A man emerged from a shadowy corner of the office, pushed the black worn leather of his trench coat to both sides with his hands, and lowered himself onto the chair across from the elder. He ran a hand over his short, black hair and then rubbed at the black stubble covering his jaw. Blue eyes sparkled, reflecting his carefree grin. He leaned back in the chair and rested his black combat-style boots on the desk, crossing one foot over the other as he laced the fingers of both hands together behind his head. "Sounds like she might be the one, Des."

Desmond's lips pursed and he stared with disgust at the boots propped on his desk, but he didn't tell the man to remove them. "Is the word of one technician enough to make that call?" he asked.

"That is entirely up to you, old friend."

"I'm not sure that it is. Up to me."

The man smiled and waited, apparently comfortable letting the older man deliberate for however long it might take.

After about thirty seconds, Desmond gave an exasperated sigh and shook his head. "Very well," he said. "Proceed with the next phase."

The man removed his boots from the desk and sat forward in his chair. "Are you sure? Because once I move forward, there's no turning back."

"I am aware of that, Marius." The elder raised one

eyebrow, then nodded once. "Yes, I'm sure. She is the one. You may proceed with the next phase of the plan."

Marius stood, dipped his chin in silent acknowledgement, then strode from the room.

46

Luna saw Gage approaching from the corner of her eye but didn't turn to greet him.

Instead, she focused on a pebble she'd selected from a small pile in her hand, examining the fine black lines webbed across its surface before letting it slip from her fingers onto her palm and replacing it with a pink stone peppered with sparkling pieces of quartz.

"Hi." He spoke softly from beside her.

"Hi." Silently, she congratulated herself for delivering the greeting in a neutral, almost bored tone.

"Mind if I sit down?"

Luna shrugged. "I don't care what you do."

Gage stood for another few seconds, then sat close enough that their legs touched. Luna shuffled a tiny bit to break the contact, her heart skipping a beat as she did so.

"Sorry 'bout the other day," Gage said.

"Which day?" She let the pink stone fall back into the pile on her hand and picked out a brown stone, holding it between thumb and forefinger as she raised it to the light.

Gage grunted and she threw the pebble. It sailed over the water and arced into the stream with a light *plop*.

"I deserve that." He took a deep breath and let it out in a sigh. "I've been an ass."

"Not the word I'd use." Luna looked down at the stones in her palm once more. "Ass doesn't begin to describe what you've been toward me lately."

"You're right."

Out of the corner of her eye, Luna saw Gage's head lower. She took her time selecting another stone, then threw it into the water.

They sat in silence for the next few minutes, Luna pretending Gage wasn't there while she tossed stones, and Gage sitting beside her without speaking.

"Guess we probably shouldn't have kissed." From the corner of her eye she saw Gage's head snap up and turn toward her.

"Why do you say that?"

Luna shrugged, still not looking at him. "Things were fine between us. Before that."

"Things are still fine, Lune. We're just having a little misunderstanding, is all."

"Little misunderstanding?" She trained her gaze on him. "I see you on the street and you won't wave to me."

"I must not have seen you."

She laughed, her eyes widening. "Oh, you saw me. Plus, you used to come over every day so we could hang out. I can't remember the last time that happened."

"I have school and you don't. And after school's out," he shrugged. "I assume that you're busy doing things—"

"Liar."

Gage frowned.

"Then there's the whole council meeting fiasco." She

shook her head and turned her attention back to the stones in her palm. "You and your cousins sat on the other side of the gallery and spent the entire time ignoring me, whispering to each other about me."

"We did not."

"I saw Glanis look my way, then whisper something in your ear. You saying she wasn't talking about me?"

Gage's lips pursed.

Her eyes met his, the sight of him blurry through sudden tears. "You wouldn't even look at me, Gage."

His expression softened. He looked at the ground once more.

"That was the worst day of my life, and I couldn't count on my best friend to be there for me."

Gage looked up, his expression hardening. "Worst day of your life?" He laughed. "What about it being the worst day of mine, Luna?"

"What?" Luna blinked. "How can you say that? The council was called to debate if I could be a trader or not. I don't see—"

"That's right." His bitter laugh conveyed frustration. "Unless it's about you, you don't see anything, do you?"

The words struck her like an open hand across the cheek.

"I swear, Luna, sometimes I just want to—" Gage paused, mouth opening and closing without any words coming out. Then he closed his eyes and shook his head. "You know what? You're right. That day was about you, and I should have been more sympathetic to what was happening." He opened his eyes to meet her gaze. "But it wasn't just about you." He paused to let her speak.

Luna stared at him.

He sighed. "It's about all of us. The other kids who will get to choose, and how the process goes."

"No it wasn't," she said. "Sure, those issues might exist. But that specific council meeting was about me. Me and my friend, who suddenly wants nothing to do with me."

"Luna—"

"No." She stood, letting the stones fall from her open palm. "I don't know why you came here—"

"To tell you—"

"Yeah," she cut him off. "To tell me how the village should behave. To mimic your daddy and say the words you think everyone wants to hear about a grown-up topic that might matter to the village but only stands in the way of me being who I want to be."

Gage reached out to touch her hand, but she jerked it back and began walking away.

"Luna."

Something in his tone made her stop and stand in place, her back to him.

"I love you."

Long moments passed. Luna did not turn to face him.

"That's the thing, Gage," she said. "I love you, too. And that's what makes all of this hurt so much more." She paused, feeling an impulse to turn back, but stopped herself and remained locked in place.

She took a deep breath.

Let it out.

And then walked down the small slope and away from the river's edge.

47

Malena adjusted her jacket and leaned forward to rap her knuckles twice against the door. Then she stepped back and waited.

A few seconds later, the door opened and the elder of agriculture frowned at the sight of his caller. "Madam Mayor."

"Madam Mayor?" Malena raised one eyebrow. "We are suddenly so formal away from the council chamber, Ben?" The elder's eyes flitted toward the ground for a second and then moved back up to meet Malena's. He shook his head and opened his mouth to speak, but Malena laughed softly and continued speaking. "That's fine. I guess I should have expected a cold reception. After you betrayed me in the last council meeting."

"Betrayed you?" The elder's expression hardened. "I hardly think that's how it went down, Mal. You knew I had concerns about—"

"I knew nothing of the sort, Elder." Malena said the word as if it tasted bad in her mouth. She took a breath, readied herself to continue speaking, but then paused. "I'm sorry. I didn't mean to come here and attack."

The elder snorted but said nothing.

"May I come in and discuss this? In private?"

Ben shook his head. "My mind is made up, Malena. I don't see what further talking will accomplish. Maybe it would be better if—"

"Your mind was made up once before, Ben." She raised one eyebrow. "But you didn't seem to have a problem with suddenly changing it. I think I'm entitled to an explanation as to why a solid ally suddenly became an adversary, wouldn't you agree?"

The elder considered her for a moment and then his expression softened. "I'm not an adversary, Mal, but Tasker made some good points. Very good points." He stopped speaking, then stepped backward, motioning for her to enter the house. "Yes, I suppose you should come in so we can clear the air."

"Thank you, Elder." Malena smiled. "I appreciate that."

MALENA DRAINED THE LAST BIT OF TEA FROM HER CUP and leaned forward to set it on the table. Then she turned to face Ben, her gaze blank as she stared at him.

Ben stared back. Long minutes passed and neither spoke.

"Okay, then." Malena let out a light sigh as she got to her feet and reached for her jacket, which was draped over a chair to one side. "It looks as if there's nothing I can do to change your mind on this, Ben."

"There isn't."

She slipped one arm into her jacket and then the other.

Then she hitched her shoulders to adjust the garment, gripping the bottom of it with both hands to help her complete the action. "I'm disappointed. More than words can say."

"This doesn't make us adversaries in all things." Ben leaned forward and began to rise.

"No." Malena reached out and placed a hand on the man's shoulder, applying gentle pressure. "Don't get up. I can see myself out."

"Don't be absurd," he began. "I know how to be a proper host—"

"Please." The tone of her voice hardened, matching the pressure she exerted on his shoulder to keep him sitting. "This will be better if you stay sitting."

Ben frowned. "What will be better? What are you talking about?"

With her right hand, Malena reached into the left breast pocket of her jacket and withdrew a thin, silver cylinder the shape and size of a fountain pen. She held it up so that the tip was in front of the elder's eyes. "I hate to have to do this, Ben, but I need your support in this council vote. Since you won't give it to me freely ..."

"Malena? What are you—"

There was a *pop*, accompanied by a small flash of light from the tip of the cylinder. Malena saw Ben's pupils constrict in response to the sudden stimulus, and his expression went blank. She continued to watch, waiting until his pupils slowly returned to their normal diameter. Then she stepped back and returned the cylinder to her pocket.

"Your vote will match mine," she said.

"My vote will match yours," Ben repeated the words.

"You will stand and defend my daughter's right to become a trader."

"I will." The man's expression remained neutral, his

eyes staring forward at some point that only he seemed capable of seeing.

"You will also do your best to convince the others who turned on me to do the same."

There was a long moment of silence.

"Ben?"

The elder's head jerked and he seemed to return to normal. He looked at Malena, frowning slightly but nodding his head. "Yes, of course, Mal." The cadence of his speech sounded natural, too. "You can count on me to support you on this."

Malena considered him for a couple of seconds, then she smiled and nodded. "That's good to hear, Ben. I appreciate it."

"Would you like some tea?" Ben tried to stand but then sank back down into his seat, obviously dizzy from the effort. "Give me a minute and I'll get you some."

"No, I'm fine, thanks." Malena adjusted her jacket and moved toward the front door. "I really must be going."

"But you just got here."

"I have a few more visits to make before I call it a day." She reached for the front door handle and turned it. "Thanks again, Ben. I appreciate your support."

"Always," was all he said as she opened the door and closed it behind her.

———

MARIUS WATCHED FROM AROUND A CORNER TWO blocks away.

When Malena exited the elder's house, he waited for her to disappear from sight, then checked his watch and began a timer.

When it reached five minutes, he left the shadows and made his way to the elder's front door and knocked.

Muffled sounds of shuffling could be heard from within. Marius smiled.

The door opened and Ben frowned. "Who are you?"

Marius extended his hand and shook it, letting the gemstone bracelet twinkle in the limited light. "Trader business, sir."

"Oh." Ben nodded but his expression remained dubious. "What business could you possibly have with me at this hour of the night ..."

"Marius."

"Nice to meet you, Marius." He extended his hand and Marius shook it.

"I'm sorry to call on you so late, but I just got in and don't plan on staying long."

"You bring a message?"

"Indeed."

"You should take it to the mayor, then. That's how things normally work—"

"This message relates to crops. Specifically grain mold."

"Oh, dear." Ben stepped to the side. "Come right in."

Marius entered the house and scanned the room.

"Please." The elder motioned toward the couch. "Grab a seat. Can I get you something to drink?"

"Thank you, no." Marius sat down, positioning himself on the edge of the couch seat, and turned to face the elder, who took a chair beside him.

"Where has the mold struck?" Ben asked. "Is there danger of it being transported in harvested stores, or is it still in the fields?"

Marius reached into an inner pocket of his trench coat and withdrew a gold metallic cylinder. Except for the metal it was made from, the device was identical to the one Malena had used. He leaned forward, resting a forearm on one knee, as he held the device up in front of the elder's face.

"What's that?" Ben frowned at the device.

"I'll show you." Marius activated the device and there was another flash of light and a *pop,* like a light bulb striking concrete and breaking.

Once again the agriculture elder's pupils constricted and his expression became blank. Marius paused, watching the other man's eyes until his dilated pupils returned to normal.

"What did Malena command you to do, Elder?" Marius asked.

"To support her in the upcoming council vote."

"Anything else?"

The elder shook his head.

Marius snorted. "Waste of a good mind flash." He considered the elder for a long moment and then continued. "Very well. From this moment forward, I want you to ignore the instructions that Malena gave you."

"Okay."

"Instead," Marius leaned back and draped one arm over the back of the couch. "This is how I want you to proceed."

48

Luna looked up as the door to the house opened and her father entered.

His eyes met hers and he smiled, winking before he turned to remove his jacket and hang it on one of the hooks by the door.

"Well?" Malena asked from where she sat in the living room area, a book resting on her lap as she watched her husband remove his outerwear. "Have you heard from Jack yet?"

"I have." Will removed his boots and made his way to the couch, letting himself drop down onto it with a sigh and a smile. "Apparently it was a pretty good meeting."

"Pretty good? As in, Tasker accepted the deal?"

Will paused for a second and then smiled, his head nodding in the affirmative. "Yep, he went for it."

Mal let out a long breath of relief and leaned back in her chair. "That's great. Did he add any other conditions?"

"Nope." Will leaned back and crossed one leg so that his right ankle rested on his left knee. "The terms were laid out with exceptional clarity. He accepted them without trying to make a single change."

Luna grinned and Will chuckled. "Your plan was perfect, and you were right, Luna. The offer was exactly what he was after all along."

"I'm glad," Luna said. "I figured all he wanted was a chance for Gage to become a trader, but I also wasn't a hundred percent positive that would be enough."

Malena snorted and shook her head. "That's all everyone wants now. For their child to be a trader."

"Well, too bad." Will ran one hand through his short, cropped hair. "Now that it has been chosen twice in a row, by the first two eligible to go through the process, it's bound to be a very long time before the position will be offered again."

Mal nodded, crossing her arms and leaning against her husband on the couch.

"I don't get why it's suddenly so important to everyone," Luna said.

"It isn't sudden," Will said. "The trader role has always been one of contention. Having the ability to move between villages—coming and going as one pleases—endows us with a tremendous amount of power."

Luna frowned. "I've never thought of it that way."

Malena smiled. "You'll see as you progress. Everything taken out and brought in is controlled by traders. Products, food and drink—"

"And information," Mal added.

"Yes." Will raised one eyebrow. "And information. Controlling the flow of resources in and out of the protected zones conveys tremendous responsibility—and a significant temptation to use the role for personal gain."

Luna considered her mother's words and nodded. "I guess that's true. But Dad has never done that, has he?"

Will smirked. "Of course I have."

Luna frowned.

"I do it every time I make a decision. You will, too. There are times when I have to refuse buying items and selling others. Flooding one village with too much product could result in depriving another of a valued resource. You've seen me tell people that I will only take so much of something, no matter how much they beg me to acquire more, right?"

"Yes."

"Left to their own, people are always greedy and selfish."

"Not always," Mal said.

"The number of people who aren't are so small that they don't count." Will said. "As a trader," his gaze turned to Luna, "it's best to think of people as always selfish."

She nodded.

"There are those who would sell all their food for money, even if it meant their family would go hungry because of their greed."

"That can't be true." Luna shook her head.

Malena laughed. "You'll see it happen, and way more often than you'd imagine."

Luna sat in silence, considering her parents' words.

"The biggest responsibility a trader has," Will continued, "is to ensure that each village possesses the resources they need to continue existing. Sometimes it means bringing in extra supplies to one village on your route while limiting that same supply to another."

"And the same goes for information," Malena said.

"That's right," Will agreed. "People love to talk, and

they all chat it up with the trader when she or he comes to visit. Some information is necessary to bring from one village to another, while other bits of knowledge are not."

"Like Stylar crossing the line?" Luna asked.

"Exactly." Will pursed his lips and nodded. "I heard that bit of gossip right away, out of ten or twelve people's mouths when I crossed in. I must decide whether that information is something I will share with other villages and, if so, exactly who I will share it with."

"And?" Luna asked. "What did you decide on that topic? Will you share it with other villages?"

"No." Will shook his head. "I will mention it to my elder, though. Then I'll proceed how she decides. She will hear from the other traders and, if more than a few people have done a similar thing across the total population of villages, she may decide it's an issue to address. But if it's an isolated incident," he shrugged, "then it probably won't be shared with anyone."

"Even if it isn't divulged," Malena said, "the information will be documented and stored in case the same sort of thing happens in the future."

"That's right," Will agreed.

"I still don't understand why parents want their children to be traders now, even with the extra responsibility."

Will considered his daughter for a few seconds and then nodded. "That's okay, sweetheart. You'll come to understand as time goes on and you gain experience. For the moment, just remember this. There are some people who are never happy with what they have in life. Those people want more, and they do whatever they can to get it. Tasker is such an individual. He wants to run the village because he thinks it will make him happy and more powerful. And that's why he wants his son to be a trader."

Luna considered her father's words carefully before speaking again. "But that's not going to happen, is it? He won't gain power when Gage becomes a trader."

Will shrugged. "Some. Maybe as much as he wants. But that's a problem for the future, not right now."

"Maybe I shouldn't have suggested the idea of making Gage a trader," Luna said.

"Of course you should have." Malena reached forward and patted her daughter's leg. "It was a good idea. If it wasn't, we wouldn't have done it."

"It gets us past the current dilemma," Will said. "And makes sure you can become a trader."

"But it could cause problems later," Luna said.

Will laughed. "Problems are unavoidable, my girl. We'll deal with them as they happen. That's the best we can do sometimes."

Luna nodded slowly, not convinced her father was correct but uncertain what made her doubt him.

49

It was late when Will returned home.

Without turning on any lights, he quietly unlocked the door, doffed his jacket and boots, and made his way to the bedroom.

Malena stirred from her sleep as he sat on the edge of the bed. "You just getting home now?"

"Mhm."

"What time is it?"

Will glanced at his wristwatch. "Ten minutes after three."

"Yuck."

"I know." He removed the watch, set it on the nightstand, and slipped under the covers.

"I'm cold," Malena said. "Come cuddle with me."

Will slid closer to his wife, wrapped his arms around her, and rested his chin lightly against her shoulder. She was facing away from him but shifted backward so their bodies were touching.

After a few silent minutes, Malena's body relaxed and her breathing became slow and rhythmic. Will felt her body twitch lightly every few seconds, as it often did when she slept. Will closed his eyes but couldn't go to sleep.

Some time later, he heard Malena's breathing alter again and she stirred. "Can't sleep?" she asked.

"Not yet."

Malena rolled onto her back, head turning to face her husband. "Want to talk about it?"

"No, no," he frowned. "Go back to sleep. You need it more than me, anyway."

"Too late," Malena snorted. "I'm already awake."

Will chuckled and propped his head against the palm of one hand as he watched her. "Are you nervous?"

"About what? Tomorrow?"

"Yes."

Malena smiled and shook her head. "I haven't been nervous in a council meeting for years. Being there is as natural to me as arriving in the village surrounded by excited buyers is for you."

Will smiled.

"I know. Tomorrow's important. But we've done the work. Everything will turn out how we want it to."

"You're sure you have the votes?" Will asked.

"More sure than we usually are."

"How many 'special' visits did you end up having to make?"

"Six."

Will frowned. "That's a lot of councillors to nudge, Mal."

"It was necessary. Sometimes the suggestion wears off. If that happens, I wanted to make sure there was still a majority who voted our way."

"That's just it," Will said. "It could wear off before the vote. For all of them."

"I've never seen such a simple compulsion fade that soon. Sure, if I'd tried to make them do something complex or that went against their morals, then yes, it could be an issue. I kept it basic and in line with something they often do."

"Vote with Malena."

"Exactly." She smiled. "None of the nudges will fade. I'd be surprised if we didn't have a hundred percent success."

"Okay."

"Besides," she turned her back to him and snuggled her body against his once more, adjusting her pillow with one hand before letting her head sink into it. "Flashing them was only a backup measure. With Tasker on board and supporting us, they will all naturally vote the way we want."

Will wrapped both arms around Malena.

After a few seconds, he felt her body tighten. "You didn't find anything wrong out there tonight, did you?" she asked.

"No," Will said. "I didn't find anything wrong at all."

"Good. Then go to sleep."

They lay quietly for a few minutes.

"It's just," Will began.

Malena sighed and then laughed. "My husband, the worrier."

"Planner," he corrected.

"I guess."

"I think about things that could happen."

"Yes," she agreed. "You certainly do think."

A long pause.

"And I'm glad you do," Malena added. "It's better to come up with scenarios and prepare for them before they occur. Fewer surprises that way."

"Thank you."

Malena flipped onto her back again. "It's just what?"

Will thought for a few seconds and then responded. "As the years pass, this is all getting more challenging to hold together. They will become immune to the flashes eventually."

"I know."

"And the more people there are, the greater the odds that someone will try and pull something we haven't considered or planned for."

"You're absolutely right," Malena agreed.

"Luna becoming a trader is key. We've been working toward this since the day she was born, and if this moron Tasker somehow manages to screw it up ..."

Malena reached out and gripped her husband's hand, giving it a squeeze as she did so. "We've got this, Will. There's nothing to worry about."

Will pursed his lips, his mind going over all the steps and turns they had taken to get here, and considering each individual issue that could sabotage their plans. Finally he nodded and gave Mal's hand a quick squeeze back. "You're right. Everything will be fine."

"Good," Mal said. "Then I'm gonna sleep."

"Yes, that's a good idea."

Malena rolled over.

"I might not sleep, though."

"No surprise there, husband." Malena chuckled. "As long as you can manage to stay awake in council tomorrow."

"I'll drink lots of coffee."

She chuckled again.

Less than five minutes later, Will heard her breathing slow down and become rhythmic as sleep claimed her.

50

Luna was lying on the grass, arms behind her head and eyes closed, when a shadow blocked the warm sun from her face.

"We need to talk."

Recognizing the voice, Luna furrowed her brows and spoke without trying to disguise her annoyance. "Go away, Glanis."

The shadow remained. After a few seconds, Luna scowled and opened her eyes to stare up at Gage's cousin.

"Fine." Luna rolled to one side and stood up, tilting her head back to meet the other girl's eyes. Like most of her family, Glanis was both taller and broader of frame than others her age and sex. Although younger than Luna, the girl towered over her by three or four inches.

"What do you want?" Luna asked.

Glanis glared for the space of a few heartbeats, using the silence as a tool to intimidate before she spoke. "Stay away from him."

"Who? Gage?"

Glanis sneered. "Don't play stupid with me, Luna. Of course Gage. Who else would I be talking about?"

Luna smiled sweetly. "If it wasn't Gage, then that would have been my next question."

Glanis's eyebrows tightened and her cheeks flushed. "I'm not joking. As of now, the two of you are off-limits."

"Off-limits?" Luna considered the order. "That's not a phrase you could come up with on your own, Glanis. Who sent you to tell me this?"

She scowled. "I speak on behalf of the family. That's all you need to know."

Luna raised one eyebrow. Since day one, the Lee family had outnumbered any other group in the village, and they had used that to their advantage as often as possible. Although they weren't exactly bullies, every so often they would attempt to use their numbers to gain an advantage of one sort or another. Overall, the Lee family's size and strength was an advantage to the prosperity of the village, but it was also true that they'd managed to be a pain in everyone's backside at some point or other.

Despite the drama they would sometimes add to life, one thing was certain with the Lee family. Their loyalty was to the family, first and above everything else.

"Did you hear me?" Glanis puffed herself up and took a step forward, leering down at Luna as she did so.

"Relax." Luna held a hand in front of her, almost touching the other girl, but not quite. "I heard you."

"And?"

"And what?"

"You gonna leave Gage alone?"

Luna's eyes narrowed as she felt a stab of anger at the other girl's tone and posture. "You can't tell me what to do."

Harsh laughter. "I can. I did. And you'd better listen."

263

"Or what?"

Glanis raised one eyebrow and reached out, grabbing the fabric of Luna's shirt at the neck line.

"Hey! Let go of me."

Glanis twisted the handful of cloth and jerked hard. Luna stumbled forward, her chest touching Glanis's fist.

"Get. Your hands," Luna snarled, "off of me. Or I swear I'll—"

"You'll what?" Glanis laughed. "You think you wanna play with me, little girl? I'm tempted to snap you like a—" The girl's brows lowered, her lips pursed, and her free hand reared back to become a fist.

A sudden blast of anger washed over Luna. She tried to take a step back, pulling hard but still remaining locked in the other girl's grip. The fist hovered for a second and then streaked toward Luna's face.

"No."

Luna knew the word had come from her mouth, but it sounded distant, as if spoken from the other side of the street. At the moment she said it, there was a bright flash and a sudden *pop* that echoed in the space between her and the other girl. Luna saw Glanis freeze and the pupils of her eyes widen, exploding outward so that the colour of her irises almost disappeared.

Luna fell backwards, suddenly off-balance from being let go. She regained her balance, and the rage she had felt a moment before vanished as suddenly as it had appeared. An eerie silence filled the air.

Glanis stood stock still, staring forward, her face empty of expression, her hands hanging loosely at her sides.

"Glanis?" Luna said.

No reply.

Luna frowned. "Glanis," she repeated, her tone no

longer questioning but instead commanding the girl's attention.

"Yes." The word was faint as it tumbled from Glanis's lips.

"Are you okay?"

Again, nothing.

Luna considered the other girl for a long moment. Then she sighed. "Leave me alone."

"Okay."

Luna frowned. "And don't threaten me. Ever again. Do you understand?"

"I understand."

Luna waited for Glanis to say more. When she didn't, Luna shrugged and walked away.

GLANIS BLINKED, STILL CONFUSED AS SHE SLOWLY became conscious of her surroundings.

She looked around, turning slowly.

"What am I doing out here?" she asked out loud. A vague memory flitted through her mind. She had been speaking to someone. Saying something. She shook her head, unable to recall any more than that.

After another few seconds, Glanis took a deep breath, turned and began to walk slowly toward home.

51

Luna walked through the village back streets, paying no attention to her surroundings as the encounter with Glanis cycled through her mind.

What was that popping sound, and why did Glanis suddenly stop dead in her tracks? Right in the middle of throwing a punch!

Luna turned a corner, subconsciously directed toward the Town Hall, where the council meeting was scheduled to begin soon.

Glanis had just ... frozen in place, unresponsive, as if in some sort of trance, or under a spell. And her eyes! Luna could still see the blank stare and the huge black circles of the girl's pupils. She had only ever seen that when she was younger, when she and Gage had decided to sit in the dark, letting their eyes adjust, before flicking the lights back on and staring into a mirror, laughing as the pupils of their eyes went from large and dark to small, pin-hole sized dots in response to the sudden brightness.

For the fifth or sixth time, Luna considered turning around, going back to make sure the girl was okay. Her pace

266

slowed and she came to a stop, frowning and shaking her head before beginning to walk forward once more.

"She was fine," Luna murmured. "I spoke to her and she spoke back."

"That doesn't mean she was fine," a man's voice said from her left.

Luna spun toward the speaker, letting out a small gasp of surprise. "I'm sorry," she began. "I didn't see anyone—"

Then she recognized who it was and froze, mouth half-open and eyes wide.

It was the man in the black leather trench coat, leaning against the wall of a house with arms crossed and body language conveying a relaxed posture.

"You," she whispered.

"Me," he agreed.

"What are you doing here?" she asked.

"Same thing I've been doing for a while now," he smirked. "Following you."

Part of her screamed to run away, to put distance between this man and herself. But the other part—the curious portion—encouraged her to stay. *He's not that close,* her mind said. *Find out what he's up to. You can always run if tries to grab you.*

The man chuckled again. "Stay or go? I can see the conflict on your face, little one."

"There's no conflict," Luna snapped. "And don't call me that. I'm not little."

"I could call you Dove."

"How do you know that name?"

"I know a lot of things. And you'd be very interested to hear about most of them, I think."

Luna frowned.

"I'm not here to answer questions, Luna." He pushed

himself away from the wall but didn't come any closer to her. "I need to ask you something. And it's pretty important."

"Who are you?" Luna asked.

His head tilted to one side, then he shrugged and answered: "Marius."

"Are you a trader, Marius?"

Marius narrowed his eyes and then laughed.

"What?"

"A strange man who's been following you for weeks finally makes contact and you're not scared." A wry grin spread across his face. "Instead you stand there, all brave and defiant, questions tumbling from you as if you're in charge of things and I have no choice but to do as you wish."

"Should I be scared of you?"

"Of course."

Luna took a step back, her leg muscles tensing in preparation to run.

Marius's smile widened. "You should always be scared of the unknown. Hasn't your dad been teaching you exactly that?"

"I don't like you following me around. If you don't stop, I'll—"

"You'll what? Do to me what you did to the Lee girl?"

Luna felt her breath catch in her chest. "I don't know what you mean."

"Sure you do." Marius ran a hand through his short black hair, then shook his head as he watched her, the expression on his face disapproving. "It took her six full minutes to snap out of it. I mean, sure, she was gonna hit you, so you had the right to defend yourself. Still, six minutes was a long time to shut her down, don't you think?"

"Shut her down?"

"Ahh," he smiled. "You have no idea what you did to her, do you?"

"I didn't do anything."

"Of course you did."

Luna pursed her lips, then shook her head.

Marius raised one eyebrow. "Is this is the first time you've ever flashed anyone?"

"Flashed?"

"Of course it is. That makes sense." He stuck out his hand. "Hand it over."

"What?"

"The tag."

"Tag?"

"Yes, girl, the tag."

Luna frowned. "I don't know what you're talking about."

"Don't play with me," he snapped, his expression darkening as he took a sudden step forward, before catching himself and stopping. He raised a hand in a calming gesture. "Hold on. Don't run away. I'm not gonna steal it. Actually, you know what?" He took a slow step backward. "If you promise to put it back from wherever you borrowed it, I'll let you keep the thing."

"Thing? Seriously, mister, I have no idea what you're talking about."

Marius scowled. "You're starting to get on my nerves, girl. Just put the tag back and don't use it again. You're lucky no one in the village saw you—"

"Listen," Luna interrupted. "I don't know what a *tag* is and I certainly don't have one."

Marius considered her for a long moment. Then one eyebrow rose. "You're telling the truth."

"Yes I am."

The man rubbed his face with one hand and sighed. "I must be slipping, then. Another must have been there and flashed the girl when she was going to hit you. I didn't see a remote flash, but there was brush and big rocks around, so I guess it's possible that I missed it."

Luna opened her mouth to tell Marius no one else had been there, but she thought better of it and said nothing.

Marius stared at her, eyes searching hers. "Unless," he mumbled, "you flashed her without a tag ..."

Her eyes flickered at the truth of his statement, and he caught it immediately.

"Damn," he muttered. "This makes you ..." He frowned. "I never believed such a thing possible."

"I don't know what you mean."

A quick, harsh laugh escaped the man's lips. "Of course you don't. How could you?"

Marius stared at her.

Luna stared back.

Without another word, Marius nodded once, turned on his heel, and began to walk away.

"Wait." She took a few steps toward him but stopped when he glanced at her over his shoulder.

"It was nice to meet you, Luna."

"What are you doing here?" she called out.

Marius laughed and shook his head. "Don't worry. I'll answer another question or two when next we meet."

"When will that be?" she called as he disappeared around the corner.

Luna sprang into action, running to the corner of the street where Marius had been only seconds ago. She rounded the corner and skidded to a halt.

The street beyond was empty.

52

LUNA ENTERED THE TOWN HALL AND MADE HER WAY to the stairwell, taking the steps two at a time.

She reached the top of the stairs and pressed her lips together in frustration. The audience chamber was completely filled. Even the aisles were clogged with people who were willing to stand in discomfort rather than avoid missing today's council meeting.

Her eyes skimmed the crowd, looking for a friendly face. She noted the large group that was the Lee clan sitting together as usual, but it appeared as if Gage was not with them. Thinking that was odd, she continued to skim the gallery.

Then she spied something that made her eyes widen. Gage was here, after all, sitting on the far side, directly opposite from where the rest of his family was situated. He was looking directly at her and raised a hand in greeting, smiling as he made a beckoning motion with one hand while the other pointed at the seat beside him, signalling that he would save room for her if she joined him.

Luna wove her way through the crowd, smiling politely

at those she recognized and asking others to excuse her as she navigated the throng of tightly packed bodies. When she was close, Gage closed his wide-spread legs and slid to one side, creating an empty portion of bench for her to sit on.

"Hiya." She did her best to sound friendly as she sat.

"Hi."

"Thanks for saving me a seat."

"No problem." He smiled. "Well, it was a bit of a problem. I had to spread my legs and puff out my shoulders to make it seem as if I needed all the extra space. It got a few grumbles and groans, but I managed to pull it off."

Luna laughed as she imagined the scene. "I appreciate it. I was afraid there wouldn't be any room and I'd have to wait outside until the meeting was over to find out what happened."

"That would have been terrible," Gage said. "Considering how important this session is to you, I thought you'd be one of the first people here. You sleep in or something?"

Luna's smile faded. Part of her wanted to share the details of her encounter with Marius, but she knew it wasn't a wise thing to do. "I got sidetracked."

Gage frowned and opened his mouth to say more but clamped it shut as whispers and shushing sounds drifted through the crowd and eyes began to focus on the councillors now entering the main chamber below.

53

Silent and sombre, the councillors filed into the chamber, each moving to their chair and standing quietly behind it while waiting for everyone else to do the same. When all were in place, the village leaders took their seats in unison. No one spoke. All sat with hands clasped together on the table in front of them and waited as they faced the empty Speaker's chair.

Less than a minute after the councillors had sat down, another door opened and the Speaker emerged. He moved to the chair that was his to occupy and turned to face the assembled crowd.

"All rise," he said.

There was a muted rustling of cloth and sharp sounds of wooden chairs sliding against the floor as everyone on both levels came to their feet.

"Be advised," the Speaker spoke the words with a formal timbre in his voice, "that all who have business in this village should now come forward to assemble and be heard. Let council now come to session." The Speaker stared out at the councillors and then looked up to the gallery. Satisfied with what he saw, the man nodded once, gathered a handful of robe in each hand, and lowered himself into the large wooden chair. "You may be seated."

The Speaker waited for silence to return, then looked toward Malena and dipped his head in acknowledgement. "If there is no objection, Madam Mayor, then I will dispense with normal procedure and initiate the business at hand myself."

Malena nodded. "Of course, Mr. Speaker."

The Speaker reached for a sheet of paper resting on a side table to the right of his chair. "The first order of business is to conclude a contract." He stood and silently read over the document and then looked up when finished. "Will Reymont and Tasker Lee, please stand."

Both men stood.

"I hold in my hand," the Speaker began, "a legally binding agreement that requires each of your signatures. Do either of you want me to read the entirety of it out loud for purposes of entering the full text into the public record?"

Will smiled and shook his head. "I do not, Mr. Speaker."

"Nor do I," Tasker replied, his expression flat and serious.

"Very well. Come forward and sign the document to make it official and legally binding."

The two men made their way to the Speaker's chair. Will accepted the paper and placed it on the small table. After reading it over, he withdrew a pen and scrawled his signature onto the bottom of the page. He stepped back and Tasker Lee took his place, repeating the process with a loud scratching of pen against paper.

The Speaker retrieved the document, examined the signatures, then looked up and nodded at each man in turn.

"The deal is struck, and the agreement created declares the following." He held the paper up to chest level and turned to face the gallery. "When Tasker Lee's eldest son, Gage, comes of age, if he chooses to be a trader he will be accepted into the profession without reservation or condition. By signing this note, all parties involved agree that there is nothing that can negate or reverse this decision as it has now been signed."

Luna frowned and looked at her friend. Gage stared down at the Speaker, a smile on his face as people around him turned to stare and whisper to each other.

"That's ridiculous," a voice from nearby said.

"The first two kids we have that come of age *both* get to become traders?" Another voice. "Who's going to carry on with the other professions if everyone is allowed to pick the same role?"

The Speaker reached for his staff of office and used it to tap the floor loudly to call for silence. When the murmuring had died down, the Speaker licked his lips and stared at the sheet of paper in his hand for a long moment. Then he set it on the side table and looked up at the gallery. "I am sure that many of you are concerned about this bit of news and what it might mean for the village, specifically the other professions."

There was another murmur from the crowd. The Speaker allowed it to go on for a few seconds before he raised one hand and silence returned.

"I can assure you," he said, "that all children will not choose to become traders as they come of age. We all knew that there would be unforeseen complications with the process that we created, and that we would deal with them as they occurred. This happens to have become one of those complications. In order to address the issue, council has agreed to the following." He nodded at the two men in front of him. They turned away from him and went back to their chairs. "From this point on, the position of trader is no longer available until the rest of the professions have been chosen. Once the remaining professions have at least one new young adult, then the trader profession will open up for choosing once more. That may take some time, but it is the best solution, and council has agreed to it outside of chambers."

There were more grumbles, and the Speaker tapped his staff for silence.

Once things had quieted down, the Speaker sat in the chair of his office and leaned the staff against one of the arm rests. Then he retrieved another piece of paper from the table and held it in the air. "There is only one other item on today's agenda." He looked up from the page and met Malena's eyes. "Madam Mayor, please introduce the issue at hand, make whatever statement you deem appropriate, and then call for a vote."

Malena stood. Her gaze drifted toward Will. He nodded and she smiled. "Mr. Speaker." She looked back to the Speaker and began her address. "At her Choosing ceremony, Luna Reymont selected the profession of trader. She was accepted by the trader representative, yet the village challenged the validity of both her choice and the entire Choosing process."

"That was certainly not the case, your honour." Tasker Lee came to his feet, face red and brows furrowed. "We simply wanted to make certain there were no existing loopholes in the Choosing process. Specifically with regards to the trader profession. At the time of Choosing, trader was not an accepted profession on our village list. I think we all agree that it should be, and that was the reason for delaying Luna's acceptance."

"Regardless of Mr. Lee's current story," Malena sniffed, "the council voted to discuss the matter further and extra time was given. Now that time has passed, Mr. Speaker, and I am standing before you to call a vote on the matter. There are two items to vote on. Number one. Shall we add trader as a sanctioned profession to the village roster and include it for children as they come of age in the Choosing ceremony?"

"I think the first order of business already tipped our hat as to how this vote will go," the Speaker said, as he motioned toward Jack. "Deputy Mayor, vote first and record the votes of the remaining councillors, if you please."

Jack stood. "I vote yay." He sat and recorded his vote on a piece of paper.

"I vote yay." Tasker Lee spoke the words in a loud voice.

The next few minutes passed with each councillor standing, declaring their vote, and then taking their seat. Will stood and declared his support with a "yay," then sat and watched his wife as she stood and cast the final vote.

"I vote yay, Mr. Speaker." She remained standing.

"Excellent." The Speaker smiled. "Mr. Deputy Mayor, please declare the official tally for all to hear."

Jack stood, a smile on his face as well. "The vote is unanimous, Mr. Speaker. The village votes yay, in the affirmative, for making trader a recognized profession."

"Very well." The Speaker picked up a pen and recorded the vote result in a worn notebook from his little table. He looked up and motioned toward the mayor with a wave of his pen. "Now let's get through the second vote and be done with today's business, shall we?"

"Thank you, Mr. Speaker." Malena stood tall and

straight, wearing a confident expression. "Now that the trader profession has been accepted, please vote if you agree that Luna Reymont should be allowed to become the village's first trader, as she chose in her ceremony. I will begin by voting yay."

Malena sat and turned toward Tasker Lee. The man stood. "I also vote yay." He spoke the word and looked at Malena, a smile on his face as he fulfilled his part of their bargain.

She dipped her head once in silent thanks, then looked past Tasker to the next councillor, a devoted follower of Tasker in all his council dealings and one of the people that Malena had visited with her device to ensure she would vote in favour of Luna, regardless of the deal they'd made with Tasker Lee.

The woman stood. Malena saw the woman glance toward her ally, but Tasker kept his back to the woman, continuing to stare at Malena with a smile on his face. The woman looked back to the Speaker, licked her lips, and cast her vote.

"Nay."

The gathered crowd began to murmur loudly. Malena's smile slid away, her eyes flashing with confusion toward the councillor who had voted against her daughter—against both her ally, Tasker Lee, and the compulsion that Malena had placed upon her.

The next councillor stood. Another ally of Tasker.

"Nay."

A loud throbbing began to pulse in Malena's ears as anger flooded into her. Her eyes met Tasker Lee's.

His smile widened, and he bowed at the waist as behind him, one of Malena's own stalwart allies voted against Luna being accepted as trader.

54

Luna watched as, one by one, the councillors stood and cast their votes.

Each was a "nay."

Halfway through the ordeal, she stood and looked down at Gage. "Let's go."

Gage was staring at the politicians below, mouth wide open and eyes narrowed in confusion. Slowly he looked up at Luna and blinked.

"It's not gonna happen." Luna was surprised at the calmness in her own voice. "I don't need to see any more. Let's get outta here."

"It's not over yet," Gage whispered. "There's still a chance that—"

"No."

Luna didn't shout the word, but the gallery was so quiet that it sounded as if she had. Heads turned, annoyed expressions melting as they realized who was speaking, replaced by looks of compassion and sympathy.

Without waiting for Gage to stand, she began to make

her way toward the exit. There were grumbles and muffled protests as people were jostled by her passage, but Luna didn't acknowledge them. Instead, she moved with purpose, not caring if anyone was disturbed.

"Sorry. Oops. Pardon me. Yeah ... excuse us, please." Gage's whispered apologies sounded from behind as he followed.

Luna reached the steps and began to descend. Faint but clear, she heard another called vote of "nay." The word felt like a slap in the face, another nail in the coffin of her hopes for the future. One that would never come to pass.

Luna pushed open the front door with both hands and went around the front corner of the building. She leaned against the wall and bent over at the waist, elbows resting on her knees as dizziness churned in her head and nausea in her stomach.

"I think I'm gonna puke," she mumbled.

"It's okay." Gage's hand touched her shoulder and remained there.

"Don't touch me," she muttered.

Gage ignored the command. "Should I hold your hair back?"

She made a jerking motion with her shoulder, trying to push his hand away. "I said. Don't." Her voice rose with each word. "Touch. Me."

The warmth of his palm against her shoulder disappeared and she saw his feet take a step back from her.

"Go away."

After a pause. "No."

She made a groaning noise. "Gage, please, just go aw—"

"No." The tone of his voice became deeper, more adamant. "Listen." His voice softened. "I know you're hurting. And that I'm partly responsible for it."

She laughed.

"But you're my best friend. I'm not gonna abandon you right now. You shouldn't be alone."

Luna closed her eyes as a gurgling sensation began to roil in her stomach. She groaned. "Oh, god."

"Whoah. You don't look so good."

Luna dropped to her knees and retched loudly, moaning in pain as her stomach surrendered its contents and spewed them onto the ground.

SHE HEAVED AND RETCHED LONG AFTER THERE WAS nothing left to bring up. Her stomach muscles burned and the back of her throat felt hot and raw.

"Come on," she whispered, letting out a grunt of pain as she rolled away from the mess that she'd made and came to rest on her back.

After a few seconds, Luna opened her eyes and blinked. She frowned in confusion at the silhouettes above her until they materialized into the distinct forms of her parents, standing over her, looking worried.

"Hi," Luna said.

"Hi," Malena replied.

"Is the voting over with?" Luna asked.

"Yes, it's over." Malena declared with a sigh.

"And the outcome? They voted unanimously against me being a trader, right?"

"No ..." Will said.

"I mean, when you take out family and the obligatory vote that Tasker promised to cast in my favour."

Will's eyes hardened, and he nodded his head once.

Luna laughed. "Even Mom's and Uncle Jack's allies voted against me. What a friggin joke."

"We'll get to the bottom of this, Dove," Will said through gritted teeth. "And when we do, people are going to pay. I promise you that."

"Will." Malena spoke sternly.

"What?" Will turned toward her. She gave a slight shake of her head.

"I'm angry."

"We all are," Malena agreed. "But that's no excuse for losing our calm in public."

"I'm not sure I agree."

Mal rested a hand on Will's shoulder. "Please don't say anything that might make matters worse."

Luna sat up, accepting her father's hand as she got to her feet. "How could it be any worse, Mom? I chose a profession—something the law was supposed to guarantee was my right—and the adults overturned it. Everything this village stands for is a joke."

Malena's expression darkened.

"I'm not the only one saying that, am I?"

"No."

"Tasker played us," Will snarled. "Before the week is out, I promise I am going to—"

"You're going to what?" Tasker's voice sounded from behind the trader.

Will spun to face the man, fists clenched at his sides. "This is a private party, Lee," Will growled. "Move along before I lose control and do something I shouldn't."

"Whoa, whoa." The councillor raised both hands in a calming gesture. "Cool your jets, man. Why're you mad at me?" He smiled, the expression mocking despite his tone. "I did as promised and voted for Luna."

"Your allies were supposed to vote for her, too," Malena said.

"Really?" Tasker frowned. "I don't recall seeing that in the conditions set out in our contract."

"You son of a—"

Tasker laughed. "Don't be mad at me. I didn't realize it was my responsibility to pass the message along. I thought you'd spoken to the rest of my friends."

"Please," Malena snorted.

"Besides," Tasker raised one eyebrow and jutted his chin in Jack's direction. "I didn't see any of your traditional allies voting in favour of the girl becoming a trader, either. The count was clear, and against you." He shrugged. "I did what you asked me to. Don't blame me because the rest of the village didn't."

Luna observed the exchange in silence, eyes drifting from one man to the other as each spoke in turn for a few seconds, before she noticed Gage standing off to one side, his expression filled with disappointment and concern as he watched her.

"Well," Tasker shook his head and turned on his heel. "I came over to offer my condolences and see if there was anything I could do to help. But it looks as if you're not in the mood to consider being helped at the moment." He began to walk away. "Perhaps when you cool down a bit. You will be training my son to be a trader soon, after all. It makes sense that our families be closer than they've been in the past."

Will's eyes flashed with anger but he held his tongue.

"Come along, Gage," Tasker called out to his son. Gage stood where he was for a few seconds, then gave Luna a timid smile—maybe of encouragement, although it was impossible for her to know for sure—and followed his father.

55

LUNA WAS UP BEFORE THE SUN THE NEXT MORNING, moving about the barn, doing chores. She was on her way to fetch another pail of water when she saw the familiar shape of Gage lumbering up the driveway.

Part of her wanted to turn around and retreat inside the barn, but instead she sighed and set the pail on the ground, turning it upside-down. She sat down on it while she waited for her friend to reach her. Gage's eyes were fixed on the ground as he walked. He came to a stop and looked up, prompting Luna to suck in her breath and frown.

"Oh, Gage."

"Yeah, I know." Gage made a wry face, the dark purple and yellow surrounding his left eye hitching upward in response to the expression. "I've never been very good at keeping my mouth shut, have I?"

Luna stood and reached out with one hand, her fingertips lightly touching the most swollen part, near the bottom of his eye. "Did your dad do this to you?"

Gage gave a snort and nodded his head once.

"What did you do?"

"Spoke up against the family."

"In my defence?"

"Sort of." Gage shrugged. "I told him that if you weren't allowed to become a trader, I would refuse to be one as well."

Luna laughed. "You told him that?"

"Mhm."

Her hand returned to her side. "I'm sorry that happened."

"I'm not." Gage grinned once more. "I'll just add this experience to the list of exciting and crazy things that've occurred during the past few weeks."

Luna used her toe to flip the pail upward. As it rose in front of her, she reached out and gripped the handle in mid-air. "I've got a few more buckets of water to haul. Wanna help?"

"No."

Luna raised one eyebrow. "But you will?"

"Of course."

She laughed. "Good. Let's go."

GAGE TIPPED THE PAIL AND DIRECTED THE FLOW OF water into the large bin on the ground of the chicken coop.

Luna reached into the smaller pail tucked in the crook of her left arm, grabbed a handful of dried corn, and threw it onto the ground in front of the chickens. The white and black feathered birds scurried forward, heads darting to pluck corn from the ground while positioning their bodies so as to keep others from getting any of the morning meal. Gage finished emptying the pail and set it down. Then he leaned on the fence and watched her.

Luna looked up at him, smiled, and focused on the contents in her pail of grain. "I do appreciate you standing up to your dad for me," she said.

"It was the right thing to do."

"I'm surprised your dad hit you. That's only happened once or twice, right?"

Gage laughed. "Yeah, I was too. But I get it. He's been under a lot of stress lately."

"I can relate."

"I think a lot of us can."

Luna tossed another handful of corn, took a step forward, then tossed another. Neither spoke until the bucket was empty and she stepped out of the enclosure.

"I'm really sorry," Gage said.

Luna hung the pail on the corner post. "I know."

"I never meant for any of this to happen."

Luna laughed.

"You don't believe me?"

She shook her head. "Of course I believe you." She slipped her arm through his and began to lead him toward the house. "Life was simple and easy before the idea of being a trader was raised."

Gage grunted. "That does seem to be where it all started to hit the manure pile, isn't it?"

"We've been friends for a long time. This isn't the first time our parents have fought over something."

"You're right. Still, this seems like a bigger deal than the other times."

Luna laughed. "It's a huge deal, but I'm not sure you're thinking of it the way I am."

"What do you mean?"

"It's not so much the argument over who gets to become

a trader. It's that the adults are the ones discussing it. We were supposed to have a choice."

"Well, we don't seem to be involved in deciding anything, do we?"

"No," Luna sighed. "We don't."

Luna released her grip from Gage and took a seat on the porch. Gage sat across from her.

"One of us could go against our family," Gage suggested.

"Why only one?" Luna's eyebrows rose.

"You're right. We both could."

There was a moment of silence as each considered the possibility. Then both broke out into laughter at the same time.

"Oops," Gage was first to stop laughing. "Sorry about the noise."

"Please." Luna rolled her eyes. "If Mom and Dad are still sleeping it's time to get up anyway. The chores are done."

Gage laughed for a second then stopped and frowned.

"What?"

He shook his head.

"Come on. Tell me."

"It's just," he paused for a second. "No matter how things turn out, I don't think there'll be many moments like this between us from now on."

"Yeah." Luna felt sadness wash over her. "You're probably right."

The front door squeaked and the screen door slammed. They turned to see Will standing in the doorway.

"Morning, Dad."

Will's expression was blank for a moment. Then he

smiled. "Morning, Dove." He dipped his head toward Gage. "Gage."

Gage raised one hand in greeting.

Will's eyes narrowed as he noted the young man's blackened eye. He opened his mouth to say something, but then paused and gave his head a slight shake. "Wanna help me with the chores?"

"Nope."

The trader frowned. "Why not?"

"Because," Luna batted her eyelashes and smiled. "They're already done."

Will's smile returned. "Well, then. How 'bout I make us some breakfast?"

Luna stood. "Sounds good."

"I should be going." Gage stood as well. "You guys have a great day. Thanks for the talk, Luna." He moved toward the porch steps.

"You not hungry?" Will asked.

Gage stopped and threw the man a look over his shoulder. "I am, but I figured—"

"You've been eating our food since before you could talk, lad." Will smiled. "There's no need to stop now." He opened the door and beckoned with one hand.

Luna stepped past her father and entered the house. Gage waited for another few seconds, then followed his friend inside.

56

WILL TOOK A SIP OF HIS COFFEE AND CONSIDERED THE figure of Thomas approaching along the driveway. He lowered his cup and let it rest on his lap, enjoying the feeling of faint warmth through the fabric of his jeans.

As he got closer, Thomas smiled and raised a hand in greeting.

Will returned the gesture.

"Good afternoon," Thomas called out.

"Hi there." Will set his coffee on the side table and stood. "Luna isn't here right now, but she should be back in an hour or so."

"That's okay. I'm not here to see Luna."

"No?"

The tower technician shook his head and came to stand at the bottom step. "You're the guy I was hoping to chat with."

Will considered Thomas for a heartbeat, then he smiled and motioned toward the seats on the porch. "Then grab a chair. Can I offer you some coffee?"

"That'd be great, thanks." Thomas bent his knees and

lowered the toolbox in his right hand to the ground. Then he climbed the steps and took a seat opposite from where Will had been sitting.

"Cream or sugar?" Will asked.

"Black is fine."

Will disappeared into the house and returned a few minutes later with a carafe and an empty mug. He set the mug on the rectangular table between the chairs and poured steaming liquid into it until it was almost full.

"Thanks so much." Thomas reached for the cup, gripping it with both hands as he raised it to his mouth. He blew lightly across the coffee's surface, then took a tentative sip and smiled. "Merciful Aatun, how I've missed coffee."

"Missed it?" Will sat and refilled his cup from the carafe.

"Unfortunately, coffee is a luxury that I haven't been able to afford for a few months. I need the money to buy tools that I've put off getting as long as I could. Expensive tools, but necessary." Thomas grinned. "And working the towers has kept me so busy that I've not had time to visit friends and borrow a cup."

Will chuckled and stood once more. "That's no good. Hang on a sec." He went back into the house.

Thomas sipped his coffee.

A few minutes later the screen door opened and Will stepped back onto the porch with a small burlap bag in his hand. "Here." He dropped the bag onto the table, with the telltale sound of unground coffee beans shifting around inside as it settled on the hard surface. "Take this with you."

"That's very generous of you, Will," Thomas shook his head from side to side, "but I couldn't."

"Sure you can." Will sat and retrieved his coffee cup. With a grin, he raised it to his lips. "I'd hate to hear about you falling off a tower because you were too tired to focus on the climb." He took a sip and Thomas laughed.

"Thank you kindly," Thomas said. "I'll mark it down and repay you when I'm able."

"No need. It's a gift."

Thomas touched his hand to his chest in a gesture of gratitude, then took another sip of coffee and smiled as he looked around. "It's nice and peaceful out here, away from the town."

Will snorted. "If only that were true. My brain is swirling from the chaos that's been stirring in this village the past few weeks. I can't get away from it, even with the distance."

"It has been a crazy time," Thomas said. "I wonder if the other villages will follow suit?"

"What do you mean?"

"As their children come of age and begin to choose. Will they bicker and fight about the choices made, too?"

"If they are able, then yes."

"Always politics." Thomas sighed.

"Yes," Will agreed. "I don't know if it will make a difference, but I'm going to recommend we address the trader option before the next Choosing happens anywhere."

"That little addition did seem to add a lot of drama to the whole affair."

"Indeed." Will ran a hand through his hair. "I'm going to recommend we leave it off the table altogether for the next few ceremonies."

"Once word gets out that it's an option, taking it way could cause trouble too, right?"

Will raised one eyebrow. "Once word gets out, yes."

"Ahh," Thomas smiled. "I guess the other villages only

learn about things from traders, right? If they don't mention it, then no other villages will know."

"I wish that were the case. But elders send correspondence to each other." Will shook his head. "There will be no keeping this a secret."

"Well." Thomas raised his cup in a silent toast. "I'm glad I don't have to worry about complicated things like that." Thomas leaned back in his chair. "I've no children, at least not yet." His eyebrows furrowed and he tilted his head to one side. "You should have all this stuff figured out in another twenty years or so, right? In case I do have kids soon."

"Maybe," Will laughed. "Who knows?"

The conversation lapsed, and the men sat without speaking for a few minutes.

Thomas broke the silence. "I'm sure it stings now, but Luna will be happy as a tower tech."

Will took a sip of coffee.

"And who knows how it will affect the village?" Thomas continued. "Maybe even all the villages, however many there are out there."

Will frowned. "How what will affect the village?"

"Her ability to speak with Aatun. If she can do so at her age, there's no telling how well she'll be able to communicate with the goddess as she gets older. We are all very excited to see how it turns—"

"You mean she can communicate with the Deandria?" Will asked, referring to the individual towers that communicated with tower technicians, emitting basic signals and information when they required repair or maintenance. "She has figured out how to interpret the beeps and whistles to some degree?"

"No," Thomas shook his head. "I mean, sure, she can

understand the Deandria. But she can speak with Aatun herself." Thomas frowned. "Real conversations with the female avatar. Words used. In her dreams ..."

Will frowned.

"You didn't know?"

Will stared at the tower technician.

"I thought she would have told you," Thomas continued. "Or Elder Baker would've visited to discuss the ramifications of such a blessing."

"The elder?" Will's frown deepened. "Desmond knows about this, too?"

"Of course." Thomas's expression conveyed his surprise. "I'm sure he's told Malena. Maybe you were out of the village when he did so. Although that doesn't make sense, because it's pretty exciting news and he should've shared it with the both of you."

Thomas continued to speak, but his voice faded into the background as Will's mind began to consider what this revelation might mean.

To their family.

And also the village.

57

When Luna came through the front door, her Uncle Jack was standing at the kitchen table, back to her, arms moving as he spoke. Malena and Will sat across from him, focused intently as they listened to whatever it was he was talking about. In unison, her parents' eyes shifted to rest on her.

Jack stopped mid-sentence and half-turned to look at her. "Heya," he said.

"Hi." Luna removed her jacket and hung it on the empty wall peg. "Whatcha talking about?"

"The village," Will said.

"That's what I figured." Luna took a seat at the table between her dad and uncle. "It's not a very cheerful place at the moment, is it?"

"Human nature rears its ugly head," Jack mumbled.

"What do you mean?" Luna asked.

"People love to find something to worry and gossip about."

She frowned. "Do they?"

Will laughed and Malena smiled.

"What?" Luna's brows furrowed.

"It's cute to hear the genuine puzzlement in your voice," Will said. Luna opened her mouth to say something but he held up one hand and gave a slight shake of his head. "I'm not criticizing or trying to embarrass you, Dove. Truly, it has never been something that you need concern yourself with. But now that you're in the thick of it, there's no way to avoid seeing people for what they truly are. As a group, people tend to be simple creatures who worry about all the wrong things and waste their time, and that of everyone else around them, gossiping and sowing discontent."

Luna considered her father's words and then smiled. "That does seem to describe things, doesn't it? And as bad as that sounds, I'd give most anything not to be the subject of everyone's attention at the moment."

Malena reached out and patted Luna's hand. "It might feel uncomfortable right now, but it won't last."

"You think so?" Luna raised one eyebrow.

"I'm certain of it. A short time from now, everyone will lose interest in this drama and go looking for something else to worry about."

"It's actually sort of neat," Luna observed.

Jack snorted.

"Oh no. Not all the attention and drama. I mean, how calm the three of you seem about the whole thing."

A bark of laughter escaped Malena. "I'm not sure how calm your father or uncle are. If it weren't for me I'm pretty sure they'd be coming up with some creative ways to teach these people to keep their noses out of our business."

"Who says we aren't?" Will smiled and batted his eyes. Malena shook her head and the two brothers laughed.

"Well." Jack stood and looked Malena. "I guess we've done enough talking for now. The two of us are due at a council meeting in twenty minutes. Shall we head out, Madam Mayor?"

"I suppose." Malena leaned over and kissed Will, then got to her feet. "What will the two of you be up to for the afternoon?" she asked.

"Not sure," Luna shrugged. "I can't train with Dad, so maybe I'll just read or something."

"Reading sounds good," Will said. "But that's not likely in the cards for me today."

"No?" Malena raised one eyebrow.

"I might have to head out soon."

"Head out?" Luna's brows furrowed. "As in, leave the village?"

He nodded.

"Already?"

"Blame this village full of meddlers," he smiled. "I think it best if I report everything that's happened here to the trader hall. Sooner than later."

"So you can head any trouble off before similar things spread and begin to happen in other villages?" Luna guessed.

"Exactly. You're gonna make a great trader."

"Maybe."

Will's eyes flashed. "There's no way I'm gonna allow Tasker Lee and his cronies to stop you from—"

"Uh, uh, uh." Malena interrupted him. Will's frown deepened for a second as their eyes met. Then he nodded once and smiled. "Okay, you're right, Love. I'll keep my passion to myself."

"Passion." Jack smiled.

"Anger can be described that way." Will slapped his brother's leg with the back of his hand.

Jack laughed again as he dodged the strike as best he

could and made his way to the front door. He reached for Malena's jacket and helped her put it on, then grabbed his own and draped it over his forearm.

"There's roast chicken in the fridge," Malena said. "Snack on that for lunch and we'll figure out what to cook for dinner when I get home."

"Good luck," Luna said.

"Love you." Will waved.

"Love you, too." Jack mimicked his brother's tone and opened the door, making an extravagant sweeping motion with his other hand to indicate that Malena should exit before him. The two stepped out into the morning sunlight and closed the door behind them.

"Gonna read inside or out?" Will asked.

Luna turned to look out the window. "I suppose I should enjoy the weather. Before the snow comes."

Will laughed. "Snow? What are you talking about? It never snows here."

She looked back at her father and smiled. "You're right. I had this dream a while back. And snow was on the way."

"A dream?"

Luna nodded.

"Is that where you see Aatun as well, in dreams?"

Luna's eyes narrowed as she considered her father.

"Thomas stopped by the other day and mentioned that you could talk to the tower A.I."

"All the techs can, Dad."

"No." Will shook his head. "All of them can hear the commands and status updates. But none of them actually see a woman claiming to be the goddess herself."

Luna stared at her father.

"Is it true? You've actually seen and spoken with Aatun?"

"Yes. But only in my dreams."

"I see."

Luna frowned. "I'm pretty sure I told you about this."

Will shook his head slowly.

"Mom, then. I must have mentioned it to Mom."

Will sat on the couch across from Luna and ran a hand through his hair. "How many times have you seen her?"

"Only once."

"Are you sure?"

Luna nodded.

"And when did it happen?"

"A few weeks ago."

"Can you narrow it down more than that?"

Luna shook her head, then paused. "Yeah, I think I can. It was right before the Choosing."

Will's eyes narrowed. "You're sure about that?"

"Absolutely."

"In a dream, right?"

Luna laughed. "Yes, Dad, in a dream. You don't think I was climbing a tower all by myself and happened to turn around to find a woman standing up there with me?"

"You didn't tell me how or where you met her at all. Until right now."

"Oh. That's right, I didn't. Sorry."

Will stroked his chin, something he did when he was thinking hard about a topic. "What else did she say?"

Luna furrowed her brows and pretended to think about the dream. The truth of the matter was she clearly remembered the entire incident. But something told her the information that Aatun had shared was for her alone. She waited for a few more seconds and then shook her head. "I can't remember much about it. Most of my dreams fade from memory pretty quick."

Will grunted.

"She was pretty," Luna offered.

Will scowled but said nothing.

"You think it means something?"

"I don't know." Will sighed. "I suppose not. It makes sense that kids would have a dream like this at some point. The towers and barrier are very real things to you. And you are able to hear the audio cues for repair and diagnostics. It wouldn't be much of a jump for that creative brain of yours to start dreaming about Aatun. The villagers have created a religion around her, after all."

Her father's words raised questions in Luna's mind, but she thought it best to sit quietly and hope this line of questioning ended soon.

Will nodded slowly as if reading her thoughts. "Okay. I suppose it's likely nothing."

"What is?"

Will smiled. "Exactly."

"Do you really have to go, Dad?"

Will's expression remained serious and he did not reply for a few seconds. Finally he smiled and met his daughter's eyes. "Sorry, what were you asking me?"

Luna laughed. Her father disappeared when deep in thought, but she couldn't blame him; she did the very same thing herself. "I asked if you really have to leave the village so soon."

Will nodded. "'Fraid so, Dove." He stood. "But don't worry. I won't be gone very long."

"Quick trip to report stuff to the traders and then back?"

"That's right." His tone still sounded distracted to Luna's ears. "Quick trip and back."

58

Elder Baker stepped through the front entrance of his house and smiled, closing his eyes and inhaling deeply through his nose. "Fresh bread and roast chicken," he said out loud. "How delightful."

He hung his coat up, removed his shoes, and made his way to the kitchen. "Something smells wonderful, Agnes," he called out. "Is company coming, because if so, I forgot who it—"

The elder saw who was sitting at his dining room table and froze, his smile turning to a scowl.

His wife Agnes sat at one end of the table, hands folded and resting on the table. Marius sat at a chair reserved for guests, his plate mounded with golden roasted chicken, fluffy white mashed potatoes topped with caramel-coloured gravy, and assorted vegetables of differing vibrant colours.

The man took a forkful of chicken and chewed, his mouth opening every third chew to make a smacking noise that seemed to fill the room. He set his fork down and reached for a thick slice of bread from the tray in the centre of the table. He used the dull knife in his other hand to slather butter on the bread's steaming white surface.

"I'm sorry, Desmond." Agnes shook her head as she met her husband's gaze. "I told him that in this house we wait for everyone to arrive before eating, but his manners ..." She shook her head again in obvious disgust.

"There he is." Marius looked up from his bread and smiled at Desmond, ignoring Agnes's words as if she hadn't spoken at all. "We waited as long as we could, but everything was in danger of getting cold." His eyes slid to Agnes and paused before looking back at the elder. "I didn't think you'd want to make us all eat soggy food on your account. *That* would be terrible manners to your guests. So we started without you. Hope you don't mind?"

Desmond sighed, made his way to the head of the table, and sat.

Agnes began to dish food up on a clean plate.

"It's delicious, by the way." Marius smiled at Agnes and raised his knife in salute.

Agnes ignored the compliment, her attention focused on a spoonful of carrots.

Desmond reached for the wine bottle, lifted it to pour himself a glass, and frowned as he realized it was almost empty. He upended the bottle and a trickle of red wine dribbled into his glass.

Marius watched the spectacle and nodded as Desmond set the bottle down with a thud. "I'd love some more, thanks."

"Unbelievable." Agnes's anger was clear in her tone. "This cannot continue, Desmond. I will not have this man—"

Marius chuckled, shaking his head as he continued to stare at Desmond.

Desmond lifted his hand in a placating gesture to his wife and pondered the man at their table for a long moment.

Marius smiled as he took a big bite of bread and chewed with his mouth open.

"I'm glad that you've enjoyed our hospitality, Marius," Desmond said.

"It's been fairly decent."

Desmond pursed his lips, then smiled. "I must admit that I'm very disappointed by what I've seen from you so far."

Marius's eyebrows furrowed, and his smile disappeared.

"I thought you had special talents and were here to use them."

Marius set the knife down beside his plate. He stared at the food, chewing what was in his mouth as he listened.

"Instead, you eat my richest foods, drink my finest wines, and sit around doing nothing, day in and day out."

Marius swallowed the food in his mouth and reached for the napkin in front of his plate. He raised it to his lips and wiped the grease from his mouth. Then he held it over the plate and let it drop onto the uneaten food before pushing the plate away.

Desmond detected a sudden change in the air around Marius, an aura that made him seem dangerous.

Agnes stared at Marius with wide, frightened eyes.

Desmond still felt angry, but a tinge of apprehension made his stomach quail as well.

"I told you." Marius spoke the words slowly. Quietly. "That these sorts of things can not be rushed."

"I remember," the elder said.

"The best way to ensure success," Marius continued to stare at his plate, "is to wait until the trader leaves. Without his protection, the girl will be vulnerable." He looked up and met Desmond's eyes. "That's when I make my move. Not before."

"Yes," Desmond drawled the word. "You've made your strategy perfectly clear."

"Then why"—Marius's hand came smashing down on the table with enough force to make the silverware and plates rattle—"are you going on about this while I'm trying to eat?"

The elder stared at the man for a long moment, his features calm. "Will left the village late last night."

Marius stared at Desmond.

Desmond stared back.

"He did?"

Desmond nodded.

Marius's scowl transformed into a smile, and he spread his hands out. "Excellent." His chair scraped the floor as he stood and pushed it away. He turned toward Agnes and dipped his head in a small bow. "The meal was delightful, Agnes. You're a wonderful cook."

Agnes glared back.

He moved toward the front door, motioning with one hand at Desmond. "Don't worry, old boy. There's no need to get up and see me out. I've got work to do."

Husband and wife sat at the table. A few seconds later, they heard the front door close.

"Thank Aatun he's gone." Agnes breathed a sigh of relief. "He won't return, will he?"

Desmond shook his head and stood. "More wine, darling?"

"Yes, please."

The elder walked past his wife, reaching out to touch

her shoulder as he did so. "Now that he's gone, I can actually grab us a bottle of good stuff."

59

Luna stood in the middle of a large, sunlit field. Clouds drifted across the light blue sky, and cool wind wafted over the tips of the long, greenish-brown grass all around her, making it wave back and forth as if dancing to some unseen music.

She turned slowly and smiled, taking in the view with gratitude in her heart. After a complete rotation, Luna stopped, and her smile became a frown.

"Where am I?" she asked out loud.

Confused, she turned again, her eyes searching the land as far out as she could see, hunting for familiar landmarks in hopes of determining her location. She turned twice more with no success, then came to a standstill once more.

"And how did I get here?" Luna heard the confusion in her own voice as she spoke the question.

"You seem to be drawn to interesting places."

The voice behind her sounded familiar. She turned, and her eyes widened. "Hello again," she said.

Aatun stood less than three feet away, dressed in a flowing gown of spun gold that sparkled as it caught the sunlight and reflected it back. The goddess of the towers smiled, her smooth, pale skin blemish-free and perfect as she dipped her head in a silent greeting.

"I feel as if I should bow," Luna frowned. "Should I?"

Aatun laughed. "There's no need for such things, child. No need at all."

"Where are we?"

"Your mind has created a place that exists in reality, although it lies far from your village."

"How is that possible?" Luna frowned. "That my mind can create a real place in my dreams which I know nothing about in real life?"

Aatun's smile softened, conveying amusement. "Understanding how is not always important, child. There will always be things that are mysterious and unexplained."

"That's not an answer."

"It is," Aatun paused, amusement dancing in her eyes. "Perhaps not the answer you desire, but that will also often be the case in life."

Luna considered the goddess's words.

"This place is called Yama's meadow."

"Who is Yama?"

Aatun grinned. "A king who existed long ago. Who may still exist." She shrugged. "You cannot stay here long, Luna. Do your best to become familiar with the landmarks that surround you."

Luna's first impulse was to ask why, but she noted the smile on Aatun's face and, instead of speaking, nodded and did as she'd been instructed. Minutes passed in silence as she turned, doing her best to take note of all the details of the land, both far away and close.

She smelled something and paused, turning back toward the goddess with a frown. "Is that smoke?"

Aatun's smile faded, replaced by a look of sadness as she nodded her head. "It is."

"But—" Luna looked around her in confusion. "I don't see anything burning."

"No."

"Then where's the smell coming from?"

"It is time to wake up, child." Aatun raised one hand and made a motion between them. "Remember this place. You will be glad you did someday."

"Wait." Luna felt a tingling sensation and her vision began to blur. "I'm not ready to go. Please. I have questions."

Aatun's smiling form began to vibrate and shiver. "You and your questions, girl. Never lose that spirit of yours."

Luna opened her mouth to say more, but the goddess was gone.

AND A SECOND LATER, SO WAS LUNA.

60

Luna sat up in her bed and sniffed.

"I can still smell smoke," she muttered, as habit made her eyes flit toward her door.

The light from the bottom gap in the door appeared fuzzy, with wisps of whiteness curling upward.

Luna rose from bed and moved to the door, pulling it open with a sharp yank. She stuck her head into the hallway and looked right, toward the lit stairwell.

The lights were on downstairs.

"Mom?" she called.

"Luna?" Her mother's voice.

"What are you doing?"

The clap of cabinet doors being closed with more force than usual came from the kitchen.

Luna waited a few more seconds, then sighed loudly and made for the stairs.

When her foot was on the bottom step, she looked toward the kitchen area and frowned. Her mother was fully dressed, wearing her jacket, and was placing items into a red plastic box on the counter, filled with what looked like medical supplies.

"What are you doing?" Luna asked.

Malena glanced at her daughter over one shoulder, eyes doing a quick up and down, and then she turned back to the box in front of her. "Get dressed and throw your jacket on."

"Where are you going?"

"We," Malena said. "There's been an accident on Main Street."

"What kind of accident?"

"I'm not sure." Malena dropped a pair of scissors into the box, picked up the box, and turned to face her daughter. "But your Uncle Jack called on the phone and said to get first-aid things and get there as fast as we could."

"On the phone?" Luna frowned. The phone always meant it was serious. Only three or four people had access to an old-fashioned land-line phone. Communication on them was saved for the gravest emergencies. "Do you smell smoke?"

"No." Malena frowned, then closed her mouth and inhaled through her nose. One eyebrow rose. "Maybe, now that you mention it."

"I saw it under my bedroom door."

Malena shook her head. "If there was smoke in the house, the smell would be stronger. What I detect is so faint that the smell is there and then gone almost before it registers."

"Then where's it coming from?"

Malena's eyes widened and she grabbed the box with both hands. "The village."

Luna followed her mother to the door and opened it, following Malena quickly onto the porch and shutting the door behind her. Both women looked toward the village and stared.

Orange light flickered and columns of black smoke rose high into the air, illuminating the buildings of the village in an eerie light as flames danced along the wooden structures.

"Damn it," Malena swore under her breath and ran down the steps. "Let's go, Luna. Do your best to keep up."

Luna stared at the sight in the distance for a second longer, then started after her mother at a run.

61

THEY FOUND JACK STANDING ON THE SIDEWALK opposite the Agriculture Hall, jaws clenched as he watched the structure burn. People had formed a line along the length of the street and were passing pails of water to a large man—Tasker Lee's brother—who threw the water onto the fire and then tossed the empty to someone else.

Despite their efforts, it was clear the blaze was out of control.

Luna and Malena stopped beside Jack, Luna breathing heavily and Malena gasping as she bent over, resting her hands on her knees to help her recover from their run.

"The Ag Building is a goner," Jack said, bringing the mayor up to speed without needing to be asked. "Seems it started here and spread along that side of the street only." He met his sister-in-law's gaze. "So far."

Malena straightened, eyebrows furrowing as she took in the scene. "Any casualties?"

"None that I know of," Jack said. "The closest residence buildings were evacuated before they caught." He nodded toward the line of people. "And no one is running around screaming or crying, so I'm taking that as a sign no one has bought it."

"What else needs to be done?" Luna asked. "How can I help?"

Jack shook his head but then looked at his niece and stopped. "There's a group throwing water on nearby buildings to prevent them from catching fire. Head to the Record Hall and help out there."

"No," Mal shook her head.

Luna opened her mouth to protest, but Jack spoke first. "She's an adult, Mal, and wants to help."

Malena's eyes tightened at the corners but after a second she pursed her lips and nodded. "You're right." She met her daughter's gaze. "Go help at the Record Hall. Make sure it's good and soggy. We can't lose our history."

Luna nodded and turned.

Malena reached out and gripped her daughter's arm, pulling her into a fierce embrace. "Be careful, Dove."

Luna returned the hug. "I will, Mom."

"I love you."

"I love you, too."

Malena released her and Luna jogged away.

———

Gage was in the water line when Luna and Malena arrived at the Agriculture Hall. His arms were already sore from passing pails full of water toward the fire, but he kept working with the others as he watched his friend arrive and look in his direction.

After a few minutes, Luna turned and jogged away.

Gage frowned.

"Take it."

He reached out and accepted the next pail, moving it to his right hand and passing it along while he continued to watch his friend leave the area.

As she was turning out of sight, Gage frowned.

A man dressed in a long black trench coat appeared from the shadows and followed Luna.

"Come on!" the voice shouted again. "Wake up, Gage!"

"I've gotta go." Gage set his bucket on the ground and took off, running as fast as he could as angry calls sounded from behind him. As his mind pushed his body to run faster, another part wondered who the stranger in the trench coat was.

And why was he following Luna?

Luna was halfway to the Record Hall when a hand grabbed her shoulder, causing her to stop and turn.

Her first thought was that a villager was stopping to ask for help, but when she saw who it was, her eyes narrowed and she tried to step backward. The hand gripping her held her firmly in place.

"Hey there," Marius smiled down at her.

"What are you doing?"

"Taking you somewhere safe."

"What?"

"That's why I'm here, Luna. To make sure you don't get hurt."

Luna frowned.

"This way." Marius tried to turn her in the opposite direction.

"No." Luna gave a sharp twist of her shoulder and

managed to break free of the man's grip. She took a step back.

"Come on," he said. "We don't have time for any of this."

"Who sent you to watch me?"

He smiled. "Really? Your home is burning down and you want to ask me questions?"

"I'm not going anywhere with you."

"Well, that's just not true."

Luna stood and stared at him for a long moment. Then she turned and began running with everything she had.

She'd taken fewer than ten strides when Marius had her once more, this time gripping her by the collar of her jacket, yanking backward to halt her movement. Luna unzipped her coat and wiggled her shoulders, trying to shed it and break free. She felt it falling away and leaned forward to begin running ... only to feel her hair being grabbed. "Ow!" She tried to twist away, but there was a flash of pain in her scalp and she froze.

Marius looked down at her, grinning as he held her by the hair. "You're like a wild kitten. Now behave yourself and come with me."

Luna sensed an opening and took it. She raised her right foot and stomped down as hard as she could onto Marius's foot, expecting a grunt of surprise and the grip on her hair to disappear.

But instead of feeling her heel squash into the softness of his foot inside the boot, something hard pushed back and a jolt of pain lanced up her foot and into her knee.

Marius's hold on her remained strong.

"Steel-toed boots, lass. Now come on. I'm trying to help you—"

Luna opened her mouth and did the only thing she

could think of. She screamed as loud and shrill as she could. She saw the man's eyes widen in surprise as her call split the air like a siren. When her breath had been used up, she took another and screamed again, and then again. Hope filled her. Someone would hear and come to her rescue. She took another deep breath ...

And doubled over in surprise as Marius punched her hard in the stomach. She fell to the ground, panic splintering her mind as she realized she could no longer breathe, let alone scream. Her eyes widened as she struggled to get a lungful of air. She could feel her body trying, mouth opening and diaphragm moving in an attempt to pull air in, but it wasn't working. She heard a clicking sound and realized it was coming from her own mouth. She looked up at the sky, paralyzed by desperation and fear.

Marius's face appeared in her line of vision. "Don't worry," he smirked. "Just knocked the wind outta ya. You'll be able to breathe in a bit."

His face disappeared and Luna felt herself being hauled from the ground and slung over Marius's shoulder. Now all she could see was the ground behind him.

"Shoulda done this from the start," Marius muttered. "Less fuss and muss."

Luna felt her breath slowly return as he began to carry her off.

62

Luna couldn't tell exactly where they were going, but her limited view of ground switched first from paving stones, to grass, and finally gravel.

"Where are you taking me?" she yelled.

Marius ignored her as he continued to walk.

She guessed it was fifteen or twenty minutes later when Marius finally stopped walking and lowered her to the ground. She stood, looked around, and frowned.

"What are we doing at the edge of the village?" she asked.

Marius stared at her, a dangerous expression on his face. "Answer me."

He reached into his pocket and withdrew a trader bracelet. The multicoloured gemstones glinted in the moonlight as he slipped it over his left wrist. "Are you gonna behave yourself from now on?"

"Are we leaving?"

"This would be easier if I could nudge you," he continued. "But something tells me you're immune to that." He paused. "Although I suppose it is better if you remain in full control of yourself. We might have to run."

"Answer me," Luna felt fear rising up in her stomach. "Are you taking me through the barrier?"

Marius smiled and held out his hand.

Luna took a step back, but it was too late. His hand snaked forward and gripped her with his full strength. She tried to twist away but couldn't slip out of his vise-like hold on her.

"Let's go." He began dragging her toward the line, now twenty or so feet away.

"I don't want to!" She tried to drop to the ground, but his grip on her was sure. He dragged her forward without slowing his pace.

"Please. Don't make me go."

"Quit your whining." Marius didn't look back as he spoke. "You know we're both safe while I wear the bracelet."

Luna struggled and tore at his hand, digging her feet into the gravel and feeling tears in her eyes as she slid steadily toward the line. Beyond the line, the sun was peeking over the horizon and sending orange-gold rays to light up the fields beyond.

Luna huffed and then frowned as she heard something behind her. She turned her head just in time to see Gage close the distance between them. With a loud shout, he raised his clasped hands over his head and brought them down on Marius's wrist.

The man let out a grunt of pain mixed with surprise, his head whipping around with eyes wide. Under the force of Gage's blow, Marius lost his grip on Luna. She fell to the ground, rolling once, twice, and a third time, before coming to a stop and getting to her feet.

Gage and Marius remained locked together, Gage gripping the man by his wrist. Marius snarled and pulled backward. He freed his arm, but there was a snapping sound followed by glittering sparkles as the gemstone bracelet broke away from his wrist and the stones tumbled to the ground in a spray of glassy colour.

"You idiot," Marius snarled.

Gage dropped into a crouch, smiling as his fists raised to a protective stance near his face. "Not going anywhere now, are ya?"

Marius reached into his jacket, and his hand gripped the hilt of a knife. Then he paused, shook his head, and withdrew his hand without the blade. "You're not worth the mess, pup," he muttered, hands hanging loosely at his sides as he strode toward Gage with a seemingly careless gait.

Luna knew Gage could fight. His family were the security specialists for the village, and he'd been raised fighting with his cousins and aunts and uncles. He was not the best in the Lee family, but only his father and uncle could best him in the recent matches that Luna had watched.

Gage took a step back as Marius approached, but then seemed to make a decision and stepped forward with purpose, his right hand cocking back and then streaking forward for the man's face. Luna knew there was no way Marius could dodge or block it—

But that's exactly what he did.

Gage's fist was a blur of motion, but Marius's head moved faster, narrowly avoiding the blow as her friend's fist breezed past his opponent's ear.

Gage darted back quickly, a frown on his face.

Marius grinned and then winked, his hands still at his sides.

Gage moved forward to get within striking range.

Marius shuffled backward, his feet silent on the gravel. Gage took a large step forward to close the gap, but Marius retreated with ease.

This went on for several seconds, Gage pushing forward and Marius moving back. Luna frowned, wondering why Marius was retreating.

Then her eyes fell to the ground, widening in sudden understanding.

"Gage, stop!" she called. "He's trying to get you close to the line."

Gage's eyes flicked to the ground.

"Get back!" Luna shouted.

Gage dropped his hands and shifted his weight to take a step back—

Marius struck forward faster than anything Luna had ever seen. In a blur, he closed the gap between himself and her friend. Equally as fast, he grabbed Gage's hand and then pulled back with a mighty heave.

She opened her mouth to call out, to scream her best friend's name—

But before a sound passed her lips, Gage sailed through the air, the whites of his eyes visible as his hand was the first part of him to touch the barrier.

There was a loud hiss, followed by a sizzle as Gage's body went through the barrier and disintegrated in a cloud of dark ash.

Luna stood with her mouth open and eyes wide. A heavy weight was squeezing her heart, preventing her from catching a breath. Unable to push air over her vocal cords, her lips silently mouthed Gage's name as a wave of pain and grief crashed over her, forcing her to her knees.

Marius watched the ash drift through the air and

disperse, then turned back to her and shook his head. "Stupid boy. He ruined my plan."

Unable to move, Luna stared as the man walked to where she knelt and stared down at her, a mocking grin on his face. He reached down, grabbed her wrist, and began to drag her toward the line.

Luna frowned. After he'd taken a couple more steps she began to fight him the same as she'd done earlier. "Stop," she whispered. "Please. Don't."

Marius came to the silver line and stopped. He pulled upwards, bringing Luna to her feet. He stared at her for a long moment, tilting his head like a curious dog as he considered her. "Well," he sighed. "I suppose we'll go with plan B, then."

"What? What's plan—" Before Luna could finish the question, Marius shoved Luna hard.

Unable to stop, she plunged headfirst toward the barrier, screaming in terror as her hand made contact with the field of deadly energy.

63

MALENA LOOKED UP AS THE DOOR OPENED.

Thomas entered first, followed by Jack.

"Anything?" Malena wiped the tears from her eyes and stood, hopeful as she met her brother-in-law's gaze.

Jack shook his head. "We've looked everywhere, Mal. There's no sign of either of them."

"Did you check the gorge? There are tunnels and sink-holes in there. Remember, there was one time little William got lost and it took us hours before we—"

"We've searched the gorge," Jack said. "More than once."

"Yes. I know. I'm sorry."

Jack came to the table and placed one hand on her shoulder. "There's still plenty of time to find them."

"I know."

Thomas remained by the door. He opened his mouth to say something, then reconsidered and closed it.

"The fires are all out?" Malena asked.

"Yes," Jack said. "The Agriculture Hall took the worst

of it. Surrounding buildings are water-damaged, but that's easier to fix than fire."

"The fire ate most of the grain?"

Jack pursed his lips and nodded.

"That's gonna hurt." She spoke the words, but there was no emotion or feeling in them.

"We'll manage." Jack stared at the floor. "Somehow."

There was a knock at the door. Malena and Jack both looked at Thomas. The tower technician opened the door, saw who was standing at it, and stepped back to make room.

Desmond Baker entered.

"What can I do for you, Elder?" Malena asked.

"Nothing, Madam Mayor." The man looked uncomfortable as he met Thomas's eyes and then looked at Mal. "I bring news."

"About?"

"The missing ... your daughter."

Malena closed her eyes and took a deep breath. Then she opened them and motioned toward the table. "Please join us."

"Thank you." The elder sat down at the table, his hands folded together. The other three joined him. "After the search parties returned ... unsuccessful," he paused and then continued. "I decided to run a weekly diagnostic report for the towers."

"Diagnostic report?" Jack frowned. "What for?"

"Well," the elder's expression became pained for a moment and then returned to sombre. "The report covers many parameters. Not only how the towers are each functioning, but also the status of the barrier."

"Status of the barrier?" Malena's brows furrowed.

"Yes." The elder nodded once more. Then he winced and continued speaking. "It seems that there was an ...

anomalous reading from the east part of the village barrier. Two, actually."

"Anomalous reading?" Malena repeated the word.

"No," Thomas whispered, one hand coming up to cover his mouth and tears springing to his eyes.

Malena caught the man's expression and shook her head. "I'm sorry, but I don't understand what that means, Elder. Perhaps you can put it in language we all know."

"Yes." The elder looked at his hands and then met Malena's questioning stare. "It means that the barrier was breached. Twice."

Malena's eyes became glassy. "You think Luna and Gage were destroyed by the barrier?"

"We don't think, Madam Mayor." Desmond said. "The data indicates that is exactly what happened."

64

LUNA OPENED HER EYES AND SAT UP ON THE COT, squinting at the sunlight streaming through the window. The sound of an axe splitting wood echoed through the thin walls of the tiny cabin where she had been for the past two days.

Luna rose and went to the window, peering out at the small path that led from the porch to a grass-filled stretch of the ancient road they had travelled to get to this place. She'd learned the hard, cracked surface, mostly grass-covered, was called *asphalt*. It stretched farther than the eye could see in both directions.

Her eyes flicked to Marius. The man stood beside a pile of wood, his shirt off and a long-handled axe in one hand as he placed a round log on top of a large stump. Then he stepped back and swung the axe downward, splitting the smaller log in two. She looked around the front yard, or at least the small portion of it visible from her window, and sighed.

She wished Gage could have seen this land beyond the barrier of their village.

She wished Gage was still alive.

Luna wiped a tear from her eye and slid to the floor, her back against the wooden cabin wall. She tried to concentrate, telling herself that now was not the time to disappear into grief and sorrow. Gage would want her to keep her head clear, to get out of this and get back to her parents. She nodded to herself and took a deep breath, pushing the sadness away. Letting anger and determination fill her instead.

Marius hadn't bothered to tie her up. Instead, he told her about the dangers that would love to find a young girl like her all alone in the Wilds. Some of the stories were pretty gruesome. Luna hadn't been able to keep a look of fear from crossing her face during a couple of his cautionary talks. Marius had laughed at her.

But inwardly, Luna had smiled. Dangerous or not, nothing could stop her from trying to escape. She was simply waiting, biding her time for the best possible moment. She knew her moment would come. An opportunity would present itself at some point. And when it did ...

Getting away from Marius was important, but it wasn't her only challenge. For some reason she couldn't understand, crossing the barrier hadn't killed her, but it had knocked her unconscious for several hours. Meanwhile, Marius had carried her away into the Wild. One thing she did know was which direction they had come from down the great broken road.

That was the way she would run.

Luna sat with her legs folded, listening to Marius split wood as she considered her plan.

Luna was pulled from her thoughts when she heard Marius speaking outside. She frowned and got to her feet to look out the window, to better see what was going on.

Marius was standing in her field of vision, the axe now resting on the chopping block as he talked. It was clear he was speaking with someone, and a second after her captor stopped talking she heard a muffled voice reply.

She moved to the far side of the window and angled herself to try to get a look at the other person, but it was no use. Whoever it was—another man, from the pitch of the voice—remained out of sight.

The two spoke for a few minutes, then Marius nodded and began to walk away. Luna watched as he strode up the pathway to the road, then turned left and continued walking.

Luna held her breath. This was the farthest Marius had gone from the house. She watched him walking on until he was out of sight.

Instinct took over. Luna rushed to the cot and retrieved her jacket from beneath it, her mind made up.

This was her chance. She was gonna make a run for it.

She heard a cough outside, followed by footsteps on the wood steps leading to the cabin's front porch.

Luna's breath caught in her throat.

The other person was coming in!

She leapt to her feet and ran behind the door, reaching for the ceramic lamp that she'd decided days ago would be the best thing to knock out Marius if she had a chance.

She waited, blood pounding at a certain spot in her neck as she waited.

The door opened.

Luna watched the floor in front of it. She saw a boot step forward ... and that was her moment to strike.

As the man took a second step into the cabin, Luna raised the lamp high, stepped up behind him, and brought it down on the back of his head, as hard as she could.

There was a loud crash as the lamp broke, shards of ceramic and golden lamp oil flying in all directions.

The man let out a startled *OOF* and collapsed forward onto the floor.

Luna was already racing for the door, ready to sprint full out to the road and take off in the opposite direction that Marius had taken.

She cast one quick glance back to make sure the man was down and wouldn't chase her, and—

Luna came to a full stop. "What the—" She frowned, stunned, as the man looked up at her with glazed eyes and a confused expression.

She shook her head, still not believing what she was seeing. "Dad?"

<hr />

To Be Continued In
Book 2 : GHOST

Oh and hey?! If you liked this book, could you please head over and leave a review for it? Reviews are a huge help to authors, and I'd certainly be thankful if you do leave one.
Thanks!

BOOKS BY TERRY SCHOTT

The Game is Life Series
The Game (Book 1)
Digital Heretic (Book 2)
Interlude-Brandon (Book 3)
Virtual Prophet (Book 4)
Shadows (Book 5)
Digital Evolution (Book 6)
Cyber (Book 7)
Fragmented (Book 8)
Resonance (Book 9)

The Blight Series
Ascension (Book 1)

Blades VR Trilogy
Scout (Book 1)
Campaign (Book 2)
Raid (Book 3)

The Advent Trilogy
The Ward (Book 1)
The Source (Book 2)
The Exception (Book 3)

The Dark Ages Series

Epoch (Part 1)

The Exigency Series
Towers (Book 1)
Ghost (Book 2)
Shade (Book 3)

ACKNOWLEDGMENTS

Thanks to Shawn, Carl, and Karen for reading this story as I wrote it. I appreciate the kind words of encouragement and feedback as I went along. I'm a challenge to encourage and support sometimes, but you three are always ready and willing to do so! Thank you so much.

Big shout of thanks to Becca Syme. Her feedback and opinions, on both writing and life, have provided me with hours of fun conversation and many awesome insights as a result... Thanks for your patience and laughter, Becca. It's been a great help so very often during my process.

Thanks also to my editor, Doreen Martens. I don't know what else I can say about her awesome speed, attention to detail, and her special ability to enhance the story rather than confuse and detract from it. Thanks so much, Doreen. You rock !

Leigh Ribak is my second set of eyes on this one and he also came up with some clutch finds! The other thing that I want to thank Leigh for is how he approached me. Very much as a fan who was offering to share some 'tiny' things that he found in order to help the product be better for all.

Thank you for that, Leigh. I'm so thankful to have met you and glad that you have been willing to help. It is much appreciated.

Thank you once again to all of my Patreon supporters! This amazing group of people read this book months ago because they choose to follow me and see stuff as it is written. They also get other perks such as exclusive stories, cover reveals, video blog posts, and interaction with me whenever they want to shoot me a message.

You gals and guys are the best.

Thanks to Zach Shank, Clayton Hopper, Dan Moran, Danny Boots, Matthew Chadwick, Nicole, Walker Klenk, Alex, Camryn Rhys, Derek McComb, Joe ,Johan Brännmar, Lisa Rivera, Mark Shaskey Jr., Natasha Macaulay, Steve Campbell, and Thom Fenix, for your continued support!

Printed in Great Britain
by Amazon